BLACKWELL

Other Books by Alexandrea Weis

To My Senses
Recovery
Sacrifice
Broken Wings
Diary of a One-Night Stand
Acadian Waltz
The Satyr's Curse
The Satyr's Curse II: The Reckoning
The Ghosts of Rue Dumaine
Cover to Covers
The Riding Master
The Bondage Club
That Night with You
Taming Me
Rival Seduction
The Art of Sin
Behind the Door with M. Clarke
Dark Perception
Dark Attraction
His Dark Canvas

Forthcoming from Vesuvian Books 2017

By Alexandrea Weis
The Secret Brokers

By Alexandrea Weis with Lucas Astor
The Chimera Effect
Magnus Blackwell Series, Book II

BLACKWELL

Hell has a new master

Alexandrea Weis
with Lucas Astor

Blackwell

This is a work of fiction. Names, characters, places, and incidents either are the product of
the author's imagination or are used fictitiously.
Any resemblance to actual persons, living or dead, events or locales is entirely coincidental.

Cover Credit: Original Illustration by Sam Shearon
www.mister-sam.com

ISBN: 978-1-944109-24-0

275

VESUVIAN BOOKS

Published by Vesuvian Books
www.vesuvianbooks.com

Printed in the United States of America

10 9 8 7 6 5 4 3 2 1

To the wonderful woman who made this book possible, Italia Gandolfo. To the Jedi Master, Luke Astor, for trusting me with his baby. To the tireless Liana Gardner for all her hard work, and to my friend, Mary Ting, for pointing me in the right direction.

Thank you for believing in me.
— Alexandrea Weis

To Italia Gandolfo, for her tireless dedication and determination. To Alexandrea Weis, for loving twisted stories as much as I do and helping bring Magnus Blackwell so eloquently into the world. To Liana Gardner for being an earth angel, and to the epic Mister Sam Shearon who brought Magnus to life with his incredible original cover illustration of the man himself.

Thank you all for making this possible.
— Lucas Astor

Table of Contents

Chapter One

A Fortunate Meeting

1886

The crunch of leaves beneath Jacob O'Connor's freshly polished shoes filled the crisp fall air. In a rush to cross the green of Harvard Yard, he dodged fellow students while struggling to pull his long black coat around his shoulders. Ahead, he eyed the red-bricked walls and white-trimmed windows of Massachusetts Hall.

When he reached the white-painted door, Jacob ran a nervous hand through his wavy black hair. "Hell of a first impression, O'Connor," he muttered, reaching for the brass doorknob. "You're already late, and classes haven't even started."

"You're not late," a deep voice spoke out.

A pair of inquisitive green eyes greeted Jacob. In a fitted long black coat and white ascot tie, the eavesdropper leaned against the red-bricked building. A lit cigarette dangled in his hand; he casually flicked away the ash.

"They haven't even begun serving drinks yet," the handsome man offered as he pushed away from the building. "Are you another of the freshman architects here for the reception?"

"I'm Jacob O'Connor." Jacob puffed out his chest, trying not to falter while the well-dressed man inspected his worn black coat and hand-me-down black shoes.

"I've heard about you. You're the sponsor from Fogle, Hardwick, and Hillman in Boston."

Jacob was painfully aware of how ratty his second-hand clothes must have appeared to the sharply dressed man. "Yes, Mr. Fogle was my mentor and got me into the Harvard Architecture Program."

The gentleman's cigarette went to the ground. "Yes, you received a full scholarship. You're the man the rest of us have to live up to."

"I am?" Jacob questioned, his voice cracking with nerves.

"Word is you are very talented." The toe of the man's shiny black shoe rubbed out his cigarette.

Jacob warily glanced around the yard. "Not talented. Perhaps just determined."

The stranger's green eyes gave him a thorough going over while the wind lifted his dirty-blond hair. "Sometimes being determined is a talent, O'Connor." He pointed to his chest. "I, on the other hand, am neither determined nor talented. I'm here because my old man insists I get an education."

From the cut of his suit to his regal attitude, Jacob figured he was another of the rich and spoiled upperclassmen he had run into continuously since settling into his dorm a few days ago. For Jacob, the campus of Harvard was teeming with affluent men whose only purpose in life was to spend their family's money.

"I heard you're an orphan. Is it true?"

Jacob nervously cleared his throat. "Ah, yes, it's true."

The rude man added a cocky grin. "And were saved from a life on the streets by your mentor."

Jacob's anger stirred. "I may not have been born into a life of privilege, sir, but I can assure you I deserve to be here just like any other student."

A raucous, maniacal laugh took Jacob by surprise. He didn't know people could laugh like that.

"I'm not the enemy, dear boy." His inquisitor drew closer. "I'd like to be your friend."

"Why?" Jacob snapped, suspicious of his intentions.

"Because unlike the rest of the rabble on this campus, I admire determination and talent." He held out a tapered hand. "I'm Magnus Blackwell."

Jacob knew the name. Everyone in New England had heard of the Blackwell family. They were practically New England royalty. Their wealth had been acquired through shipping and banking, but had switched to steel production with the construction of the First Transcontinental Railroad. Their exploits and finances had been a particular interest to Jacob's mentor, Martin Fogle. He had been trying to land their accounts for years.

After shaking his hand, Jacob took a step back. "I've heard of you."

Magnus rested his wide shoulder against the white-painted door. "It's all lies. Everything everyone says about me is a lie. If you want the truth, just ask."

Intrigued, Jacob focused his dark brown eyes on the man's chiseled features. "Are you as rich as they say?"

Magnus stretched for the doorknob. "Richer."

Jacob raised his dark brows. "Is that possible?"

"With my family, most definitely." Magnus opened the door for him. "Do you have any other questions you'd like to ask me, O'Connor?"

"I'm sure I can come up with a few more," Jacob returned with a diminutive grin.

Magnus curled his thin lips into a half-smile. "Wonderful. It will give us something to talk about during this tedious orientation reception we are being forced to attend."

"You might find my questions just as tedious, Mr. Blackwell."

"Somehow, I doubt you could ever be boring, O'Connor." With a flourish, Magnus Blackwell waved Jacob in the door. "From now on, you must call me Magnus."

"And you must call me Jacob."

"I think I prefer O'Connor. Makes you sound more mysterious."

"Mysterious? Me?" Jacob chuckled as he moved toward the door.

Magnus put his arm across the doorway, barring Jacob's entry. "Mystery is all we have, dear boy. Without it, we would be open books at the mercy of those who would rip out our pages and scatter our secrets to the winds. Always strive to keep your secrets hidden."

Jacob nodded. "Yes, Magnus."

"And I thought this was going to be another boring party." Magnus clamped his hand over Jacob's right shoulder. "What do you say we tackle this college adventure together, O'Connor. Let's take Harvard by storm."

4

Chapter Two

The Problem with Women

Walls decorated with black-and-white photographs of buildings, and a row of windows that overlooked a cement walkway frequented by students rushing to class on Harvard campus, did little to offset the stuffy feeling of the classroom.

At the head of the room, an older professor with spectacles, thinning gray hair, and a customary black robe made notations on a chalkboard. He added asterisks to his drawing of the facade of a Greek Revival structure, complete with pediment and columns.

Seated around a circular table with several other young men, Magnus and Jacob wore the school uniform of black coats, white shirts, and black ties. While Jacob avidly took notes, his textbook open in front of him, Magnus sat back in his chair, looking utterly bored.

"Reaction against the dominance of the Neoclassical movement came in the 1820s with Augustus Pugin," the professor lectured in a monotone voice. "He provided a theoretical push for the return of Gothic Revival seen in many structures designed in the middle part of the current century."

Magnus leaned over to Jacob. "When do we get to draw buildings instead of talking about them?"

"Magnus, please," Jacob urged, hiding his head from their professor.

"This professor is putting me to sleep," Magnus insisted in a soft grumble.

Jacob glared at him. "Shhh."

"Thus was coined the term 'architectural realism,'" their professor extolled from the front of the class. "And many proponents of the movement have brought a renovation to the notion of style during our time."

Magnus took a quick glance out the window, and then patted Jacob on the shoulder. "I'll leave you in charge of the notetaking, O'Connor, for both of us."

Jacob stared at Magnus, the apprehension swimming in his brown eyes. "What are you going to do?" he whispered.

Magnus just gave him a sly grin and then stood from his chair, wobbling slightly. "I'm sorry, Professor Talbert," he proclaimed in an unsteady tone. "I'm not feeling very well at the moment. I must excuse myself." Magnus placed his hand over his mouth, pretending to hold something back.

Jacob took in his performance with a profound sense of disbelief.

"Very well. Go, Mr. Blackwell." Professor Talbert sounded more annoyed than concerned.

Magnus collected his unopened textbook on Architectural Theory from the table and shoved the few blank sheets of paper he had in front of him toward Jacob.

"As I was saying," the Professor continued, as Magnus hurried toward the classroom door. "The Realist movement can be drawn from several other movements. One being Art Nouveau in the United Kingdom, exemplified by the work of Charles Rennie Mackintosh."

Jacob was stunned that Magnus could get away with such a lie. Frustrated, he casually gazed out the window. Seconds later, Jacob spotted Magnus jogging along the path. His friend slowed when he caught up with a statuesque blonde in a green dress.

Distracted from the lecture and wondering if the pretty woman prompted Magnus's sudden departure, Jacob observed as Magnus struck up a conversation with her.

Smiling, Magnus relieved the young female student of her books and waved her down the path.

Jacob kept his eyes on the couple until they walked out of sight. Then he shook his head, disgusted by Magnus's luck. With a heaving sigh, he returned to his notes.

Magnus trotted down the straight oak staircase as the afternoon light filtered through the leaded glass of his front door. Muttering when his feet hit the first floor, he imagined the tongue-lashing he would give to whoever was banging on his door.

In the entrance hall, he hurried across the pine floors to the door. Checking the belt on his red robe, he put his lit cigarette in his mouth and took in a deep pull of smoke as he combed his hands through his disheveled hair. Letting out the smoke through his nose, he yanked the door open.

He was shocked to find Jacob standing in his doorway. His friend was holding up a pile of papers.

"Today's notes from theory class," Jacob sounded angry.

"And you brought them here? Now?" Magnus threw his cigarette out on the porch.

Jacob went after the smoking bud, stomping it out with his foot. He came back to the door and shoved the papers at Magnus.

"Professor Talbert asked where you were. That's three classes in a row you've missed this week, Magnus. I can't keep covering for you," Jacob added as he marched in the doorway.

Magnus took the papers from him and shut the door. "What did you tell him?" he probed in an anxious tone.

"You were sick, what else?"

A creaking noise from the staircase announced the arrival of the reason for Magnus's absence. Dressed only in her white petticoat skirt and top, the same statuesque blonde Magnus had left class for proudly strutted down the steps, a playful grin on her lips.

When her bare feet touched the pine floor, she sashayed over to Magnus. Making sure she got his attention, she kissed his lips and then reached out to rub his ass.

The pretty woman seemed to delight in the various shades of Jacob's red cheeks. With a smug smile, she turned away. While ambling down the hallway to the side of the staircase, she accented the sway of her hips.

Magnus tried not to laugh. "As you can see, I had a previous engagement."

"Is that what you call it?"

"I call it fucking. You should try it sometime, O'Connor."

8

Magnus put the papers in his hand down on the first step.

"I prefer to wait until I've found a woman I can love," Jacob professed.

Magnus appeared heartily amused by his comment. "Have you ever been with a woman, O'Connor?"

"If you must know, yes. Two women. Neither of whom I loved."

"Thank God for that." Magnus rolled his eyes. "Otherwise, you would have been married with a house full of brats by now."

"You make love sound like a bad thing."

"Isn't it? Most women do not care for us; they tolerate us for wealth, protection, vanity, what have you, but love, never."

"You're a pessimist, Magnus."

Magnus slipped his hands into the side pockets of his robe, appearing pensive. "No, I'm a realist. As you should be. A woman is the only creature who can take away your will as well as your soul."

"But a woman can also save your soul," Jacob argued. "Love is what brings us back from the brink."

"I'll have to take your word, dear boy. I plan on never becoming a victim of that disease."

Magnus showed Jacob to the door just as the blonde returned. She offered Magnus a leering grin, and then jogged up the stairs. Both men admired her firm ass beneath her petticoat while she made her way up the steps.

"I need to get back to my previous engagement," Magnus advised, returning his eyes to Jacob. "But I will pick you up tomorrow to go to the club."

Embarrassed again, Jacob dropped his eyes to the floor. "Ah, yes. I'll be ready."

After Magnus had opened the door for him, Jacob rushed

out to the porch.

"I hope you have a hearty constitution, O'Connor," Magnus remarked, leaning against the doorway. "My father can be hard to take at times."

Jacob backed away from the door. "I'm sure it will be fine, Magnus."

Shaking his head, Magnus watched as his friend turned toward the porch steps. "You have no idea how wrong you are."

After Jacob had given him a wave good-bye, Magnus shut the door and secured the lock. Gazing back up the stairs, he grinned while thinking about who was waiting for him in bed.

With a short chuckle, he jogged up the steps, ready to get back to his eager blonde.

The Hastings Gentleman's Club was considered the most prestigious club in Boston for men from the upper class. The waiting list to get in could take years, but for the bluebloods of the city, like the Blackwells, there was no waiting list.

In the mandatory full tuxedo required by club members, Magnus and Jacob entered the fancy black leather doors of the establishment. They traveled through the crowded meeting and smoking rooms until they came to the private bar.

Dark paneled walls, red leather chairs, and burgundy carpets gave the barroom a definitively masculine feel. At the end of the room was an ornately carved fireplace with a small dark oak bar next to it. Full-length portraits of esteemed club members, who also happened to be some of the most influential men in the country, hung on the walls.

At the arched entrance, Magnus eyed the room. "There he

is."

Magnus and Jacob crossed the burgundy carpet to an older man sitting near the fireplace in a high-back chair and smoking a cigar.

"Father," Magnus greeted with a polite bow.

Reynolds Blackwell was an older version of his son. With a tall, agile body, he had fair hair, intrusive green eyes, and his face had Magnus's carved features—even his fiendish grin. His jawline was a little softer, his belly slightly rounder, and his hands not quite as tapered as his son's. Even down to the impatient way he flicked the ash off his cigar, there was no mistaking who had fathered Magnus Blackwell.

Reynolds Blackwell stood from his chair. While he put out his cigar in a brass ashtray on the table next to him, Reynolds mumbled, "Magnus. Good of you to come."

Magnus waved his hand to Jacob. "Father, I would like to introduce Jacob O'Connor. He is studying architecture with me at school."

Jacob stepped forward and extended his white-gloved hand.

Reynolds glared at his son while shaking Jacob's hand. "I am surprised my son brought you, Mr. O'Connor. He never introduces me to any of his friends. Makes me think he doesn't have any." Reynolds snapped his fingers at two empty red leather chairs not far from his.

Jacob went to one of the nearby chairs. Out of nowhere, an attendant dressed all in white appeared at his side and pushed one of the chairs closer for Magnus.

Jacob waited for the attendant to get another chair. As he stood by, anxiously darting his eyes around the room, Jacob's chair was pushed into place next to Magnus.

Magnus flipped his long coat tails behind him and had a seat.

"I never introduced you to any of my friends because I knew you would not approve."

"You're right." Reynolds directed his eyes to Jacob, who was clumsily attempting to mimic Magnus's gesture as he took his chair. "What of your family, Mr. O'Connor?"

"He's an orphan," Magnus blurted out before Jacob could speak. "Without a penny to his name."

"Then why are you with him?" Reynolds Blackwell shot back.

"Because he is the kind of rabble you never wanted me to associate with, Father."

Reynolds ignored his son's taunting. "Tell me, Mr. O'Connor, how did you find the means to attend Harvard?"

Jacob gulped as he felt the man's piercing green eyes boring into him. "Ah, Mr. Martin Fogle of Fogle, Hardwick, and Hillman was my mentor." Jacob silently cursed as his voice cracked. "He took me in and educated me when I was a boy. He got me a scholarship to Harvard."

"I know Martin Fogle," Reynolds curtly replied. "He's been trying to land my construction accounts for years. He's a wily prick, but a good architect. Are you like him?"

Jacob's stomach did a nervous flip. "Like him? What do you mean?"

Magnus casually removed a spot of lint from his pressed, black jacket. "Jacob is a gifted architect and not a wily prick, Father."

"Then what the hell is he doing with a bum like you?" his father roared.

A tense moment of silence passed, and Jacob warily glanced from father to son, convinced the two men were going to come to blows at any moment.

"You summoned me, and I invited him to come. He's never seen the inside of The Hastings," Magnus eventually answered, his voice never giving any hint as to the frustration stewing in his eyes.

Reynolds tapped his long fingers on the arm of his chair. "I am not sending you to Harvard to befriend charity cases, Magnus. I sent you to get an education."

"And so I am," Magnus insisted with a cocky smirk. "I'm expanding my horizons every day. You are the one who always pushed me to be well-rounded—just like you."

Jacob observed as the older man's eyes flooded with indignation.

Drumming his fingers on the arm of the chair, Reynolds nodded to Jacob. "Mr. O'Connor, can you give my son a moment alone with me?"

Relieved to get away, Jacob stood from his chair. "Of course, Mr. Blackwell. I'll wait at the bar."

Jacob felt all the tension in his muscles ease as soon as he bellied up to the bar. He was starting to understand why Magnus never liked being around his father. The man was intimidating as hell. Behind him, Jacob could hear their strained, lowered voices.

A bartender all in white appeared before him. "What can I get for you, sir?"

Studying the array of bottles lined up behind the bar, Jacob spotted a favorite whiskey. "Whiskey and soda, please."

The bartender turned away and selected an old-fashioned glass from a shelf.

Jacob was glad for the distraction as the bartender prepared his drink. His fingertips ran back and forth along the smooth surface of the bar. He felt torn by the encounter with Reynolds

Blackwell. In many ways, he didn't envy Magnus and his relationship with his father, but then again, he had a father. He had grown up with someone to emulate. The closest Jacob had come to a father was the mild-mannered Martin Fogle. The ambitious architect had been patient and kind, but showed little interest in the boy who shadowed him.

"Time to go," Magnus growled as he came alongside Jacob at the bar.

Jacob noticed the quivering of muscles in Magnus's cheeks, and assumed the meeting was over.

"I should say good-bye to your father," Jacob suggested.

"I would advise against that, dear boy." Magnus's voice was laced with rage. "Let's get out of here."

Before Jacob could get in another word, Magnus bolted from the bar. Sighing at the prospect of a long carriage ride back to Cambridge with a pissed off Magnus, Jacob trudged forward. He suddenly wished he'd stayed on campus and spent the evening in the library with a good book.

Magnus said very little on the long carriage ride back to Harvard. Except for the occasional grunt, he just stared out the window and kept his eyes on the passing scenery. Jacob, on the other hand, kept looking at Magnus and waiting for his outrage to erupt.

"The smug son of a bitch," Magnus finally vented as he yanked off his white gloves.

Happy to hear him speak, Jacob chuckled. "You or your father?"

Magnus cracked a brief grin, sharing in Jacob's amusement.

"I hoped, with you, he would be different."

Jacob was relieved to hear his friend's fury subsiding, and eased back against the carriage bench. "He's your father, Magnus. He wants only the best for you."

"He has never given a damn about anyone," Magnus snapped. "His cruelty chased my mother out of our home. She spent most of her life in the cottage across from the manor. They hardly spoke to each other before she died."

"Just be grateful you have a father," Jacob proposed. "If you lose him, you will be like me, an orphan alone in the world."

"That could be a good thing." Magnus snickered and dropped his gloves to the side of the bench.

Jacob was astounded. It was a wonder the two men had not killed each other before now. "Why did he summon you to the club? Is it because of your extracurricular activities?" he queried while the carriage briefly paused on the road.

"That was an excuse. We haven't seen each other in two years," Magnus disclosed. "Before applying to Harvard, I did an internship at Collier and Keene, an architectural firm here in Boston. He's remained at our family home, Altmover Manor on Mount Desert Island in Maine."

"You have a family home?" Jacob asked, surprised by the news.

Magnus briefly nodded as the carriage lurched ahead. "In many ways, it reminds me of my father. It's perpetually cold, big, empty, and reflects the lifeless heart of Reynolds Blackwell. One day, I'll bring you there."

"What does Altmover stand for?"

"Our ancestral homeland in Ireland. Or so my grandfather claimed. I've never seen it."

"Irish? You?" Jacob laughed with exuberance, delighted by

the admission. "I thought you were born of English nobility. Glad to find out you are from the same stock as me."

"We have much in common, O'Connor. That's why I like being around you. You remind me of me."

"I don't think we are anything alike, Magnus."

"Just wait. I am sure you will see it one day. We are both driven."

Jacob was taken aback by the statement. He had never considered himself driven. To him, getting ahead was the only way to raise himself up from his circumstances.

"What drives you, Magnus?"

Magnus snorted. "That's simple. To be anything other than what my father wants."

"Find a new hobby, my friend." Hoping to ease his ire, Jacob patted his shoulder. "Harboring such a need for revenge isn't healthy."

"It is to me, dear boy," Magnus griped in a haunting voice. "It is what I live for."

Jacob clucked with concern. "Such hatred will only end up shortening your life."

"Or it will give me the determination to live forever," Magnus countered.

"No one lives forever."

Magnus veered his eyes to the window and the tightly packed homes lining the busy street. "We shall see, O'Connor. I bet one of us will beat the odds."

Chapter Three

Her

"Come on, O'Connor. What harm can one party do?"
Jacob glanced at his friend as they strolled down Garden Street in the chilly Cambridge evening air. He wanted to argue the point, but the childlike smile on Magnus Blackwell's face curbed Jacob's objections.

Magnus had become everything to Jacob. What started out as a casual acquaintance had blossomed into a steadfast friendship. Magnus's life was the personification of the aristocratic world Jacob had been raised to resent. But somehow, that well-ingrained hatred had shriveled up, leaving Jacob in awe.

"Are you sure I'm invited?" Jacob asked, brushing the wrinkles out of the black tailcoat and trousers. Borrowed from Magnus's wardrobe—like the rest of Jacob's clothes—the coat was a tad long, as were the pants, but Magnus had insisted.

"My dear boy," Magnus cooed in his melodic voice that reminded Jacob of a sophisticated stage actor, "anywhere I'm invited, so are you. You're my friend and are expected to be at my side at all the society events this season, no matter how droll."

"No one knows me, Magnus. I'm a nobody."

Magnus patted Jacob's back. "What have I told you since freshman year? If you think you are somebody, so will they." He tugged on his white bow tie. "Look at me. I have done nothing of consequence with my life, am a mediocre architect at best—nothing near your talent—and I occasionally have been known to dally with one too many ladies of a disreputable nature. Still, I walk into a party, and everyone thinks I'm important. Why? Because I exude confidence." He patted his friend's broad chest. "That's what you need, O'Connor: confidence."

"And a wealthy family," Jacob added, pinching at his oversized white gloves.

"Money is nothing but a tool. You don't need it to gain success."

"Yes, but money opens doors, Magnus—doors that would otherwise be closed to someone like me."

Magnus came to a sudden halt and grabbed Jacob's shoulders. "'A man is not defined by the amount of money he leaves behind but by his worth as a human being, his contribution to his fellow man.' Isn't that what our esteemed president Mr. Charles Eliot always says?"

Jacob stared into Magnus's cunning green eyes. "You're an idiot, Magnus."

Magnus gave his friend's shoulders an encouraging squeeze. "Perhaps, but tonight, I'm an idiot on a mission, dear boy." He let go and strode away.

Jacob jogged to catch up. "What's this one's name?"

"Frances McGee. She's one of those girls attending the Radcliffe experiment."

Jacob grabbed his arm, stopping him. "Are you insane? You can't date a Radcliffe girl. They're off limits. You'll get expelled."

Magnus chuckled. Everything about the man was warm, exuberant, and affable—except his laugh. To Jacob, it was the one eerie thing about Magnus Blackwell that made him edgy.

"I'll only get expelled if anyone finds out about it." Magnus moved along.

Staring at his friend's back, Jacob felt an overwhelming sense of dread. That was not good. Magnus was always into games, challenging authority and pushing his friends to their limits, but none of his mischievous undertakings had bordered on dangerous. Not like this.

"Come on, dear boy," Magnus called from beneath the flickering streetlights. "We mustn't be late for the party."

The modest residence was like many on the outlying campus surrounding the college. Used by the professors, the homes were built for function more than appeal. Jacob looked over the plain wood exterior with its paltry display of gingerbread woodworking around the porch posts and exterior railings. The windows were small, the front door simple, and the facade almost boring.

His mind went to work rescaling the depth and dimensions of the structure, adding width to the windows and elaborate transoms to the front door, and designing a facade that was more regal and would make the home something that stood out on the block instead of blending in.

"What are you looking at?" Magnus tugged at his elbow.

"Just thinking how much better the home would look with a few adjustments," Jacob revealed.

"One day, I will have you build something for me.

Something where you can let all of those creative juices of yours flow free."

Jacob walked alongside him to the front door. "That would be a dream come true."

"Pray you never realize any of your dreams, O'Connor. What will you have left to conquer?"

"I'll make new dreams, Magnus."

They climbed the few wooden steps to the front porch. "Dreams are like a fine wine, my friend: best kept under wraps until they are just about to turn to vinegar."

"I don't see it that way," Jacob argued.

Magnus reached for the door handle. "You will, one day."

The home was already packed with students. The mixer, chaperoned by the portly Professor McCleary, was meant to allow the men of Harvard an opportunity to meet the upstanding and talented women who were accepted into the freshman class of Radcliffe. Not yet a university, the women's college was called "The Experiment" by many on campus because no one was sure how long it would last or whether Harvard would approve the school's charter.

Inside the modest home with white wainscoting and floral wallpaper, Magnus and Jacob removed their hats and gloves and handed them to a maid as they stepped through the front door. A parlor was to the right, and a dark mahogany staircase rose to the left of the entrance. In the parlor, done in green plush sofas, an assortment of young ladies were being cordially introduced to a line of men—also wearing black tails and white bow ties—by the stout wife of Professor McCleary.

Mrs. McCleary waved her white gloved hands at the men gathered around her. "Well, go on," she fussed. "Say hello to the ladies."

The demure young women were all in sleeveless gowns of white, pearl, or pale pink with dipping necklines and lace overlay. With hair piled high atop their heads, their faces were unpainted, and each lady was the epitome of refinement, sophistication, and social propriety demanded by their school. To Jacob, the women looked as lifeless as dolls, and he suspected their brains would be just as empty. The women he had met thus far at Harvard had bored him to death.

"Is she one of them?" Jacob asked, pointing to the women.

"Gracious no," Magnus chuckled. "She is not so typical." He motioned further into the home. "Just look for the woman with all the men around her, and you'll have found my Frances."

Suddenly, a raucous chortle broke out from further inside the home, taking Jacob by surprise. It sounded like a woman's chuckle, but it was unlike any laugh he had heard before—from a genteel woman, that is.

"Ah, I hear her now," Magnus murmured.

Magnus pulled Jacob along the entry hall to the rear of the home. In a living room bathed in warm candlelight, Jacob discovered a lone woman on a burgundy velvet couch. Her daring blue gown shimmered in the light and hugged her hourglass figure. She was surrounded by eager young men, their eyes ablaze with fascination.

"There she is," Magnus whispered. "The lovely Frances."

Jacob thought her features were more mysterious than beautiful. Her dark brown eyes were set close together, her forehead high, and her hair a lovely shade of honey blonde. The porcelain color of her skin stood out against the blue of her gown. With pink, elegantly carved cheekbones, heart-shaped pink lips and a dainty nose, she was everything a man would consider pretty. Her chin was the only flaw as far as Jacob could see.

21

Slightly small, it made her wonderfully curved jawline come to an abrupt end instead of complementing her features. But it was her hands that immediately distracted him. With long arms and graceful movements, her hands reminded him of a bird taking flight. They were magical to watch as she waved them in the air.

"She's exquisite," Magnus confided. "I met her at the library just after our first day of sophomore classes. I'm besotted with her. Even gave up smoking because she thinks cigarettes are foul."

"Then it must be love. What do you know about her?"

"An only child. Her father is a judge in Boston; her mother is dead. Her father has doted on her and encouraged her education. She has such brains and spirit, O'Connor. I've never known a woman like this."

Jacob surveyed the attentive men gathered around her. They were listening as she told some story, their eyes never leaving her face.

"Seems like you'll have a lot of suitors to fend off," Jacob professed. "How can you be so sure she's interested in you?"

"Magnus." Her voice was as seductive as her hands. "You made it."

Magnus turned to Jacob, grinning. "How could I not, dear Frannie."

She waved at him as he stepped into the room. "He is the only man brave enough to call me Frannie."

Magnus approached the couch while gesturing to his competitors. "I am distraught, my lady, to find I'm not the only suitor here vying for your affections."

The smirk that crossed her pink mouth was heavenly. "My affections, my dear Magnus, are still waiting for someone to arouse them."

The men around her snickered.

"I often find affections are not so much aroused, dear Frances, but enticed," Magnus returned.

Frances's smirk eased into a smile. "Different adjective, same meaning, sir."

Magnus leaned over to her couch. "Hardly. I find one best describes activities of a vertical nature, whereas the other is more for horizontal purposes."

"Of which I am sure you are quite skilled, Mr. Blackwell," she shot back.

Jacob was shocked. Such behavior was not proper for a lady, but somehow, from her, it was highly entertaining.

The men gathered around her were chuckling and elbowing each other.

Magnus touched his fingers to his lips, hiding his smile. "It's one of those extracurricular activities I pride myself on. But, unfortunately, there is no space for it on the admission form."

The men tittered even louder.

"It's a shame you can't get a Ph.D. in that. Then you can finally play doctor and be one," Frances replied, making the men around her break out in raucous laughter.

Jacob joined in with the rest of the men, laughing at the young woman's quips. She was unlike any creature he had ever met. Her brash personality, sharp wit, and ability to spar with a man won his admiration.

"Frannie, you're always such a challenge," Magnus said with a slight bow. He stood and waved to Jacob. "I have someone you must meet. Jacob O'Connor, my better half." Jacob scurried to the couch. "Jacob is a determined and talented architect student sure to set the world on fire."

Her eyes swept over him, and to Jacob's surprise, he did not see the usual hint of disdain he had grown used to when women looked at him. In Frances's eyes, he saw curiosity.

"So you are the friend I keep hearing so much about." She patted the spot on the couch next to her. "Magnus has gone on and on about you."

"About me?" Jacob's voice cracked again like it always did when he was nervous.

"Yes, he said he could not make a move without consulting you."

Jacob shifted his eyes to Magnus. "You said that?"

"Only when under the influence of alcohol," Magnus joked with a wink.

"I seem to remember it was coffee, Magnus, not alcohol," Frances corrected. "And your exact words were, 'He is what I strive to be when I grow up.'"

Magnus waved his hand at Frances. "You see, I was sober, which means nothing."

Laughing at his friend, Jacob had a seat next to Frances. "Well, Magnus has been very good to me."

Jacob was amazed at the translucent quality of her skin—the creaminess of it—and how she smelled like honeysuckle on the vine.

"Magnus, be a dear and get me some punch from the kitchen while I interrogate your friend." Frances smiled up at Magnus.

Magnus narrowed his skeptical eyes on Jacob. "Whatever she asks about me, O'Connor, lie."

Magnus hurried from the room. Jacob gulped back his sudden rush of nerves when her deep brown eyes turned to him.

The other men in the room had backed away from the couch as the din of several conversations filled the air.

"You are the only person who can tell me the truth about

Magnus Blackwell," she began.

"I have nothing but the kindest regard for my friend."

She dipped her head in agreement. "So I've heard. Excuse me for saying so, but you make a rather odd couple."

Jacob's insecurities bristled. "Why? Because he is rich, and I am poor?"

"No. You misunderstand me. I simply mean he is so outgoing, and you are so quiet. A man's past is not his future. My father taught me that." Frances removed one of the long gloves, exposing her beautiful hand. "He was an orphan, brought up on the streets, until one day a local lawyer in Boston took him in to work as a messenger. He taught my father to read, write, and was so impressed with him he eventually sent my father on to college." She nudged Jacob with her elbow. "I understand you better than you think, Jacob."

Hearing her speak his name took his breath away. It was the first time he had felt a connection with anyone other than Magnus since arriving on campus. He smiled his first relaxed smile of the evening and nodded his head.

"Thank you. I sometimes fear which part of me arrives into a room first: my circumstance or my reputation as being something of a hanger-on to my friend. Neither are what I want to be known for, but for now, such is my lot."

She patted his jacket sleeve. "Lots change. In the blink of an eye, your life can turn in a whole new direction."

"I keep waiting for that 'new direction,' but it has yet to present itself," Jacob admitted.

Magnus returned to the living room, carrying a glass cup filled with punch. When Frances saw him, Jacob noticed how her face lit up.

"You just have to have patience," she imparted, never taking her eyes off Magnus. "Patience does pay in the end."

Quickly negotiating around a few of the men in the room, Magnus arrived at the couch. His eager grin added an air of mischief to his green eyes.

"I hope O'Connor was kind while I was gone."

Frances took the punch from his extended hand and gave him a flirty smile. "Your secrets will always be safe with him, Magnus."

Jacob suddenly felt like a third wheel. He stood from the couch, eyeing the punch. "I think I will get a cup of that punch for me." He faced Frances and politely bowed. "Excuse me."

Magnus took the opportunity to sit down on the couch next to Frances. She smiled at his bravado.

"When may I come to call?" he whispered so as not to be heard by the other men in the room.

"'Call'?" She appeared genuinely surprised. "Are you so old-fashioned, Magnus. We don't need a chaperone."

"Then when can I see you?"

"There are rumors about you, Magnus. Rumors that might keep a proper young lady from spending time alone with you."

His light laughter received an annoyed smirk from her pink lips. "Now who is being old-fashioned?" His eyes pleaded with her. "Meet me at the library so we can talk without being observed."

Frances took a moment to consider his offer while twirling a loose tendril of her honey-blonde hair around her right finger.

The simple gesture mesmerized Magnus.

"Tomorrow then," she softly replied, letting go of the strand of hair. "After morning classes."

His heart soared with the promise of being alone with her. "I'm glad you like to take risks."

"Am I taking one with you, Magnus?"

Her taunt screamed for a reassuring return, but he thought better of it. Magnus stood from the sofa.

"Until tomorrow, Frannie."

Magnus knew his abrupt exit would only intrigue her. When he walked out of the room, Magnus could almost feel her eyes burning into the back of his black jacket. He reasoned getting to know Frances was going to be the highlight of his sophomore year.

Chapter Four

Falling

A closed black carriage pulled by two bay horses arrived at the curb in front of a small wood-framed house painted a light shade of blue. The driver secured the reins to the rig, climbed down from the bench and opened the carriage door.

The gas streetlights flickered as Magnus, dressed in a dashing black tuxedo with diamond studs down the front, exited the carriage. He strolled along the bricked path toward the front door of the home.

Magnus knocked with his white-gloved hand, and then removed his tall black hat.

Frances answered the door, beaming. She was wearing a pale yellow satin gown, trimmed in lace, which accentuated her perfectly curled honey-blonde hair. In her hands were a matching yellow silk pouch purse and white fan.

"Will this do?" She struck an amusing pose.

Magnus admired the way her gown accentuated her ravishing figure. "You look radiant, my dear."

The challenging smirk she sported for him was fleeting. "Why won't you tell me where we are going?" She stepped onto the porch.

Magnus shut her front door, holding back his grin. "It's a surprise."

She hooked her hand around his extended arm, and allowed Magnus to escort her down the three porch steps. "Another surprise? The other day, you surprised me with coffee from my favorite coffee shop. Last week, you surprised me with a picnic for lunch. The week before that, we had dinner at that wonderful little restaurant in Boston. What was it called?"

He strolled beside her to their waiting carriage. "Bonne Nourriture."

Frances nodded her head. "Yes, that was it, Bonne Nourriture. What other surprises can you have left?"

At the carriage, Magnus held out his hand to help her up the steps, but Frances just stood there, waiting for an answer.

Magnus released a long sigh. "To find out, you will have to get in this damn carriage, Frannie."

She gave in and placed her hand in his. "I never realized what an impatient man you are, Magnus Blackwell."

"There are many things you do not know about me, but I'm hoping to change that."

Frances curled her lips in a devious way. "Really? How do you propose to do that?"

He tilted closer to her while admiring her pink lips. "Get in."

Frances giggled and climbed into the carriage.

As he watched her, Magnus felt a wistful tug at his heart. She was everything he wanted— and more.

Their carriage stopped in front of the Winter Street entrance to the Boston Music Hall. It was the largest music venue in the city and home to the Boston Symphony Orchestra. The towering, white stucco facade with its gas-lit marquee took Frances's breath away as Magnus helped her from the carriage.

He loved observing her reaction. Things Magnus had found mundane and ordinary, he saw in a whole new way with her. Her enthusiasm was contagious, and he often considered how different his life would be with her by his side.

As Magnus turned to give their carriage driver some instructions for when to return, Frances went to the posters displayed by the entrance. Around her, women in diamonds and sumptuous gowns were being escorted by men in top hats and tails to the wide red-painted theater doors.

When he came alongside her, Magnus noticed her look of disbelief as she stared at a poster with three little Japanese maids on the front.

"We need to hurry inside, Frannie. The show is about to start."

"*The Mikado?*" She gaped at him. "You got tickets to *The Mikado* for me?"

He momentarily relished the shimmer of the gaslight in her brown eyes. "You said you always wanted to see it. Now you shall."

Frances cupped her gloved hand to his cheek. "Thank you."

He took her hand and held it tight. "Come on. Let's not miss it."

Inside the doors, the crowds were thinning out as people made their way along the deep red carpet to the theater. Ushers in red velvet uniforms with matching round box hats were handing out programs as people moved through the three large theater entrances.

Magnus took a program and handed it to Frances. He glimpsed the interior of the theater beyond the doors. Almost every seat in the large hall was taken. For once, he was grateful his family name, and his father's connections, had been able to procure tickets at the last minute to the sold out event.

Magnus and Frances were shown to their seats close to the stage by one of the sharply dressed ushers. Frances smiled as she spied the cathedral ceilings and the bright chandeliers of the hall.

They had not even taken their seats when the lights dimmed, and the orchestra in the pit below the stage began to play the overture.

Frances gave Magnus's hand a gentle squeeze as the red curtains on the stage slowly rose. The first actors appeared and Frances became entranced.

While admiring her perfect profile, Magnus's mind danced with his plans for her after the show, and the fiendish grin returned to his lips.

It was late when their carriage made the trip back to Cambridge. The gas streetlights outside of Magnus's window cast flickering shadows on the dusty road as the clip-clop of the horses' hooves carried in the air.

Frances sat a discreet distance away on the bench from Magnus, humming "Three Little Maids from School" while holding her program in her hands. Magnus removed his hat and gloves, putting them to the side of the bench. His finger tapped against his thigh in time with the gentle rocking motion of the carriage.

"You haven't stopped humming that tune since we left the theater."

Frances glanced at him. "It's very catchy."

"It *was* very catchy, Frannie." Magnus sucked in a long breath, tempering his irritation. "Are you going to hum it the entire way back to Cambridge?"

Frances playfully poked him with her fan. "You're no fun."

The gesture sent him over the edge. He wasn't sure if it was her infernal humming, the smell of honeysuckle on her skin, or the way her dress clung to her figure, but he was tired of holding back.

Magnus clasped her hand and pulled her across the bench. Frances gasped when Magnus swiftly wrapped her in his arms.

"Magnus, please," she begged, pushing against his chest.

"I think we have been old-fashioned long enough, Frannie."

Undone by the feel of her against him, Magnus kissed her hard on the lips.

At first, Frances resisted, but then she gave in to him. Magnus was in heaven as he tasted her; the heady aroma of honeysuckle mixed with the heat from her skin got him hard. He wanted to rip off her clothes and let his lips travel over every inch of her.

Right when he felt her curling into his chest—obviously eager for more—the carriage hit a pothole, and they were both tossed about on the bench, interrupting their kiss.

Frances regained her composure and took the opportunity to slide away from him.

Compounded by his escalating desire and Frances's timid retreat, Magnus's frustration took hold. "What is it?"

She hovered at the opposite end of the bench. "You've never kissed me like that before."

"It is how I've wanted to kiss you since the day we met."

Her brown eyes seethed with rage. "What else have you wanted, Magnus?"

"You know what I want, Frannie. Do I have to spell it out for you?"

Flustered by his admission, she blushed. "I'm not ready for that."

"I thought you were progressive," he teased with a leering grin.

Frances avoided his dissecting gaze while pulling her shawl tighter around her shoulders. "I still believe some things should be saved for marriage."

Bored with her reluctance, Magnus turned his attention to the window. "I don't like waiting for what I want, Frannie."

"Pressuring me won't change my answer, Magnus. I will not have sex with you until we are man and wife."

Magnus kept his eyes focused on the passing houses. "If that is what you want, my dear, then I will abide by your wishes."

A deafening silence pervaded the carriage. Magnus had already made up his mind that if she would not give him what he needed, then he would have to turn somewhere else to fulfill his needs. Until he could change dear Frances's mind, he would find other ways to indulge his fantasies.

The carriage arrived at her rental home on the edge of Harvard campus. Magnus escorted Frances to her door. Her mood had been reserved since his confession, but Magnus thought it best for her to know his true intentions.

Magnus opened her door while Frances stood to the side, clutching her program.

"Thank you for a wonderful evening, Magnus."

Magnus gave her a polite bow and waited as she stepped inside the door.

With Frances safely returned to her home, Magnus rushed from her front porch.

At the carriage, Magnus looked up to the driver. "1612 Ridge Lane."

The driver nodded and waited as Magnus climbed into the carriage before he clucked to the fine bay horses to proceed on.

The carriage jostled to and fro along the bumpy street while Magnus's temper surged. He recalled the sweetness of Frances's kiss, her skin, her smell, and he vowed to one day have her beneath him. Either under the guise of marriage or without the church's consent, he would have her.

Soon, Magnus arrived in the area of town where the faculty of Harvard lived. The houses were all the same. Cookie-cutter homes built quickly and cheaply to accommodate the growing needs of the university.

When the carriage stopped in front of a square white clapboard house with green shutters and a small garden, Magnus let out a relieved sigh.

Magnus sent the driver on his way, assuring the man he was no longer needed.

At the green door, he lifted the brass knocker and let it fall with a loud *thud*.

The flickering light from a lamp materialized in a dark

window next to the door. Knowing he'd been heard, Magnus lifted the knocker once again. After the loud knock had echoed around the still porch, he heard the lock on the door click open.

In a white shawl over her white nightgown, the occupant of the home held up an oil lamp, inspecting Magnus.

He was leaning against the doorframe. His eyes swept over her sheer nightgown. "Good evening, Maria. Is it too late to take you up on your offer?"

"I thought you said it was a bad idea."

"I changed my mind." Magnus glimpsed the dark house behind her. "Is your husband still away at his conference?"

She nodded, stepping back from the door. "He'll be gone until tomorrow night."

"I'm so very glad to hear that." Magnus pushed away from the doorframe and entered her home.

A few months later, when a torrid winter gripped the campus, Jacob entered the Gore Hall Library, eager to get a few hours of study in before bed. Inside the cramped facility, piled high with books from floor to ceiling, he spotted Frances waiting just off to the side of the front desk.

In a black duster with her pale peach dress peeking out from underneath, she feigned a smile for Jacob as she saw him approaching.

Instantly, he was worried. The fake smile only added to the sadness in her brown eyes. Sadness he knew had been placed there by Magnus. Rumors about their relationship were swirling around the campus, but Jacob knew the truth.

"Frances," he said, going up to her. "What a pleasant

surprise."

Her smirk was laced with irritation. "Did he send you to make his apologies?"

Jacob took her hand and led her away from the librarian's desk. "Did who send me?"

"Come on, Jacob. Do I look like a fool?"

Jacob stopped in a private corner, letting go of her hand. "What is it?"

"Did he send you?"

"No," he avowed. "Last time I spoke to him was this morning. He wanted me to take notes for him in our theory lecture. He said he had something to do."

She snorted. "More like he had someone to do."

"Frances, please." Jacob blushed. "You shouldn't be so ..."

"What? Truthful?"

Jacob shook his head. "I was thinking more along the lines of indiscreet, but I guess truthful is more accurate."

"How long has he been seeing her, Jacob? Tell me."

He eyed the ribbon of lace around her long neck and, for a moment, itched to touch it. In fact, he itched to touch her. Perhaps not itched, but burned like he had burned for no other woman. Ever since their meeting, he had fought to drive her from his mind. Magnus had claimed her—reason enough to stay away. However, reason never applied when a woman was involved. Jacob had once heard Martin Fogle say the fairer sex muddled all matters. Now he understood what he had meant.

"She is a dalliance, Frances, nothing more," he confessed, unable to keep the truth from her. "I know he won't stay interested in her for long. She is not you." Jacob waved his hand down her figure. "He is besotted with you, as he has told me time and again."

Frances clasped her gloved hands together. "And if I were to allow him to continue with our relationship, what guarantee do I have that another dalliance will not come along later? What about when we are engaged or even married? Can you give me such assurance, Jacob?"

He longed to tell her everything would be fine, but he couldn't. Magnus was his friend, but Frances had also become his friend, and he could not lie to one to save the other. It was not in him to be so cruel.

"He is a man, Frances. A man of means and used to getting his way. I know the woman he is seeing means nothing to him. I wish I could say he would never hurt you again, but I can't. Magnus takes what he wants, no matter who he hurts in the process."

Her eyes softened as she examined his features. "And here I selfishly thought I was the only one he has hurt. What has he done to you?"

Jacob opened his mouth to speak, and then he saw a smattering of students hurrying into the library. Glancing back at her, he took her elbow.

"We should speak somewhere in private."

Frances escorted him to the entrance. "There is a lovely little coffee shop off campus that I adore. It serves the best hot chocolate. Perhaps we could go there."

Jacob stopped at the door. "But it is so cold. I do not want you to catch a chill. Maybe we should go someplace closer."

"I'm a lot tougher than I look, Jacob. Let's have some hot chocolate and talk. I'm in dire need of a friend at the moment— someone to whom I can confide all of my troubles."

The Vieux Carre Coffee Shop was just off campus and set into a corner of a three-story, red-bricked building on Massachusetts Avenue. They stamped the snow from their feet and removed their coats, still trying to warm up after their frigid walk.

Frances admired the posters of New Orleans covering the white walls. She smiled as she took in the long, romantic balconies and quaint Creole homes.

Jacob found a black iron table for two in a corner and held out a chair for Frances. "Why do you like this place?"

"Have you ever been to New Orleans, Jacob?" she inquired, taking her seat.

"Hardly. Boston is about as far south as I have ever been." He took the chair next to her.

A waiter in a white apron, white shirt, and with a red handkerchief around his neck came to their table. Frances ordered two hot chocolates and then sat quietly in her chair, waiting for the waiter to leave.

Jacob decided it would be best to get the painful part out of the way. "How did you hear about her?"

When Frances raised her head, her eyes were bright with anger. "Men are worse gossips than women, if you ask me. Several men saw him leaving her house in the early hours of the morning. I didn't think he was stupid enough to have an affair with a professor's wife."

"He claims she initiated it."

"'He claims'?" Her eyebrows went up. "Do you believe him?"

"He has no reason to lie to me."

Frances snickered. "Whereas I am a woman, so he has every reason to lie to me."

Jacob sighed and shifted his chair closer to hers, hoping to keep the other customers in the shop from overhearing their conversation. "You must understand something about Magnus; he has the best intentions, but the worst discipline. He wants to be faithful to you, and I think he will, eventually. He is just sowing his oats. When he has matured, when he has gotten it out of his system, he will come back to you. Do not take it so personally. He cares for you more than you can realize."

Frances shook her head, appearing unconvinced. "Would you run around on a woman you care for, Jacob?"

"No, I would not. If I cared for someone, I would never hurt them. I'm not like Magnus. I have no wild oats to sow."

Her hand went to his. "You are a good man, Jacob." She gave his hand a squeeze and then let it go. "In all the time we have spent together, you have never told me about yourself."

"All the time we have spent together has been with Magnus, and I ... I can never get a word in when he is around."

Her light laugh sounded as if the pain in her heart had eased somewhat. "Yes, he does tend to suck all the air out of the room, doesn't he?"

"Like no one I have ever known."

She removed her gloves and set them to the side. "I want to hear about you, Jacob. For the rest of the afternoon, I want to talk about you, your life, and your dreams."

"What about Magnus?"

Frances waved a casual hand in the air, distracting him with its graceful motion. "Today, it is just you and me—two friends, getting to know each other and sharing some hot chocolate. Let's not talk of Magnus anymore."

Jacob secretly thanked divine providence for bringing him such an opportunity. To be able to spend some precious time with the woman who was secretly capturing his heart was more than he could have hoped.

"Start at the beginning," she insisted. "Tell me about how you came to Harvard. I want to know how Jacob O'Connor came to be seated here with me."

Chapter Five

Downfall

"**M**arriage? You can't be serious, O'Connor."

Jacob pulled at the tight ascot tie around his neck as he watched Magnus pace in front of him. "I love her, Magnus. I know when she called it off with you last year you were very angry, and I waited weeks before I asked her to dinner just like you requested, but I cannot deny my feelings any longer to you or to her."

Magnus stopped in front of the red velvet chaise that graced the corner of his grand living room. He promptly sat down and stared at Jacob. "So you haven't asked her yet."

Jacob shook his head as he stood in the entranceway. He'd been afraid of Magnus's reaction, and had waited several minutes on the front porch before ringing the bell. Magnus had moved into the modest two-bedroom home soon after their freshman year. Jacob had spent more time in the house than in his dorm room, but now he felt like an unwanted stranger.

"When do you plan to propose?" Magnus finally inquired, breaking a long spell of silence.

"Tonight." Jacob gripped the brim of his only good black hat. "I'm taking her to dinner at Marvel's."

Magnus stood up. "Marvel's? How can you afford that? It's the most expensive restaurant in Cambridge."

"I have saved some money, Magnus. My job at the administration offices does pay pretty well."

Magnus moved closer. Jacob eyed his red dressing robe and starched white shirt underneath, envying his dapper appearance even in such informal clothes.

"Do you even have a ring?"

Jacob shook his head. "We don't need one."

Magnus snorted. "Of course you need one. How could you marry a woman like Frances without a proper engagement ring?"

"It's not about the ring, Magnus. It's about the life we will make together."

His short cackle made Jacob's blood run cold. "What kind of life are you going to give her, O'Connor? She is used to the finer things. Can you afford that?"

"After I graduate, I will get a job, and then I can buy her the things she wants."

Magnus inched up to him, his green eyes ablaze. "If you have it all figured out, then why are you here?"

Jacob confronted his furious scowl. "To get your blessing. You're my friend, and I wanted to make sure you are all right with it before I ask."

Magnus turned away. His hands clasped behind his back, he strolled to the wide window in the living room that overlooked the street. "I told you when you first asked her out it was fine with me, and now that you want to marry her, I am still fine with it." He glanced back at his friend. "I'm more than fine with it. I'm pleased. You're a better man than I am, O'Connor. You've always been the better man."

"Thank you, Magnus, but I would never have met Frances without you." Jacob took a step back into the entrance hall. "I should go. She will be waiting for me."

Magnus walked up to him and extended his hand. "She will say yes, O'Connor. Not to worry."

Jacob took his hand and shook it. "Thank you, Magnus."

Magnus let go of his hand and motioned to his front door. "Go on."

With an exuberant smile, Jacob rushed to the door while Magnus looked on. Once outside, Jacob spied the carriage waiting by the curb and jogged toward it. Bursting with happiness that Magnus had been appeased, Jacob climbed into the back of the carriage, anxious to see his Frances again.

At the window, Magnus looked on as the carriage carrying Jacob O'Connor pulled away from the curb. His fists were clenched and he could feel the veins in his neck pumping with such ferocity that Magnus swore he was coming apart.

"That son of a bitch!"

How could that simpleton with nothing to his name but some second-hand clothes possibly win the heart of his Frances? She was his, meant for him, and even though they had not worked the first time round, Magnus was convinced with patience and perseverance he could make her his. But now

O'Connor had stepped in and destroyed his plans for the woman.

Magnus had spent hours plotting his attack—how he would break down her defenses and make her give in to him. He had dreamt of taking her supple body in his arms, thrusting into her, and making her cry out in pain as he broke through her maidenhead. She would have been his utterly and completely— but not anymore.

His fist came crashing down on the windowsill, sending a tremor through the glass. He had to win her back. Somehow, he was going to make sure Frances McGee ended up in his bed.

"Who was that?"

The woman's voice came from the oak staircase.

Magnus let out a long hiss between his gritted teeth. Time enough to scheme later. He had another temptress waiting for him. And even though her body was not as young or as pure as Frances's, she was no less beguiling.

"It was just O'Connor," he told the woman as he entered the hall.

Gliding down the steps, still wrapped in his bedsheet, her long brown curls were tossed about her head as her deep blue eyes focused on him.

"Did you tell him about us?"

He met her as she came to rest on the bottom step. "No. He doesn't know. No one knows." He took her hand. "Not even your husband."

She eased past him and went into the living room. "Tell me, Magnus, how many married women are you going to fuck before you finally find a wife of your own?"

He followed her into the room. "Fuck?" He grinned. "I thought you were an upstanding woman of moral virtue,

44

Constance."

"My husband may be the dean of Harvard's School of Divinity, but I am far from virtuous." She seductively dropped one shoulder of the sheet wrapped around her. "That's why I'm here. Virtue isn't all it's cracked up to be, especially in the bedroom. I like impure thoughts."

He came up to her. "Probably the reason why you like my company so much."

She dropped the sheet from her other shoulder. "It's one of the reasons."

Magnus slowly began pulling the sheet off her. His eyes grew wider as full breasts and round hips appeared. Magnus tossed the sheet to the floor and licked his lips. "I'm having several impure thoughts right now. Want to take a guess at what they are?"

She tugged at the belt of his robe. After she had pushed the heavy material away from his shoulders, she glanced down at his erection. "I think I'm starting to get an idea."

Magnus pulled off the white shirt he had hurriedly put on to answer the door. Free of his clothes, he reached for her, clasping his arm around her waist. As her sweet perfume hit his nose, Magnus became consumed with memories of Frances. Her smell of honeysuckle, the way she moved, the curve of her throat, and the taste of her pink heart-shaped lips—all of it came back to him in a tidal wave of emotion.

"What is it?" Constance asked, stroking his right cheek.

Magnus stared at the woman before him as if she were a stranger. Why was she not Frances? Why was this woman, who he had been fucking for months, not the woman he had dreamed of every night when he went to sleep?

"Do you think it is possible to remain faithful to a woman you love but still be with other women?" he queried, thinking out loud.

Her laughter was harsh and nothing like the sweet melody of Frances's titterings. "You can't fuck one woman and be faithful to another, Magnus."

"But there must be some way." He held her at arm's length. "Your husband is a man of theology. Surely, he must have discussed how men can remain faithful in spirit."

"In spirit?" Constance shook her head and wrapped her fingers around his cock. "Whether this goes in a woman or not is the difference between being faithful and being sinful."

He removed her hand. "What about if it goes in a man? Is it still being unfaithful?"

Her face fell. "You're not serious. That's an affront to God."

His malicious smile returned. "But is it being unfaithful if a man sleeps with another man and not a woman?"

Constance reached for her sheet on the floor. "You're drunk again."

He held her wrist, keeping her from collecting the sheet. "Is it?"

Her blue eyes flickered with uncertainty. "I ... I don't know."

"Guess," he directed, tightening his grip on her wrist.

"That hurts, Magnus."

"Answer the question. Would you feel your husband had been unfaithful to you if he slept with another man?"

She gasped, the fear gaining ground in her eyes. "I think I would feel hurt but perhaps not as upset as if it had been with another woman."

He let go of her wrist. "Why?"

Constance inched away from him. "Another woman would be a threat to our marriage, but a man?" She shrugged. "He could never marry him."

"So he would have remained faithful, technically."

"Technically?" Constance snatched up her sheet. "You're talking nonsense, Magnus. I'm going home."

While Constance wrapped the sheet around her curvy figure, a surge of victory made Magnus's cock grow hard. There was a way to satiate his lust but remain faithful to his Frances.

"Don't go," he purred, winding the end of the sheet around his hand. "We haven't finished with our fun."

Constance was relieved to see his lust returning. She allowed him to unravel the sheet from her body. Once naked, she snuggled against his muscular chest.

"I guess I could stay a little while longer."

He led her to the red velvet chaise. "We've never done it here."

She giggled as she reclined on the chaise, spreading her legs temptingly apart.

Magnus raised one side of his mouth with a sly smile. "Turn over."

Constance arched a dark eyebrow, amused. Flipping over on her stomach, she raised her hips for him.

He pulsated with energy as he saw her exquisite ass moving back and forth. His hand slid into her folds. Magnus ran his finger over her clit, getting her good and wet for him. Constance was panting and rocking as he brought her closer to release. When he knew she was about to come, he traced her wetness between her butt cheeks.

"I have a new game in mind."

"Don't stop, baby," Constance begged.

Magnus ran his tongue between her butt cheeks, preparing her. His thumb worked his saliva into her while his other hand reached for her folds. He pinched her clit and Constance groaned.

She was so ready he could barely hold back. Magnus hooked his arm around her waist and held her tight. When he pressed the tip of his cock between her butt cheeks, Constance began to struggle.

"Magnus, what are you doing?"

He pushed into her, and whispered, "I'm being faithful."

Chapter Six

Finding Fate

Magnus stepped from his carriage outside of Trinity Church, located in the Back Bay of Boston, and raised his eyes to the massive tower. The Richardson Romanesque design—named after its builder Henry Hobson Richardson—reminded Magnus of something out of a Friedrich Nietzsche nightmare with its clay roof and polychrome, rough stone exterior, and heavy use of arches along the facade.

"Oh, it's so beautiful." The honey-blonde behind him gazed up at the church. "I heard all the elite of Boston belong to this church."

Magnus patiently smiled into the innocent, blue eyes of his date. She was another Radcliffe Experiment. This one he'd met after getting lost in the Gore Hall Library. He was supposed to meet up with a classmate to collect a few papers he had paid to have written for him but, instead, ended up chatting the evening away with the bubbly freshman.

"Linda, perhaps we should go inside," he suggested.

Linda giggled—she did that a lot—and then gathered up the skirts of her pearl and pink dress. The ostentatious outfit was made of yards of folded fabric, topped with layers of lace, and even had a matching hat that Magnus thought resembled a capsizing boat.

They climbed the steps to the three gothic arches that marked the entrance to the church. Magnus kept an eye out for any of his classmates from Harvard. O'Connor had told him he had invited the entire graduating class in architecture to the wedding, but Magnus knew many would not attend. They had been tolerant of Jacob O'Connor yet had never embraced him as a peer. Magnus knew many saw him as a peasant, a poor boy living among the elite because of luck and not because of his birthright. In that way, he hated his class. O'Connor was the best of men. However, as he considered the prize O'Connor had taken from him, Magnus's rage returned. The upstart had tread into territory he would one day regret. Frances could belong to no one but Magnus.

"I heard Ellie Brightfield say Frances's father, Judge McGee, invited over three hundred guests. All of the social set of Boston will be here," Linda chirped beside him.

Magnus's green eyes went over her gown. "Aren't you glad you are dressed for the occasion?"

Linda giggled yet again. "I stole it from my mother's wardrobe. I knew you would want to be seen with the prettiest girl at the wedding."

"And so I will," he replied, his voice oozing contempt. But his vicious mood was lost on Linda.

A social climber from a modest family, Magnus was well aware of what Linda wanted from him. She saw her escort as a wealthy man who could provide her with a very comfortable life. Magnus, however, had other plans.

The interior of the church momentarily distracted Magnus. Inlaid with mosaic-painted walls, high arches, and colorful stained-glass windows, the structure reminded him of the Gothic cathedrals of medieval Europe combined with the mysterious allure of some of the world's most beautiful mosques. It was an interesting hodgepodge of styles, beautiful in scope but also a bit perplexing.

Magnus gazed up at the intricate patterns painted on the ceiling, when he felt Linda tug on his arm.

"Where do we sit, bride or groom, since you know both so well?"

He gave her a kind smile. "Why don't you decide for us."

"Bride. The better people will be sitting on that side of the church."

He wanted to object. Magnus felt he should offer support to his friend, plus the pews on groom's side of the church were appallingly empty, but he said nothing. Let Linda have her moment in the sun. Come nightfall, in the confines of his bedroom, she would pay dearly for her folly.

The guests arrived in a steady stream. They strolled along the red runner between the pews to their seats. In the background, the great organ from the chancel rang out some celebratory tune, but Magnus's heart was unmoved.

The groom and his best man appeared from a door to the right of the sanctuary. Magnus felt a momentary spark of genuine emotion for his friend, but his bitterness quickly brushed the feeling away. In a gray morning suit with a knotted gray silk tie, a white carnation in his lapel, and bright white gloves, Jacob made a dashing groom.

Jacob approached his spot in front of the altar. He saw Magnus and gave a slight wave.

Magnus, being the consummate gentleman, dipped his head to Jacob. He was just glad he did not have to participate in the fiasco. Jacob had asked him to stand by him during the ceremony, but Magnus had graciously refused, citing Frances's possible discomfort.

"Did you see Abigale Hawthorne is here?" Linda whispered next to him. "She's the absolute queen of the social season in Boston."

Magnus rolled his eyes. "Yes, I know."

"Do you know her?" Linda asked, intrigued by his comment.

"My dear, I know everyone in this church, and they know me."

"I keep forgetting about that." Linda cocked her head to the side as she appraised his profile. "You don't act like the rest of them. You're not snooty."

He chuckled, amused by her insight. "I often find the people of my class to be boring and predictable. It's the ones who have had to struggle to get somewhere in the world who have much more interesting stories to tell."

"Is that why you befriended, O'Connor? Everyone says it is because you took pity on him—with him being an orphan and all."

Magnus studied the dainty curve of her jaw, her lightly painted pink lips, the blonde curls peeking out beneath her hideous hat, and the painted breath of blush on her pale cheeks. How could he describe to such an empty-headed little thing what

Jacob O'Connor meant to him?

"I did not take pity on O'Connor. I genuinely liked the man—still do. He has something I rarely see in people."

"What is that?"

"Integrity."

Linda raised her pretty eyes to the sanctuary. "My father says integrity is nothing but a poor man's capital because it is all he has to bargain with."

Magnus grinned. "Your father is right, dear girl. In the end, even integrity has a price."

The peal of the bridal procession rose from the chancel organ, silencing all conversations around them. Magnus stood and gazed down the long aisle to the back of the church, waiting for the arrival of his obsession. For that is what she had become to him. Ever since the evening O'Connor had arrived on his doorstep announcing his intentions to marry Frances, Magnus had been obsessed with making her his. He had convinced himself it must be love, and such love could never be denied.

After the long procession of bridesmaids wearing lovely heather gowns with sprigs of heather in their hair, the congregation waited for the arrival of the bride. When she appeared on the arm of her father, the esteemed Judge McGee, Magnus was overcome.

She was the most beautiful woman he had ever seen. With a tapered waist, bows at the shoulders, and a cathedral train, the silk brocade dress shimmered in the morning light coming through the church windows. Her bouquet of honeysuckle and white roses matched the white lace roses sewn into the fabric of her dress. As she approached, Magnus was mesmerized by the glowing smile on her face. She was radiant, pure, and the epitome of feminine beauty. He ached for her to be walking down the aisle to him instead of Jacob, but his resolve returned as she glided past him, dipping her head in acknowledgment. One day, she would wear that smile again, but it would be for his benefit and no one else's.

"What a beautiful bride," Linda whispered. "I bet that dress cost a fortune."

Magnus rolled his eyes. Pretty little Linda was getting on his nerves.

The reception was at the judge's residence on Mount Vernon Street in the trendy neighborhood of Beacon Hill. Their carriage, pulled by two sleek black horses, arrived in front of the Federal-style mansion. Composed of red brick with black decorative shutters, the opulent home had an odd array of Corinthian pilasters on the second and third-floor facade. The first floor had recessed bricked arches ornamented with Chinese fretwork balconies in iron. There was even a garish, octagonal cupola. All in all, he found the architectural mingling of styles off-putting.

"She grew up here?" Linda took in the stately home. "And she thinks she will be happy with your poor architect friend?"

Magnus took her hand and helped her from the carriage. "Love does strange things to people."

"I doubt it will last," Linda conceded. "I had a friend who married for love. He was a banker with little family money. They only stayed together for a year."

"What happened to your friend?" he asked as they climbed the steps to the front door.

"She's the mistress of a Rockefeller."

Magnus chuckled. "Well, that is a step up."

Inside the home, they were guided down a long entrance hallway by a butler who showed them to the gardens. A variety of wide flower beds that catered to the Victorian fascination with large, showy plants greeted them. Purple irises, pink and white peonies, trees of red roses, purple crape myrtles, and fastidiously trimmed Royal Empress Trees lined the walkway.

Linda all but squealed with delight. "How lovely."

Magnus was not taking in the colorful summer foliage. His eyes were scanning the guests for any signs of the bride.

"So glad you could make it, Magnus," a robust voice called.

When Magnus turned, he saw the very round figure of Judge McGee extending his hand. The judge's bright red cheeks reminded Magnus of two cherries.

Magnus gave his hand a firm shake. "Judge, good to see you again." He gestured to Linda. "My escort, Miss Linda Paddington of New York."

"How's your father, Magnus?" The judge patted his protruding belly beneath his red, silk vest.

"He's well. I just spent some time with him back at our family home on Mount Desert Island."

"I've heard he means to renovate the estate there," the judge confided.

"Yes, Father has great plans for the old manor house there. He wants to add on to the family home—make it much grander than the current one. He has architects working on the plans as we speak."

"What about you?" The judged nudged him. "Why don't you plan the construction? You are, after all, soon to be a graduate of the architecture program like my son-in-law."

"But I lack O'Connor's talent, sir. He will be a much better architect than I will."

"Oh, I see Eliza Benniger," Linda spoke up. "I must go and say hello. If you gentlemen will excuse me."

Magnus and Judge McGee bowed their heads as Linda scurried down the few brick steps that led to the gardens at the rear of the home.

The Judge eyed the girl's bouncy step, and then his deep brown eyes returned to Magnus. "I was sorry you and my daughter did not make a match of it. I think she would have been happier with a man who can keep her rather than a man who will struggle to do so."

Magnus gritted his teeth. "O'Connor will do right by her."

The judge's chubby face suddenly took on a grave appearance. "I know he is your friend, Magnus, and I would be lying if I said I was happy about the match, but Frances loves him. I could not deny my permission when I saw how happy he made her."

"You did the right thing," Magnus assured him. "Imagine the scandal if you had withheld your consent. They were determined to do this—better to let them go through with it. Who knows where it will lead."

The judge's deep chortle turned a few heads. "You sound like a man who can see into the future and tell their fortunes."

Magnus simply smiled. "If that were the case, I would be telling my fortune, not theirs."

Judge McGee gestured to his lavish gardens. "Enjoy yourself, Magnus. And give my best to your father."

The judge waddled away to mingle with his other guests. Magnus went to the only place in the garden he yearned to be: the bar.

The three quick flutes of champagne Magnus downed

helped to ease the burning in his gut. But the annoying feeling reignited with a fury when he saw Jacob and Frances coming toward him, hand in hand.

"Magnus." Jacob held out his hand. "So glad you are here."

Frances leaned in and pecked his cheek. She smelled of her honeysuckle perfume. Her lips were warm and tender on his skin. Magnus went to reach for her just as Frances pulled away.

"We are so glad you could share this day with us," she said in her musical voice.

Magnus got ahold of himself. "I would not have missed it for the world."

He could tell by the way Frances was wringing her hands together she was uncomfortable. She had always done that with him right before an argument about something that had troubled her about his actions, usually his actions with other women.

"I must find a place for the photographer to take our wedding picture. He says he must have a certain light," she remarked with an elusive smile. "Jacob, I know you would like to have a long visit with Magnus, but please don't forget about our other guests."

As she turned away, a hole formed in Magnus's heart, a large black hole that he knew only her presence would fill.

"So how was Mount Desert Island?" Jacob inquired. "Did you speak with your father?"

Magnus peered into his friend's warm brown eyes. "Yes, he wants me to take a position in his architectural firm after graduation next year. They are currently working on the designs of the new estate."

"Lucky dog." Jacob rubbed his gloved hands together. "I haven't even gotten a bite from any architecture firms."

"What about Fogle, Hardwick, and Hillman? I thought you

were going to go back to them?"

Jacob shrugged. "I am if I have no other offers. But they will bring me in as a draftsman at half the wages of an architect. With a wife and house to keep up, things will be tight for a while." He clamped his hand around Magnus's forearm. "What I wouldn't give to be in your shoes, building such a grand estate. Oh, the things you will get to design, to see constructed. I envy you."

Magnus thought of what he envied about his friend's life, especially the wedding night ahead of him. "You have much to be thankful for, O'Connor. You never know, you may get to build that grand estate one day."

"We shall see." Jacob viewed the reception around him. "Did your father say anything else?" His eyes returned to his friend. "I know you said the two of you rarely got along."

Magnus snorted. "We still don't get along. I have been seriously thinking about getting away for a while. Perhaps putting a little distance between me, my father, Boston—all of it."

Jacob appeared surprised. "Really? But we start back to school for our senior year in just a few short weeks. Where would you go?"

Magnus ran through a list of cities in his head, trying to come up with an answer. Since his Frances had taken another for a husband, the idea of getting away seemed even more intriguing. He did not know if he could stand by and watch as their happiness played out before him. Perhaps a little distance was just what he needed.

"New Orleans," slipped out before he could stop it.

"New Orleans?" Jacob balked. "Since when? You've never mentioned that city before."

Magnus watched as Frances glided across the lawn, smiling and laughing with her guests. "It's something newly acquired. I've always had a fondness for all things Southern, and the architecture there is worthy of some study."

Jacob shook his head. "Wish I could join you, Magnus."

"So do I, O'Connor."

"When will you leave?"

Magnus spotted Frances across the gardens laughing with a small group of women. The sunlight danced in her hair, and her angelic features twisted his gut into a million knots. "As soon as I can make the arrangements. Best to get some wild oats sown before my senior year begins. After graduation, I will be too weighed down by the responsibilities of life to have such a vacation."

Jacob reached out his hand. "Sow some wild oats for both of us, my friend."

Magnus smirked. "That I will do. As a gentleman, you have my word."

Magnus had consumed too much champagne. His head pounded, and his vision was blurred. Every bump and jolt of the carriage only compounded his discomfort.

"I think she looked radiant," the still perky Linda chimed in next to him.

"That is open to interpretation," he muttered.

"I never did understand why she broke it off with you and went with O'Connor. She could have had so much more with you."

He turned his glassy eyes to her. "She had a different set of needs than I."

"Needs?" Linda scrunched her blue eyes together. "What

needs?"

"There are things a man needs to do with a woman."

Linda sat back in her carriage seat, holding her pink, silk pouch purse in her lap. "Are you talking about sex?"

He nodded. "If you like."

"Sex is a sin before marriage, Magnus. I plan on saving myself for my wedding night like Frances did."

The thought of Jacob O'Connor getting the prize he deserved made the pounding in his head even worse. "There are ways to save your virginity for your wedding night, Linda, but still enjoy yourself. You and I can both remain faithful to our future spouses."

Linda frowned. "We shouldn't be discussing such things. It's not proper." She sat for a moment and then gazed up at him. "What ways?"

Magnus grinned. He loved the curious gleam in her eye. It was so seductive. "It's hard to explain." He shimmied across the bench to her side. "But I could show you."

The wheels of debate spun in her little head, making Magnus grow hard at the thought of having her naked ass bent over the chair in his bedroom. She would be such a tight fuck.

"What would I have to do?" she eventually posed with an inquisitive lilt in her voice.

"Do?" He took her hand. "Nothing. I will do everything." Knocking his hand on the top of the carriage, he waited for the slot behind his driver to open.

"Yes, sir?" the driver queried.

"Change of plans. We won't be going to Ms. Paddington's hotel. Take us back to my home."

The driver with the bushy black eyebrows curtly nodded and then shut the slot.

"Are you sure we can do this, Magnus?" Linda sounded more childlike than ever. "What if someone finds out?"

The change in her tone aroused him. "No one will know. You will enjoy it, my dear. No need to worry. You are in the best of hands."

Chapter Seven

New Orleans

Hotel Monteleone on Royal and Iberville Streets in the heart of the French Quarter offered glorious views of New Orleans from Magnus's fifth-floor balcony. The alluring smells of Creole food cooking and the tempting calls of the street corner merchants, selling anything from voodoo remedies to children's toys, delighted Magnus. Gazing out every morning over the terracotta-tiled rooftops of the Creole cottages and townhomes gave Magnus an uncanny sense of peace. New Orleans had turned out to be just what he had needed.

He had arrived two weeks before and spent most of his days walking the quaint city streets, entranced by the unique architecture. The tightly packed homes, wrought-iron balconies, and the mixture of Caribbean, French, and Spanish architectural styles had enthralled him. Magnus had dined in the numerous outstanding restaurants, watched the powerful ships maneuver the rough currents of the mighty river, and soaked in the unhurried Southern elegance of a city unfettered by the demands of the modern world. But just when Magnus was making plans to return home to Boston, a new diversion presented itself.

He walked into the Carousel Bar one night after attending an evening of Mozart at the French Opera House when he heard the most irritating laugh—like a donkey stuck in the mud. In a corner booth of the bar, decorated with gold-framed mirrors and bright lights to resemble a carousel, were three gentlemen with their heads together and an assortment of empty glasses on their table.

"Who is that? The odd-looking gentleman with the rather long face," Magnus requested of his bartender as he removed his white gloves.

"Mr. Wilde, sir. He's from London."

Magnus took his usual seat at the round bar. "Rather loud for an Englishman, isn't he? I thought they were the quiet sort."

Jasper rolled his gray eyes. "This one is Irish, sir."

Magnus put his gloves and top hat on the bar. "Which would explain the drinks on the table."

Jasper selected an old-fashioned glass from a shelf. "Do you want your usual whiskey soda, Mr. Blackwell?"

Magnus was about to say yes when a tall, lanky man with a long face and short dark hair bellied up to the bar. "Give the man a Sazerac on me, Jasper," the intruder said with a familiar brogue.

Magnus confronted the stranger's dark brown eyes. "Thank you, Mr. ....?"

"Wilde, Oscar Wilde. And you're Magnus Blackwell of the Blackwells in New England."

"How did you know that?"

"I heard one of the hotel staff mention your name. I met your father once when I was in New England a few years back. He was looking to invest in some speculative ventures in the publishing world. He was very amicable to my ideas, but then I had to return to England unexpectedly and never got the chance to follow up with him. Reynolds Blackwell was a gracious man."

Magnus softly snickered. Gracious was not the word that came to mind when he thought of his father. Satisfied with his explanation, Magnus motioned to the seat next to him. "What is it you do in England, Mr. Wilde?"

Picking at the sleeves of his gray dinner jacket, Oscar sat down. "I am currently the editor of a magazine—*The Woman's World*. We publish fiction pieces, recipes, and general informative articles for women."

Magnus observed as Jasper rinsed two old-fashioned glasses with absinthe. "I would gather I'm the wrong sex to have ever heard of it."

Oscar chuckled, tossing his head to the side. "It's total rubbish. I just work there to pay the bills until I can pursue my other venture, writing."

Jasper filled the glasses with ice and then poured cognac and added three dashes of Peychaud's Bitters to the glasses.

Magnus directed his attention to his new acquaintance. "What do you write, Mr. Wilde?"

"Please, call me Oscar. We are two gentlemen of the world, are we not?" He patted Magnus's right shoulder. "I write poetry for now, but I'm looking for an idea for a novel. One of the reasons I'm in New Orleans. Such a city is ripe with stories. And I needed to get out of London for a while."

Jasper was adding lemon peel garnishes to their drinks when Magnus posed, "What drove you from London?"

Oscar laughed or more guffawed in his bray-like style.

Magnus grinned, entertained by the sound.

"My nagging wife, two small boys who never stop crying, bill collectors, overbearing parents, the list goes on and on." His dark eyes sized up Magnus. "I've watched you in this hotel for almost two weeks now. I suspect you have no wife, no children, or parental expectations to fulfill. So why are you here, Mr. Blackwell?"

Jasper set their drinks before them. Magnus examined the deep pink color. Lifting his glass, he toasted his newfound friend. "You must call me Magnus, Oscar. Like you, I am looking for some new experience to distract me from my life back in Boston."

"'Experience is the name men give to their mistakes,'" Oscar returned.

Magnus tipped his glass to Oscar's. "Then I am here to, hopefully, make a great many mistakes."

Oscar raised his glass. "To making those mistakes together, my friend."

Sipping his strong drink, Magnus surmised he had found a kindred spirit in the outgoing Oscar Wilde.

After draining his Sazerac in one gulp, Oscar slapped his glass on the mahogany bar. "Tell me, Magnus, what have you seen of this fair city?"

Magnus went into a detailed description of the architecture he had admired, his river cruise to Algiers Point, the quaint shops he had browsed, and the enticing dishes he had sampled at various restaurants.

After his recounting, Oscar seemed genuinely appalled. "You mean you have come all the way to New Orleans and not sampled her true carnal pleasures?"

Magnus stared into the man's small eyes, grasping his meaning. Resting his drink on the bar, he slyly smiled. "I've heard of the establishments on the edge of the Quarter that cater to such 'carnal pleasures,' as you put it, but I have not visited any of them."

"Why not?" Oscar pressed. "I thought it was the first thing most American men do when they come to this city."

A fleeting image of Frances crossed his mind. "It's not my style."

Oscar leaned into him, a wide teasing smile on his long, aristocratic face. "My friend, I would like to take you to a place I have discovered. It is unlike any other in this town and caters to a select group of men."

"What select group of men?"

Oscar pointed to his glass as he looked up to Jasper. "The very wealthy kind."

As Jasper sprang into action, concocting more Sazeracs, Magnus thought of Frances in her wedding dress. He felt his cock stir with desire for her, and he was infused with interest to see what delights New Orleans could offer. He had heard of its famed brothels and their ability to cater to all tastes. He just hoped they would be willing to cater to his.

Three Sazeracs later, Oscar had shoved Magnus into a carriage and ordered the driver to Basin Street. He had not expected the drinks to hit him as hard as they did, but as the carriage bumped over the stone-covered streets, Magnus listened to Oscar describe his experiences at Mahogany House.

"It's run by Simone Glapion, a real character. She's Creole.

Down here that means she is a mixture of African, French, or Spanish blood. I have a hard time keeping up with all the terms for mixed-bloods in this part of the world, but somehow, it is important to these people. Most of the women she employs are octoroons—women with only one-eighth African blood." Oscar raised his black eyebrows. "She has men too if you prefer. Not a lot of madams offer men."

Magnus kept the effrontery from registering on his face. "I prefer women." He perused Oscar's casual dinner jacket and white dress shirt and wished he had changed out of his formal tails and trousers. They seemed a bit overstated for where they were going. "How long have you been going to this Madam Glapion?"

"A little over a week now." Their carriage jostled to a sudden stop, interrupting him. "I first came to her when she was a priestess. I wanted to see an actual voodoo ritual performed, and she is said to be the best in the city for such spells."

"Voodoo?" Magnus furrowed his brow. "What is that?"

The carriage door to Oscar's right opened, and their driver ducked his head inside. "We're here, sirs."

The driver's light coffee-colored skin made Magnus rethink what Oscar had told him about all the mixed-blood individuals found in New Orleans. He had heard stories about slave owners using their female slaves as concubines before the Civil War. Now he was being taken to a house where the descendants of those atrocities were prized as treats to be enjoyed by white men of means.

"The African slaves brought voodoo over when their people were transported to the New World," Oscar related as they stepped from the carriage. "The religion incorporates aspects of Catholicism, invariably taught to the slaves by their owners here in the South, but it still has a central core based on their African heritage. Madam Glapion is a high priestess of the religion. She is famed in the city for casting spells for the rich and powerful." Oscar reached into his jacket pocket and withdrew a few coins. "There was only one other high priestess said to be more powerful than Madam Simone, but she died a few years ago. Her name was Marie Laveau." Oscar handed the coins to the driver.

As the very tall driver bowed his bald head to them, Magnus began to foster a new appreciation for the people of this strange city. They were as mysterious and as filled with secrets as he was.

"Mahogany House," Oscar announced as he waved his hand to the residence before them.

Magnus was mystified by the ostentatious structure. Made of white marble, it was square with a slanted roof of red terracotta tiles, and stained-glass windows rose from the first floor to the fourth. Two red-bricked chimneys flanked the house, and the leaded glass door had a leaded glass, fan-shaped transom above. The steps were also white marble and shined beneath the five gas lanterns made of brass that ran along the front porch.

"Eye-popping, isn't it?"

Magnus shook his head. "If one didn't know it was a whorehouse, one might suspect it was a church."

Oscar patted his back, urging him to the front door. "Yes, but here the sinners do a hell of a lot more than pray."

At the door, they were greeted by a young black man wearing a green velvet livery. As the man took Magnus's hat and gloves, he saw Oscar's eyes size up the young man's small ass. He had seen enough to guess that Oscar had not come to this particular whorehouse for the women.

When Magnus raised his head, he was once again stunned by what he discovered. Furnished with tear-drop chandeliers, potted ferns, and rich red velvet mahogany furniture, the entrance parlor had vaulted ceilings, white marble floors, a gold-painted fountain in the center, and rich paintings of assorted Rubenesque women in numerous naughty poses covering the walls.

"Well, well, my dear Oscar has returned."

The voice was deep but still very feminine. When Magnus saw the beautiful woman in the white lace gown coming toward him, he was entranced by her high cheekbones, mesmerizing green eyes, creamy skin the color of café au lait, and thin red lips.

She moved like a cat, graceful but with purpose like a huntress. Her slim hips seductively swung from side to side while her long black hair casually wrapped around her slender shoulders. In her hand was a long walking stick, but she did not use it as a cane; she carried it almost like a staff.

"Ah, Madam Simone, I have brought you a new customer," Oscar announced. "This is Mr. Magnus Blackwell."

The stunning woman drew closer, and Magnus was intrigued by her beauty. If she was an example of the octoroon Oscar had mentioned, Magnus was indeed willing to sample this rare delight.

"Mr. Blackwell. I'm Simone Glapion." She dipped her head. "Welcome to Mahogany House."

Magnus stepped forward, bowing formally to the woman. "Thank you, dear lady, for having me."

When he rose, her green eyes were all over him. Never before had he felt so intruded upon by a woman's gaze. It was as if she could see to the very depths of his soul.

"I've been raving about your beautiful girls to him," Oscar mentioned while his eyes veered to the young man standing dutifully at the front door.

"Not my boys?" Madam Simone asked.

Oscar directed his attention back to her. "Magnus isn't into men. He wants something young, fresh, and very pretty, no doubt." Oscar shrugged. "It's what all American men want."

Madam Simone banged her stick on the marble floor, and almost instantly, two young, smooth-chested men wearing only gold brocade short trousers appeared at her side.

"Do you want these two, Oscar?" Madam Simone asked. "I've had them waiting just for you."

The desire radiating from Oscar's dark eyes almost made Magnus sick. He had known men who had taken other men for lovers, and he had not railed against it, but he preferred the feel of a woman's ass to a man's.

Oscar cupped the young men's asses with his hands as if testing the merchandise before trying it.

Seemingly satisfied, he raised his eyes to Madam Simone. "You know me too well, dear lady."

She motioned to a mahogany stairwell just to the rear of the entrance parlor. There were clusters of grapes carved into the thick banister and a red runner climbed the central portion of the steps. "Your usual room is waiting for you on the third floor."

Giving Magnus one last lusty grin, Oscar toddled off up the stairs, dragging his young playthings with him.

"He is easy to satisfy," Madam Simone admitted. "You, on the other hand." She pointed her long cane at him. "You I cannot figure out."

Magnus became distracted by the dragon's head carved into the handle of her walking stick. The dragon's eyes appeared as if they were inlaid with pearls of the most iridescent hue.

Magnus pointed to the handle. "What are those stones in the handle of your cane? Are they pearls?"

Madam Simone held up the stick. The curved shaft was carved to resemble a dragon's tail with thousands of tiny scales. "This isn't a cane. It's a baton juju." She lovingly stroked the marbled wood that had ribbons of black and dark brown running through it. "They are used by voodoo high priestesses—like me."

Magnus admired the flashing eyes of the dragon, and for a moment, he swore the stones changed to a light rose color. "It's very beautiful. How does one acquire a baton juju?"

"You have to earn it. Your power and ability determine the type of baton juju you are given. I received this baton juju as a gift from a most powerful priestess." She caressed the handle. "This cane is very special. It's imbued with the essence of the Sang Noir Tree. It's a tree that grows in the center of the local Holt Cemetery. Located outside of town, the cemetery is for poor blacks of New Orleans. The blood of the dead is said to give the tree its power."

"And the stones?" He glanced up at her. "They appear to change color."

"The stones are changeling stones. They reflect the heart of the owner. Pearl means peace, red stands for anger, and pink stands for love. The wood from the Sang Noir Tree gives the stones their power."

Magnus was amused by the story. "What power?"

She handed him the stick. Intrigued by the offer, Magnus grasped the handle. The light weight of the piece surprised him. Then, he felt the tingle in his arm. It spread upward and quickly overtook his muscles. Magnus felt stronger, euphoric, and drunk with a strange power. He believed he could do anything, and conquer anyone. While admiring the cane, the eyes of the dragon changed. At first, the color was a pale pink, but then quickly turned to blood red.

71

Madam Simone appraised the handle. "There is a deep anger in you. I thought I sensed it."

Magnus suspiciously eyed the woman. "Most men are angry for some misdeed or another committed against them."

She yanked the stick away. "Your anger is not from a loss of power or money but for a lost love. Your concept of love anyway. It's not true love."

The instant loss of the power was almost debilitating. Magnus stepped back and came to his senses. "What was that? The cane made me feel ..."

"The power of the baton juju is for those who know how to use it for good. Your intentions are far from that."

Anger bloomed in his gut. "How would you know what is in my heart, Madam Simone?"

She patted the handle of the cane. "I don't, but the baton juju does. If there was love in your heart, Magnus, it would not create anger or instill the need for revenge like the cane revealed. When you are filled with love, you wish others only the best and mean it."

Magnus had no answer for her. Instead, he focused on the changeling stones in the dragon's eyes on the handle. They were once again pearly white.

"The stones are pearl for you because you love everyone, I suppose."

She shook her head, and her light, lilting laugh resonated throughout the vast parlor. "The stones are pearl for me because I learned a long time ago that anger is not the answer. I leave it for the universe to determine the fate of others."

"I can't do that," he growled. "What if I don't want to leave the fate of the one who wronged me up to the universe?"

"Then what you give out, you will get back." She held up the walking stick once more. "That is the power the Sang Noir Tree gives the changeling stones—the ability to radiate out the heart of the bearer and return the feeling into their life."

"So if I were to hold your baton juju and radiate love instead of anger, what would happen?"

"Then it would bring to you the love you feel," Madam Simone replied.

A thought struck Magnus. "Could your magic cane bring back an object I loved? Or perhaps a person?"

"Anything is possible. The powers of the baton juju change with each owner." Her eyes perused the fancy carved handle. "It is said that many a powerful mambo have used this cane to perform great feats of magic: reverse plagues in the city, change the outcome of battles, or make some men great while destroying others."

"Many would kill for that ability." Magnus managed to curtail the excitement in his voice. "Have you ever used your power in such a grand way?"

"My magic has only been small in scale: to change the luck of the destitute, or heal the wounds of the sick. I have no desire for momentous follies. It's not my way."

Magnus snickered, feeling as if he had just been conned. "That's the reason the dragon's eyes stay pearl with you, isn't it, Madam Simone? You wish for no conflict to come into your life." He motioned to the parlor. "Or your business."

"When you run a brothel in the city of New Orleans, you try to generate as much peace in your life as possible."

Amused by her comment and feeling more at ease, Magnus allowed himself to laugh. Letting his ramrod posture relax a bit, he nodded to Madam Simone's baton juju. "How did you become a voodoo high priestess?"

She came alongside him and took his arm. "It's in my blood. I was born with a veil over my eyes. In the African culture, it means a child will become a strong high priestess or what we call *mambo asogwe*. At least that's what my grandmother professed." She ushered him deeper into the brothel. "My grandmother raised me. She taught me how to speak to the spirits. She also taught me how to run a business."

They proceeded to an open door to the right of the richly carved stairs. "Did she teach you how to run this business?"

"I am the granddaughter of a plantation owner and the daughter of a rich New Orleans businessman, Mr. Blackwell. Women of mixed blood are good for two things in this town: fucking and voodoo."

She brought him to a cozy sitting room. With a green marble fireplace, oak-paneled walls, a few built-in bookcases, and more mahogany furniture upholstered in pale yellow damask, this room was more to Magnus's liking. Above the mantel, a long formal portrait of Madam Simone caught his eye. In it, she wore a white beaded gown with the long walking stick at her side.

Madam Simone waved her stick to a pair of wingback chairs set before the fireplace. "Please, sit."

Adjusting the long tail of his coat, Magnus had a seat. He watched as Madam Simone took the chair across from him and set her stick against the side.

Magnus was distracted by the handsome cane. He became preoccupied with the things he would do if he ever possessed it. Images of Frances flashed across his mind. Perhaps ...

"What can I get you to drink, Mr. Blackwell?"

Magnus snapped out of his contemplations. "Magnus please, Madam Simone. I would love a whiskey and soda."

From the corner of the room, one of the bookcases moved

to the side and a young woman, naked from the waist up and wearing only a white petticoat, entered the room. With flowing brown hair covering her breasts and brilliant gray eyes, Magnus was immediately attracted to her.

"Whiskey and soda for the gentleman, and bring me a sweet sherry," Madam Simone told her.

The beauty disappeared into the open bookcase before Magnus could get a good look at her.

"Now tell me why you are here, Magnus," Madam Simone began as she set her hands on her lap.

"Why else does a man come to a brothel, Madam?"

"Some come for conversation, some to fuck, others to forget. But you are here for none of those reasons." She sat back in her chair. "I told you when you came in the door to my establishment I could not read what you wanted. I usually pride myself on being able to tell what a customer wants before he wants it."

Magnus ran his thumb over the wooden armrest of his chair. "My tastes are very specific."

"In how you want a woman to look or how you want her to act, Magnus?"

"It's what I want her to take," he flatly reported. "How I want her to take me."

Madam Simone was very quiet for a moment as she studied him. "I understand."

Just then, the young girl carrying their drinks on a silver tray returned to the room. When she kneeled next to Magnus's chair, he got the opportunity to admire her beauty. With golden skin, perfectly carved features, full red lips, and a long, supple neck, Magnus's cock roused when he settled his eyes on her round, firm breasts. He took his drink from the tray, but his eyes never left her as she went to Madam Simone's chair and served her sherry.

"I like her," he announced over the rim of his glass. "Can I see more?"

Madam Simone nodded to the girl. "Evangeline, take off your clothes and let the gentleman see all of your assets."

Without hesitation, the young woman placed the tray on the floor and began to ease the long white petticoat from around her hips.

Evangeline stepped out of her petticoat, and Magnus licked his lips. She had slim hips, a tiny waist, and her legs were supple and long. As she approached his chair, he took a sip of his drink, but he didn't taste the alcohol; he was too entranced by her.

The woman stopped before him, and he put down his drink on a small table to the right of his chair. Standing, he put his hands on Evangeline's waist and spun her around. When his eyes landed on her perfectly curved ass, his cock grew hard.

Madam Simone snickered at his reaction. "Will her ass do, or do you need bigger?"

Magnus glanced up at the madam. "It will do, but is it untouched?"

"Does that matter to you?"

He nodded. "I prefer it that way."

"Evangeline is one of my straight fuck girls. She's not been taken up the ass before. It will cost you extra to deflower her in that way. Fifteen dollars instead of ten."

Magnus slapped Evangeline's ass. "Fine."

Appearing bored, Madam Simone nodded to the girl. "Take him to room fourteen. And use the coke oil, Evangeline. It will make things easier on you."

"Coke oil?" Magnus questioned.

Madam Simone raised her small glass of sherry to her lips.

"Cocaine mixed with lavender oil. All my ass girls use it. Numbs the pain and allows your cock to go in smoothly."

"What if I don't want her to have it?"

Madam Simone's green eyes registered a brief look of surprise. "If you want rape, Magnus, that will cost you more. A lot more."

The tinge of warning in her voice made Magnus decide he would not push the issue. As long as he got the girl's ass, what did he care what she felt? "This current arrangement is fine."

Madam Simone sipped her sherry and waved to the girl. "Go."

While Evangeline led him to the door, Magnus kept his eyes on her lovely ass and marveled at how it jiggled as she walked.

"Every room has a bathroom with hot and cold running water, Magnus," Madam Simone called from her chair. "I suggest you use it before you return. We'll talk when you're done with the girl."

Outside in the hallway, Magnus felt the excitement building in his loins. Coming to New Orleans was turning out to be the best decision he'd made in a very long time.

Chapter Eight

A Dangerous Game

Evangeline had been better than Magnus expected. Her ass had been so tight he could barely keep from coming as soon as he entered her. She put up some resistance, but not much. Magnus had taken his time with her, making sure to get his money's worth.

After freshening up, Magnus returned to the private sitting room with oak paneling to find Madam Simone and Oscar with their heads together around an old book.

"How was the girl?" Madam Simone asked, never glancing up from the open tome on her lap.

"Very nice," he admitted, coming into the room. "Have you any more like her?"

"Plenty. I assume you want a fresh one every time."

Magnus nodded. "Yes."

78

"You'll ruin all my whores, Magnus. Once they take it from behind, they won't want to do it any other way."

"Not after I'm done with them," he quipped.

Oscar chuckled as he stood from kneeling beside Madam Simone's chair. "You are a nasty little devil, aren't you?"

"I like what I like." Magnus straightened out the cuffs of his white dress shirt.

"Never figured you'd be into the back end of a woman," Oscar went on. "You always struck me as an upstanding kind of man."

Magnus went to the wingback chair across from Madam Simone. "I used to be. Only fucked married women and whores until I met a woman who made me want more."

"What happened?" Oscar probed. "Did she not approve of your back door approach?"

Magnus scowled. "She married my best friend."

Oscar's obnoxious bray filled the room. "Be thankful you got rid of her so easily. Never marry, Magnus. I am married, and it is nothing to admire. 'Men marry because they are tired; women, because they are curious: both are disappointed.'"

"It is not so much that she is married but who she married that slighted me."

"And who was it?" Madam Simone grilled.

"A poor architectural student with no name or fortune," Magnus disclosed. "He was also a very good friend. I introduced them."

Oscar clapped his hands. "Oh, how magnificent. You have been revenge fucking every woman you've met since then." He tilted his head, questioningly. "But why up the ass?"

Magnus wiped something out of the corner of his right eye. "I haven't given up on getting her back. And when I do ...." He grinned.

"You will be as pure as the driven snow," Oscar concluded. He went to the fireplace and rested his elbow on the mantel. "You are a divine character, Magnus. I should put you in one of my books. I would love to capture your cruelty and that odd sense of control you so carefully project."

"What story would there be in a man who hides his sins from the world to impress the woman he loves?" Madam Simone chimed in. "I see that every day in my establishment. Married men are my biggest customers." She closed the book on her lap.

"Yes, but sin is the only truth we have in this world," Oscar argued. "Without it, there would be no need for truth."

Madam Simone snickered. "Without it, I would be out of work."

Magnus rolled his thumb across his fingers, considering Oscar's words. "But what if a man could wallow in sin yet still live a seemingly truthful life. What if he could hide that sin and keep it from those he cares for. What would be the truth, and what would be the fallacy?"

Oscar glanced up at the portrait of Madame Simone above the mantel. He waved his hand at the painting. "Wouldn't it be wonderful if we could hide all of our sins in a painting while still being able to appear untainted by sin to the rest of the world."

Magnus chuckled. "Sin doesn't show, Oscar."

"All sins show," Madam Simone corrected. "Eventually, everything we do mars us in a way. Every sin taints the soul."

Magnus raised his eyes to her. "What makes you say that?"

She held up the black leather bound book in her lap. "Sin can mark the soul. All the evil we do may not show on the outside, but on the inside, our souls blacken. A lie here or there may register as a black spot or two. A grudge can cause a scar, or

80

a heinous crime could create a vast tear. I have seen such souls, and they are very ugly indeed."

Oscar feigned a shiver. "I hate to think of my insides turning into the mess you describe, Madam."

She stood from the chair. "You'll see your soul when you die, Oscar. All will be revealed then."

"How do you know?" Magnus demanded.

Madam Simone went to a bookcase next to the mantel. "I've seen it." She pushed the book back into an open slot. "I can see spirits. They exist among the living—hang about and watch over those they loved. In the afterlife, the sins we created are worn like badges of dishonor on the soul."

"Now that is creepy!" Oscar gazed about the room. "Are there any here now?"

Madam Simone laughed at him, and Magnus could not help but join in.

"Spirits are seen the clearest during the time of ritual," she explained. "When I perform my voodoo ceremonies, I see the spirits of the dead very clearly."

"Could we see these spirits?" Magnus inquired.

She shook her head. "Only those who possess the sight can see them, Magnus."

He stood from his chair. "Yes, but could I come and see one of the ceremonies? I would very much like to learn about your voodoo. How you conduct your ceremonies and what you see?"

Madam Simone rested her hand on her hip, weighing his interest. "Is this more for curiosity, or do you have another purpose? Perhaps winning back that woman you want so badly?"

Magnus tossed his head to the side. "Maybe a little of both."

"Careful, Magnus," Oscar warned. "What you may see can never be unseen."

"What I may see, my friend, will be worth it. Especially if it can get me what I most desire."

Madam Simone walked right up to him, her green eyes peering into his. "Come to Bayou St. John tomorrow just after sundown. I will perform a special ritual for you there."

"Bayou St. John? Where is that?"

"All the drivers in the city know how to get there. But you must tell them I instructed you to go there. They will not take you unless they know you have the permission of the high priestess."

"Can I come?" Oscar excitedly begged.

Madam Simone glanced over at him. "There will be no eager young men dancing at this ritual, Oscar. You might get bored."

"It's strictly for research, Madam. I might want to write a story about voodoo one day."

She directed her eyes to Magnus. "Bring Oscar then but no one else. It's not a circus."

Magnus nodded in agreement. "Tell me, Madam, are you going to cure my soul of sin?"

"'Nothing can cure the soul but the senses, just as nothing can cure the senses but the soul,'" she extolled.

"Oh, I must remember that line," Oscar chirped. "Might have to put it in a book one day."

Magnus smiled at his friend. "One day, I might have to read one of your books, Oscar."

"When I write one I will be sure to send you a copy, especially if you are in it."

Madam Simone went back to her chair and collected the baton juju resting against the arm. "Gentlemen, if you will excuse me, I must see to my other customers."

Both men politely bowed as she exited the room.

"You must have charmed her while I was busy upstairs, Magnus." Oscar came across the sitting room to his side. "I've never been invited to one of her rituals before."

Magnus scanned a few of the titles of the books in the bookcase closest to him. "It might be amusing."

"'Amusing'?" Oscar patted his shoulder. "Hell, we will be the envy of everyone in the city. Madam Simone is considered by many to be a very powerful high priestess. This should be good."

"I'll be surprised if it is nothing more than some hokey words, beating of drums, and a few naked women gyrating about."

Oscar guided Magnus to the door. "I've seen some strange things in my life, but this religion and the people who practice it are not to be crossed."

Magnus stopped at the door and cocked a dark eyebrow at Oscar. "You sound like Madam Simone. 'All souls are blackened by sin.' You don't really believe in this stuff do you?"

Oscar's face darkened. "I never disbelieve in any religion, my friend. Because you never know; the one religion you never believed in could rise up one day and bite you in the ass."

Magnus shook his head and ambled out the door. "Spoken like a true omnist."

"All writers are omnists," Oscar called behind him. "We'll pray to anybody as long as it gets our books published."

Chapter Nine

Deeper

The bright morning sunshine peeked through the curtains of Magnus's hotel room window. He climbed from his bed, pulling his dressing gown around him, and stepped out onto his grand balcony to take in the late morning activity in the French Quarter.

French bread and blocks of ice were being delivered to the restaurant down the street, and merchants pushing carts with vegetables and coffee beans called for customers to sample their selections. His stomach rumbled as he eyed the carts with the colorful produce progress along the street. His head throbbed from the alcohol and activities of the night before, but as recollections of the conversations with Oscar and Madam Simone came back to him, Magnus felt that itch of curiosity grab hold.

His brief introduction to voodoo had left him hungry to learn more about the religion, and he knew there was no better spot on earth to do research than New Orleans. Plotting out his day, he rushed back to his room and went to his wardrobe. Invigorated with a new sense of purpose, he began to dress.

In the lobby, he strode to the hotel restaurant, eager to find Oscar. If he was going to do research, he needed someone well-trained in the mechanism.

"God, how can you look so chipper at ten A.M.?" Oscar complained when Magnus sat down at his table.

Oscar's brown eyes were rimmed with circles, his face looked haggard, his black hair was a shambled mess, and Magnus could have sworn he was still wearing the same dinner jacket he had on the night before.

Removing his hat, Magnus waved down a passing waiter. "You look like you slept in your clothes."

Oscar raised his head, wincing as the sunlight hit his eyes. "Jasper and I got into a heated discussion about brandy after I left you last night."

"Jasper?" Magnus questioned.

"The bartender at the Carousel Bar in the hotel. He kept serving me different brands of brandy until I passed out. The cleaning staff in the bar woke me up this morning."

A black-tie waiter appeared at the table and gave the two men a slight bow.

"Bring me a coffee with chicory." Magnus pointed to Oscar's nearly empty cup of coffee. "Bring him two more."

"What are you trying to do, wake me up?"

After the waiter smirked and turned away, Magnus stared into Oscar's bloodshot eyes. "I want you to help me today. I need to learn about voodoo."

Oscar furrowed his brow. "Why for God's sake? We're going to see a ritual tonight. Isn't that enough?" He picked up his white coffee cup. "Madam Simone gave you the highlights. What else do you need?"

Magnus sat back in his chair. "To see if it actually works."

Practically dropping his coffee cup back in its saucer, Oscar broke out in a fit of laughter. "You're joking. Seriously? For what purpose?" He paused and waited for Magnus to reply, but his companion remained very tight-lipped. As a thought hit him, Oscar's face brightened. "You want to get revenge on your friend and the woman he stole from you, don't you?" He clapped his hands and held them to his lips, smiling. "Do you honestly think some African mumbo jumbo is going to get back the woman you love?"

Magnus never said a word but held Oscar's gaze. He was never one to discuss his plans with anyone. He had even kept a lot of things from O'Connor during their time together, mainly his feelings for Frances.

Shaking his head, Oscar picked up his coffee cup. "What you are thinking is not only stupid, it's—"

"An adventure, Oscar," Magnus cut in.

Oscar's brown eyes burned with anger. "It's dangerous, Magnus." He pointed his finger to the white linen tablecloth. "These people believe, really believe in voodoo in this town. I've heard stories and seen the fear in some men's eyes when they tell their tales. This stuff is not to be trifled with."

"I'm not trifling," Magnus insisted. "I'm simply gathering information. I want to know more about it."

The waiter returned to their table, carrying three white cups of coffee on a round black tray. After he had placed a cup in front of Magnus and two in front of Oscar, he asked for the gentlemen's breakfast order.

"Just the coffee," Oscar declared.

"Scrambled eggs and toast for me," Magnus told him.

Watching their waiter saunter away, Oscar reached for a fresh cup of coffee. "I will give you until I finish these two cups of coffee to change your mind."

"And if I don't change my mind?" Magnus debated.

Oscar rolled his eyes. "Then I'd better switch from coffee to gin."

Once outside, Oscar took Magnus to the row of carriages parked down from the hotel entrance. The enclosed black carriages had the hotel's *M* logo in gold on the side. They were led by two fine bay horses and driven by men wearing long black coats, tall black hats, white ties, and white gloves.

Magnus skeptically waited as Oscar inspected the faces of the drivers. When he found the man he was looking for, he called to Magnus.

"Magnus, meet Cleitus LeBlanc." He waved up at the driver, who clutched the long black reins. "He's the driver who educated me about voodoo when I arrived in the city. He's quite knowledgeable on the subject."

The round-faced, dark-skinned man looked warily from Magnus to Oscar. "I did as you asked me, sir. I took you to all the places known for voodoo in N'awlins."

Oscar opened the door to the carriage. "And you did a fine job, my man." He pulled his billfold out from his jacket pocket. "I would appreciate it if we could show my friend what you showed me." Removing a five-dollar bill from his billfold, Oscar passed it up to the driver. "For your trouble."

Cleitus's eyes grew wide as he held up the money. "Hop in. I can take you on a tour, sirs."

The carriage made a short trek to the north edge of the French Quarter along Rampart Street.

When the carriage came to a stop by a plain strip of land, Magnus tilted closer to Oscar. "A barren field?"

Oscar waved away his remark. "Wait. When I was here, I saw wondrous things."

Cleitus opened the door and folded down the steps. "This here is Congo Square," he told Magnus as he exited the carriage. "The Mayor of N'awlins gave it to the slaves in the city some years back."

Oscar joined Magnus on the street along the stretch of land.

"When the French passed somethin' called the Code Noir, the slaves were given off every Sunday from work. But the slaves weren't given nowhere to congregate to celebrate their voodoo religion. So after the slaves was chased off the levees around the city and out of the public parks, the mayor designated Congo Square for the blacks in the city to celebrate their religion."

"Where are all the dancers I saw here last time we came, Cleitus?" Oscar all but whined. "The place was absolutely teeming with people."

Cleitus chuckled. "I brought you here on a Sunday, sir. Today's Wednesday. All the dancers are workin'."

"Oh, you should have seen it, Magnus." Oscar waved his hands about in the air. "There were drums and people dancing, caught up in the frenzy of the music, and others were singing. It was quite moving."

"Watchya see nowadays is more performance rather than rituals down here in the square." Cleitus waved to a row of fancy houses sitting on the other side of the square. "A lot of the madams come here and hire the dancers to perform in their houses. Some hire the girls for their customers."

"Do you believe in voodoo, Cleitus?" Magnus inquired.

Cleitus bowed his head, nodding. "Yes, sir, I do. I've seen some strange things done by priestesses in this city."

Oscar stepped closer. "Like what?"

"I've seen cursed men curl up in agony and die. And men who should be dead from disease get up and survive. Ain't no explainin' how any of it is done. I just know it's true. The strongest high priestesses are very powerful."

"Like Madam Simone?" Magnus pressed.

Cleitus's eyes flickered with understanding. "If you know Madam Simone, then you know the most powerful mistress in the city, but she ain't the queen of voodoo."

"Queen of voodoo?" Oscar laughed. "For heaven's sake, you mean to tell me there is royalty associated with this religion?"

"Yes, sir." Cleitus nodded. "Ms. Marie was the queen."

Magnus cast his gaze to Oscar. "What do you mean by was?"

"She been dead some years now. But I can take you to her. Even in death, Ms. Marie can still grant favors."

Oscar's face lit up. "Well, take us to her. I'm English. We simply adore meeting royalty."

They did not have to travel far to see the queen of voodoo. Cleitus took them to the famous black gate of St. Louis Cemetery Number One.

When Magnus emerged from the carriage, he was disappointed by the size of the cemetery. He thought it would be bigger. But the residents of the city had learned long ago to make use of small spaces, and though the occupants of the cemetery inhabited houses of the dead built above ground, the tombs were tightly packed together with only small pathways left to negotiate.

Cleitus stopped before a modest rectangular tomb built out of limestone and painted white. Offerings of candles, flowers, small handmade dolls, and even money lay scattered around the entrance of the mini-mausoleum.

"Marie Laveau rests here," Cleitus said with reverence as he made the sign of the cross over his chest. "She still hears and sees all."

Magnus inspected the tomb. "What made this woman so famous?"

Oscar moved toward the tomb and reached out to caress the limestone. "She was born a free woman of color in 1794. She was a hairdresser known for her psychic abilities and powerful magic, or what they call *gris-gris.*"

"How do you know so much about her?"

Oscar smiled. "I already took the tour."

"Ms. Marie was also a skilled healer and a voice for the poor and destitute in our city," Cleitus added. "A lot of people outside of N'awlins don't know about her charity work. She cared for the sick, fed the poor, and spoke out for the underprivileged. She was a devout Catholic and went to mass daily, but she wholeheartedly believed in voodoo—and business."

"She had a home on St. Ann Street. A gift from a grateful client," Oscar related. "There, she worked her magic."

"And along Bayou St. John," Cleitus corrected. "Ms. Marie's ceremonies on the bayou are legendary."

"Can we see this house of hers?"

Oscar stepped away from the tomb and picked up an old

piece of red brick from the ground. "It's a voodoo temple now. A place where you can buy ritual implements, herbs, potions, and have spells cast." He made an X on the side of the tomb. "If you are listening, dear lady, I could use your help with my book." He raised his eyebrows as he held out the piece of brick in his hand to Magnus. "It can't hurt."

Magnus took the brick fragment from his hand. "What do I do?"

Oscar motioned to the tomb. "Draw an X and ask for her help."

"But you must only ask for good things," Cleitus reported. "Ms. Marie gets angry if you ask for bad."

Magnus held the brick fragment above the tomb about to make his mark. "How angry?"

Cleitus stepped closer. "Bad vibrations go out, bad things happen. If you want good in your life, send out good."

"And if I want bad?"

Cleitus took the piece of brick from Magnus's hand and dropped it on the ground. "Then you don't want this." He wiped his hands together. "I'll take you to Ms. Marie's house now, and then the tour is over."

Cleitus hurried toward the front gate. As his footfalls carried throughout the peaceful cemetery, Oscar patted Magnus on the shoulder.

"Well done. I told you these people believe in this religion, Magnus. No need to anger them."

Magnus wiped the brick dust from hands. "I thought you said this was going to be an informative tour. So far, all I have seen is a few myths and not a whole lot of magic."

Shaking his head, Oscar tipped his hat to the side of his head. "You're not supposed to see the magic, Magnus. You're supposed to believe in it."

The house on St. Ann Street let Magnus down even more than the cemetery. The dwelling was nothing more than a simple, one-story Creole cottage with a gabled roof and built to the front property line. With two front doors, small windows, and a plaster-covered facade painted pale green, it was hardly the residence expected of a voodoo queen.

Staring out the carriage window at the structure, Magnus muttered, "In my experiences, religion is about pomp and circumstance." He reached for the door handle. "But this ..."

"What do you expect from a religion born out of poverty and suffering?" Oscar asked. "The world is a very different place than what you are used to, my friend."

Magnus froze, his hand still on the carriage door. "Meaning what, exactly?"

Oscar moved forward. "You live in an ivory tower. You are the few." He nodded to the cottage outside. "That is the many. How much longer do you think it will be before those with nothing rebel to take away from your kind?"

Magnus snorted with contempt, showing every inch of his privileged upbringing. "You forget it is people like me who build railroads, invest in progress, and fund programs so people like that," he motioned to the cottage, "can survive." Magnus was about to push the door open and exit the carriage when Oscar held his arm.

"Your perception of power is merely a shell, Magnus. With a blink of the eye, someone like this Marie Laveau can change your destiny. You need to respect what we are doing here and not project your aristocracy like some malodorous perfume."

Magnus shook off his arm. "Why, I'm surprised at you, Oscar. Was that respect you were giving those two young men last night at Madam Simone's, or your contempt?" He leaned in closer to Oscar and dropped his voice. "Don't ever think you can question me or my motives. I will crush you if need be."

Oscar sat back, momentarily stunned. "You really are a bastard, aren't you?"

Magnus shoved the carriage door open. "Bastard? Hardly. Admit it, Oscar. You will always admire me. I represent all those nasty little sins you never had the courage to commit."

"The former home of the voodoo queen was converted into a voodoo temple," Cleitus explained as he held the French doors at the entrance for the two men. "People come here for spells and medicines."

Tables of different colored wax candles, tightly bunched herbs wrapped with red and black ribbons, tiny brown bottles of pre-made magical potions, an assortment of bells, drums, skulls of dead animals, and even a few books written about voodoo filled the simple, square room just inside the doors. Perusing the items, Magnus smelled the wands of sage, read a few of the spells written on the bottles, and inspected an animal skull or two, trying to figure out the species.

"'Before performing any voodoo spell, be warned,'" Oscar read from one of the books. "'Every voodoo spell has its risk. Even love spells can be risky. A spell can bind your soul to the soul of the one you wish to possess, harm, love, or destroy. Never use on someone you don't want to be bound to forever. A spell binds you because it is an oath to the spirits that the energy formed by two souls coming together will be given to the universe. Renege on such a promise, and the universe shall have its vengeance.'"

Magnus returned the rat skull he had been examining to the table in front of him. "Why would the universe care about such insignificant matters?"

"The universe cares about all things, events, and people," a woman's silky voice called from the corner of the room. "Through it, we are all bound."

"Mistress." Cleitus bowed to the woman as she emerged from behind a white curtain. "They wanted to see Ms. Marie's home."

The woman wore a bright turban on her head, and her smooth café au lait skin reminded Magnus of the beautiful Madam Simone. This woman was smaller and younger, but still moved with the same mysterious grace as Madam Simone. Her brown eyes, sharp cheekbones, full, luscious lips, and peaceful face intrigued Magnus. He could see the fascination the local white men had with these women of mixed blood; their beauty was beyond compare.

"You're welcome to my mother's home, gentlemen." She dipped her head ever so slightly.

"Mother?" Oscar gaped at the woman. "You are the daughter of Marie Laveau?"

She nodded, the gold in the fabric of her turban sparkled in the sunlight coming through the French doors. "I'm her firstborn and have taken up her work as high priestess. My name is also Marie."

Oscar walked up to her, extending his hand. "Such a pleasure."

She took his hand and gripped it firmly as her eyes gazed into his. "You're a writer."

"Attempting to be one," Oscar confessed.

She held on to his hand as if entranced by some inner voice. "You shall succeed. In due time, you will be quite well known. Your stories will live on long after you're gone. Be comforted by that. Your soul shall live on in the white well of souls."

Oscar's long face appeared touched by her words. "I hope what you say comes true, dear lady."

"Don't you doubt Ms. Marie's word," Cleitus maintained while standing by the door. "She has the gift of sight like her momma."

While removing his hat, Magnus moved toward her. "Is it a requirement to have the gift of sight to be a voodoo high priestess, Ms. Laveau? I ask only because we have recently made the acquaintance of another voodoo high priestess who claims she was also born with the sight. A Madam Simone Glapion."

The slender woman snickered. "Madam Simone from Mahogany House is my auntie, sir. She is a relative of my father, Christophe de Glapion. If she were not 'of the blood,' as we say, then we would be forced to have a *haute défi.*"

"High challenge?" Oscar translated.

"A contest of power between two high priestesses. It's a dangerous time when such an event occurs. It hasn't happened since my mother's day."

"Then we are grateful the power remains *dans la famille,*" Oscar commented with a flourish of his hand.

"Indeed, Mistress Glapion." Magnus held his hat over his chest.

Marie smiled at him. "My name is Laveau. My parents were not married, monsieur. I'm a bastard, as are my fourteen brothers and sisters. But being a bastard in New Orleans is not looked down on like in the rest of the world. Here, it's simply the way of things."

"Then I am happy some corners of the globe are so enlightened." He held out his hand to her. "Magnus Blackwell, at your service."

From the moment she touched his hand, her features changed. Marred by fear, her serene countenance disappeared.

"You have many secrets, Mr. Blackwell. Secrets will be your undoing." Magnus tried to pull away his hand, but her grip tightened so he could not get free. "Your legacy will be one of hate, and when your body has turned to dust, you shall be forever trapped in the black well of souls."

She unexpectedly let go of his hand, sending Magnus backward. Oscar came forward and took his arm to keep him from falling.

"Why does he get the black well of souls and I the white one?" Oscar posed.

Marie wiped her hands together as if removing some unseen stain. "It's a harbinger of destiny. A very dark destiny."

"What is this well of the souls?" Magnus questioned.

Her brown eyes seared into him. "A place where souls are born into our world. Some are good; some are bad."

"Hence the reason I am from the white and you the black," Oscar teased.

"It would explain a few things," Magnus conceded.

"I know the darkness that surrounds you, Monsieur Blackwell, and it is deceptive. You feel it gives you strength, but it only drains you of all your goodness. You will have to fight to regain your soul. If you do not, you shall lose it forever."

Magnus was unmoved by her words. Tipping his head to her, he politely smiled. "I appreciate the advice, mistress, but I am secure in my fate. One cannot have an exemplary life without enduring a little tragedy."

She shook her head, offering him a slight smirk. Turning away, she went to a table of herbs and selected a few dried twigs. Her hands began to weave the twigs into a form.

"Tragedy is what is done to us, not what we do to others."

"I think Shakespeare would disagree with you there, dear woman," Oscar jested.

"There is one who holds something you want to possess," she called as the twigs in her hand took on a human shape.

"Perhaps there is. What of it?" Magnus replied.

She unwound some black ribbon from a bunch of herbs on the table and began winding it around the stick figure in her hand. "She can be your redemption or your demise; the choice is up to you."

"Care to elaborate?" Oscar edged in.

When she had finished winding the black ribbon around the stick figure, she held it up to Magnus. "Give it a name."

His eyebrows went up. "A name?"

"Think of the name of the one who holds what you want. Don't say it, only think it."

Magnus stared at the rudimentary doll in her hands. Suddenly, the face of his old friend floated across his vision.

"Now spit on it," Marie directed.

His eyes gauged her sincerity, and then he did what she asked. While wiping his mouth with the back of his gloved hand, she handed him the doll made of twigs.

"Keep it with you. Feed it with your hate."

He took the doll from her. "Then what?"

Her short chortle carried around the room. "That is entirely up to you."

Oscar came forward and inspected the doll. "And now you have a souvenir of your trip to New Orleans. How exciting."

"It's five cents for the voodoo doll." Marie held out her hand for payment.

Smiling, Magnus reached into his pocket and laid a five-dollar bill across her palm. "For the doll and the fortune telling." He put his hat on his head and politely tipped it to her. "Thank you, Mistress Laveau."

"*Bonne soirée,* gentlemen."

Without so much as a second glance, Marie disappeared behind the curtain she had come from in the corner of the room.

"The meetin' is over," Cleitus called as he opened the French doors to the cottage.

While climbing back into the carriage, Magnus inspected his souvenir.

"What did you name it?" Oscar asked as Magnus took the seat across from him in the black carriage.

Magnus looked out the window at the French Quarter street and scowled. "O'Connor."

Chapter Ten

A Door Opening

After a supper of Chateaubriand at Antoine's , the two men returned to Hotel Monteleone to dress for the evening's frivolities. Stepping into their horse-drawn carriage in their formal black coats, black top hats, and white dress shirts, Oscar and Magnus sat back and enjoyed the ride out of the city to the banks of Bayou St. John.

With Cleitus at the helm, their carriage traversed the bumpy road of Esplanade Avenue as the sun dipped below the tall oaks to the side of the wide street. They passed a green trolley car belonging to the New Orleans City Railroad Company on the tracks in the middle of the street. Pulled by a pair of thick silver mules, the packed trolley carried customers home after a long day in the city.

"Are you sure you want to see this ceremony?" Oscar asked,

his black top hat in his hands. "I've heard these things can get pretty wild."

Magnus stared out the window as his body swayed back and forth with the rocking of their carriage. "I'm ready for anything, Oscar."

"Yes, I believe you are." Oscar paused when the carriage hit a pothole. "I've read the natives who settled this area called the waterway Bayouk Choupic. There used to be portage between the bayou and the Mississippi River that attracted the early French explorers, traders, and trappers. The placement of Bayou St. John was a key factor in the selection of the site when the city was founded in 1718."

Magnus chuckled as he admired the flickering gas street lamps along Esplanade Avenue. "Where did you read that?"

"A pamphlet at the hotel."

"Maybe you can use our experience tonight in one of your books."

"Can you imagine the vapor-susceptible, God-fearing women in England reading about that?" He rolled his eyes. "I would be drawn and quartered."

Magnus rubbed his hand over his chin as his cruel laughter bounced around the stuffy carriage interior.

"You're a wonder, Magnus," Oscar went on. "You don't seem the least bit bothered by anything that young woman said to you today. All through dinner, you never mentioned anything about it. And here we are, riding out to see God-knows-what, and you are as cool as a block of ice. Most men would be shaken by what you were told."

"I'm not going to let the ramblings of some voodoo priestess upset me." Magnus picked at a piece of lint on his black coat. "My failure has been predicted time and again by individuals much better informed than Mistress Marie. And yet here I am still successful and determining my path."

"Who predicted you would fail?"

Magnus sucked in a breath of the humid mimosa laden air. "My father. As long as I can remember, he professed I would achieve nothing in life but misery and idleness. I have fought continually to prove him wrong. When he told me I was not smart enough to excel at boarding school, I studied day and night to get high marks in my classes. After finishing school, he predicted I would never get into college without his political connections. But I got into Harvard on my own. I worked for two years as an apprentice under an architect my father knew, and that got me into the architecture program."

"You showed him. That must have felt good," Oscar proposed with an encouraging cheerfulness in his voice.

"I didn't feel anything." Magnus spied the approaching black water of the bayou rising beyond the carriage window. "I think I stopped feeling the day my mother died. That was a turning point for me."

"How old were you?"

"Eight. We buried her and my younger brother, Edward. Typhoid fever. They were not even cold when my father shipped me off to boarding school. After that, I made sure never to let my emotions cloud my judgment." He raised his chin. "And I have stuck with that mantra until ..."

"What was her name?" Oscar tilted forward in his seat, eager to hear more about the woman who had conquered Magnus.

"Her? What makes you think it was a woman who broke through my defenses?"

Oscar was taken aback by the statement. "Isn't she the reason you're here? Haven't you been repairing your broken heart because she chose your friend over you?"

Magnus balled his right hand into a fist. "Frances did not break my heart, and she was not the one who betrayed my trust. O'Connor did that the moment he told me he was going to ask the woman I had chosen for myself to be *his* wife. On that day, he sealed his fate and mine."

Oscar held out his hands, pleading for reason. "People fall in love, Magnus. You can't begrudge a man for following his heart."

Magnus's wry smile reflected the evil in his thoughts. "I don't begrudge him love, Oscar. I just want back what belongs to me."

The carriage came to a stop, and Magnus turned his eyes to the window. "Ah, we must be here."

He was about to move toward the carriage door when Oscar asked, "What will you do?"

"Do?" Magnus paused and stared at him.

"About your friend and his wife? What will you do to them?" Oscar's brown eyes traveled the length of his face. "You are not a man to forgive and forget."

"I'll have to keep you posted on my plans, Oscar. Perhaps you can even use that in one of your books, too."

Exiting the carriage, Magnus peered out over the still, black water of the bayou. Around the higher edges of the shore, several homes were scattered. For him, the homes represented an interesting mix of the architecture so prevalent in this part of the world. A few were the classic, double-gallery homes raised on brick piers. The two-story structures had hipped roof lines and boasted covered, two-story galleries framed by columns. He was admiring a raised central-hall house composed of wood with a long front gallery that was framed by six columns when the flickering of light further along the street drew his eyes to another structure.

It was a green and white Creole colonial house not often seen in the city. Meant for country living, such homes were still found on working plantations that dotted the Louisiana landscape. Magnus smiled as he studied the structure. It had been one of his favorite architectural styles because of the clean sweeping lines and peaceful appearance. They were just the opposite of the austere, cold, and almost Romanesque home in which he had been raised as a child.

His mind whirled with fleeting images of Altmover Manor. The eight-bedroom, stone and timber box-like structure he still called home had stone ravens guarding the eaves and vast, almost lifeless rooms.

"Where is this ritual to take place?" Oscar called to Cleitus as he emerged from the carriage.

Climbing down from his seat atop the carriage, Cleitus pointed to the outline of what appeared to be a dark bridge over the water. "Bayou Bridge is where all the rituals take place."

"We must be early," Magnus said.

"No, sir. You just walk on ahead to the bridge. When they see you comin', they will light the fires." Cleitus came up to Magnus and Oscar. "I'll wait here for y'all to return."

"You don't want to join in?" Oscar questioned.

Cleitus shook his head. "No, I prefer to watch from back here. It's safer."

"Safer?" Oscar asked while putting his hat on his head. "Safe from what?"

"The spirits." Cleitus nodded to the open bayou. "The spirits come out when voodoo takes place on the bayou."

"What spirits?" Magnus probed.

Cleitus waved them on. "You'll see, sirs."

Oscar just laughed as he patted Magnus across the back. The two men set off for the water's edge, keeping the shadow of the bridge in their line of sight.

Just as they were almost there, a bright open bonfire lit up at the entrance to the bridge just ahead of them. Several people, all wearing white, came into view in the firelight.

Oscar clapped his hands at the theatrics; however, Magnus was not impressed.

The people gathered began to stomp their feet along with the slow, steady cadence of a drumbeat.

Magnus gaped around for the drummer, but he could not make out any shapes in the dark.

They were coming up to the small group when a woman all in white with a white turban on her head and no shoes on her feet stepped out of the darkness and blocked their path.

"Gentlemen, you're right on time."

Magnus removed his hat and bowed to Madam Simone. "Thank you for having us, madam. I have been looking forward to your demonstration all day."

Oscar took in the mixture of men and women beginning to move slowly together as they hummed some unrecognizable tune. "What are they doing?"

"Summoning the spirit," she explained, waving her baton juju at the group. "Songs are used to summon the deity we will worship. They're similar to hymns in the Catholic Church that are used to celebrate Catholic saints. We use songs to open the gate between the deities and the human world and invite the spirits to possess someone."

"Excellent." Oscar was as a giddy as a schoolboy. "Who are we summoning tonight?"

Madam Simone's green eyes shifted to Magnus. "For you

Magnus, I am invoking the goddess Ezili. She has tremendous power and several different roles: goddess of the word, love, help, goodwill, health, beauty, and fortune as well as the goddess of jealousy, vengeance, and discord."

"Why do you summon her for me, dear lady?"

"Because only she can redirect your path. She will either guide you to your true love, or she will lead you deeper into jealousy. The choice is hers."

"I already know my true love," he argued.

"Do you? We'll see what the goddess says." Madam Simone pointed her long stick to the side of the bonfire. "Take your places there by the fire and never leave them. The fire will protect you from the dead who will visit us."

"What dead?" Oscar pressed, his small eyes growing big with fear. "You mean like ghosts?"

"A ritual always awakens the spirits of the dead in the area." She once again directed the end of her cane to the fire. "Stay there until we are done, and they will not harm you."

Madam Simone sauntered away, clutching her long stick in her hands. Standing beside her fellow worshippers, her body began to sway, caught up in the seductive beat.

As her gyrations became more frenzied, her followers began erratically jumping about. Their bodies resembled the wild nature of the wind when enlivened by a coming storm. Words that were unintelligible to Magnus started to issue forth from the mouths of those gathered around the fire. The women's bodies were now undulating in the most seductive way. The group began to break off into couples, with the men taking a chosen woman in their arms and moving with them. Madam Simone was the only one without a partner. She stood out in front of the group; her hands raised high, and her face turned toward the heavens.

She spoke in a language that was neither French nor English, but the passion of her words needed no translation. She held up her baton juju in the air, entreating someone or something to join their group.

The dancers were getting more heated in their movements, and couples began to mimic the throes of sexual ecstasy. The song they had been singing would occasionally be interrupted by a sudden cry or scream by one of the participants.

"My word," Oscar said beside him as the light from the bonfire illuminated his long face. "We don't have anything like this back in jolly old England."

Magnus smiled, amused by his comment, but he was again distracted by the heated dance of lust taking place before him. There was something primitive about it. The song blended with the beat of drums, and the followers' movements resonated with him. Then, the air changed, and a mist formed on the water beside them, but Magnus chalked up the phenomenon to the play of firelight.

A heaviness settled in the air as if the humidity suddenly had doubled. Magnus began to feel weighted down in his limbs, and he yearned to move and free himself of the unusual feeling.

"Do you feel that?"

The tall Englishman's eyes were on fire as he remained hypnotized by the frenzied throes of the followers. "Feel what?"

Magnus did not press the issue. He felt a change in the air. It was as if he was in touch with everything around him. With his senses heightened, Magnus could taste the air and feel the thickness of it on his skin. His heart beat faster, and with every breath, the rise and fall of his chest quickened. A light film of sweat broke out over his upper lip, and he was dizzy—all of a sudden, he was unbelievably dizzy.

Madam Simone arched backward, and her eyes rolled up in the back of her head. Her face contorted in pain, but her lips still moved, still spoke that strange language Magnus could not understand.

Suddenly, the fire next to them swelled higher, the kindling cracking loudly as the flames rose upward. Oscar laughed and clapped his hands at the show, but Magnus did not find it amusing. Somewhere in the depths of his soul, he was afraid.

Then, he saw it. Beyond the group, close to the water's edge, something shimmered slightly—as if the moonlight danced on the water. The shimmer took shape, and Magnus had to blink to make sure his eyes were not playing tricks on him.

The singing of the revelers died away as the form of a woman materialized before his eyes. She wore only a nightdress that clung to her wet body. Her hair was long, dark, and hung freely down her back. Her face was luminescent as if she was part of the moon that shone above. When her black eyes connected with Magnus, he felt an uncontrollable urge to go to her.

Leaving the firelight, he headed toward the water, eager to learn more about the woman. Beyond the glare of the bonfire, his eyes were better able to take in her figure. Her nightdress was torn in places and had dark splotches on it in others. She stood at the water's edge, her feet hidden below the surface of the bayou. As he drew closer, Magnus got a better view of her exquisite face. Her pale, snowy skin glowed in the darkness, and her features were perfect except for a scar above her right lip. He ached to help her, to guide her from the water and back to the warmth of the fire.

"Are you all right?"

She titled her head to the side as she examined him. Then without saying anything, she held out her hand to him.

Chapter Eleven

The Wrong Road

That night, back in his hotel room, Magnus could not sleep. The ghost from the bayou kept appearing in his head, calling to him. Frustrated, he tossed off the covers and went to his balcony.

Observing the full moon showering down on the scattered rooftops of the French Quarter, Magnus's anger reignited. Pounding his fist on the black iron railing around his balcony, he cursed the fates that had brought him to the strange and yet fascinating city. He had hoped putting some distance between him, Frances, and O'Connor would cool his ire, but he should have known better. He was not a man to ever forget a slight, and usually, with time, his need for vengeance only intensified. Such was the case with O'Connor and Frances.

Her name brought to mind the sweet scent of honeysuckle

he would forever attribute to her. Her eyes, lips, figure, and upfront manner were etched in his soul. Just the thought of her brought his cock to life.

"Shit!" he growled.

Knowing he would never return to sleep with lust coursing through his veins, he grabbed his clothes still on the chair by his bed. There was only one place for him to be. He just hoped Madam Simone had a fresh young creature ready to satiate his needs.

The girl was young, eager, and her round ass beckoned to him. Pushing her headfirst onto the squeaky brass bed with the blue bedspread, he raised her hips. She had been prepared with the sticky oil that made his cock tingle. When he spread her butt cheeks apart, he slipped his finger into her, testing her tightness. She was fresh and untouched just as Madam Simone had said.

His cock was hard with the promise of her virgin ass. Unable to wait, he thrust into her. She cried out briefly—like most women did when he entered them in this way. Others had put up more of a fight, but this girl didn't. Pity. He liked the struggle. It quenched his lust and cooled his anger.

Magnus pounded into her, her occasional groans spurring his desire. When he finally came, he grunted into her back, resting his head against her golden skin. She smelled of soap and the pungent oil in her ass. The aroma turned him off, and Magnus quickly pulled out of her. He went to the bathroom, eager to wash off the remnants of her.

Magnus buttoned up his trousers as he headed out the bedroom door. He needed a drink, something to wash away the smell of the girl that lingered on his skin.

"How was Mona?" Madam Simone inquired when he stepped into her intimate sitting room.

She had changed back into one of her regal white lace gowns; her thick rich brown hair was piled atop her head in a fashionable coif and a single gold necklace made of glittering emeralds shone about her neck.

"She was satisfactory," he reported. "The oil she used was a bit of a nuisance, though."

Madam Simone fondled the dragon's head handle on the long cane resting next to her chair. "Better than hearing her scream."

He took the chair next to her, admiring the small fire burning in the hearth. Despite the heat of summer, the fire gave the room a certain coziness. "Sometimes the screaming adds a bit of flavor to the act."

She chuckled, drumming her fingers on the dragon's head of her cane. "You are a man playing with fire. Taking whores in such a manner is one thing, but taking a woman of character or position up the ass will eventually get you sent to prison."

"That's why I make sure to fuck married women who are in no position to complain about their treatment."

A woman wearing only a see-through petticoat entered the room carrying a silver tray with a single old-fashioned glass on it. She eased up to Magnus and presented him the drink.

"I took the liberty," Madam Simone told him. "I figured you would be thirsty after your exertions."

He lifted the drink from the silver tray and eyed the young girl's naked breasts. "I will miss this city and all of its delights."

"Are you leaving us so soon?"

He peered into his whiskey and soda. "I have to return to

school soon."

"Are you sure that is where you want to be?"

Magnus glanced up at her. "I have only one year left in my studies. I need to finish."

Madam Simone gazed into the fire. "What will you do when you are done? You don't need to work."

"How would you know that?" He raised his drink to his lips.

"I made inquiries about you and your family."

He held his glass before his lips. "For what purpose?"

Madam Simone waved off the worry in his voice. "I have no interest in blackmail, Magnus. That is not what I do. But I will offer you some advice." She paused and turned her green eyes to him. "Change your path. Where you're headed, no man should go."

"Another one of your cryptic messages, Madam?"

"You know what I'm talking about—the girl, the one you pine over; let her go. Let her be with the man she has chosen. You need to rid yourself of that hate before it destroys you."

"It's already destroyed me." He gulped back more of his drink. "What if I were to make you an offer? Perform one of your voodoo rituals for me and bring back the girl. Make her mine again. What would you charge me?"

She shook her head and stood from her chair, retrieving her long cane. "I will not change the course of love, Magnus. That goes against the laws of the universe. Love is the most powerful magic there is; no spell can break it."

His outrage stirred, and he hastily finished the contents of his drink. "I thought you were an all-powerful voodoo high priestess, and yet you tell me you can't perform such a simple spell."

"Not can't, Magnus: won't. I will not destroy love. No mortal has the right to take away such a gift."

He jumped from his chair and went to her side. "Gift?" He tossed his head back, and his maniacal laugh permeated the room. "More like curse. I made some inquiries about you as well, madam. By day, you hand out love potions and amulets to lonely rich girls looking for wealthy husbands, and at night, you make bedding arrangements for the men those hopeful young women desire. You summon spirits for rich widows hoping for news of their dead husbands and children. You are a liar, a cheat, a swindler, and are known to have several politicians in your pocket because of their propensity for women of a darker color." He threw his glass into the fire. "You stand there preaching to me of paths and righteousness when your path is more crooked and foul than mine could ever be."

Madam Simone squared her shoulders, gripping her cane. "Careful, Magnus. You do not know with whom you are dealing."

He ripped the dragon cane from her hand. "Neither do you."

The tingle from the walking stick hit his arm, and then the power cascading through him turned to rage. Like the dragon in the handle of the cane, Magnus felt he could breathe fire. His energy was boundless, and the sense of power exhilarated him. His hands pulsated as he held the baton juju. With such an instrument, he could win Frances back, and he wouldn't need the voodoo priestess's help.

"You feel it, don't you, Magnus? The power is seductive, but in the hands of the untrained, it can be a dangerous weapon." She motioned to the long cane. "Now give it back."

Magnus was on fire. He had no intention of ever letting go of the cane.

"You must give me back my baton," she warned in a voice dripping with her fury.

His eyes caught in the firelight, and he sneered at her. "Never."

Magnus would do anything to keep the power of the cane for himself. But how could he get the woman to give it up?

Madam Simone reached for the baton juju, but Magnus was too fast for her. Infused with his anger and driven by his desire to keep the magical cane, he raised the handle high in the air. Without second-guessing his murderous intent, Magnus brought the cane down hard on her head. The crack of the wood connecting with her skull was like music to his ears. He wanted to hear it again.

On the floor in front of the hearth, Madam Simone writhed in pain and clutched her head. "What have you done?"

"What I have to," he snarled, hovering over her.

Madam Simone's green eyes connected with his. "Killing me will seal your fate, boy."

Magnus raised the cane again. "Then so be it."

Wanting to silence her forever, he came down hard on her head once more. He repeated the blows, over and over, as madness gripped him.

Magnus had no idea how many times he hit her with the heavy handle, but by the time he stopped, his arms ached, and he was out of breath. What was left of the woman's head was nothing more than an unrecognizable mass of flesh, bone, and hair.

His senses suddenly returned, and he dropped the stick. The infusion of power and anger that had driven him disappeared. What had he done? How could he kill like that? Such thoughts, such actions had never been part of him before.

A flash of something on the hardwood floor caught his eye. The eyes of the dragon in the cane's handle were glowing red.

He stooped next to Madam Simone's body and studied the intricately carved handle. Tentatively, he reached out and caressed the smooth wood. As soon as his fingers touched the stick, the insurmountable rush of energy returned. Here was the instrument of his downfall. Or was it his salvation? His hand closed around the handle.

"From this moment on, I will no longer be a servant of fate."

Rising to his feet, Magnus took in the room and the woman's lifeless body on the floor. As if sent by some divine messenger, visions of fire filled his head. Instantly, Magnus knew what he had to do to cover his tracks.

Gently setting the cane against one of the chairs, he headed to the closest bookcase and gathered up an armful of books. After tossing the books into the fire, he watched as the flames rose higher. He collected more books and arranged them in a line from the fireplace grate to Madam Simone's body.

It did not take long before the fire spread and consumed her body. Grabbing more books, Magnus flung them around the room, hoping to add more fuel to the fire.

In minutes, the flames engulfed the room. Satisfied all evidence of his crime had been concealed, Magnus headed out the door. In the entrance parlor, he was relieved to find no one around. And as he stepped outside, the faint tendrils of the morning sun just touched the horizon. He thought he heard the gentle laughter of a woman all around him. He could have sworn the lilting chuckle sounded just like—

"Do you need a ride, sir?" A carriage driver appeared in front of him.

"No." Magnus gazed back at Mahogany House. "I think I'll

walk."

Strolling along the sidewalk, Madam Simone's cane swinging at his side, Magnus Blackwell felt reborn. Gazing down at the blazing red eyes of the dragon handle, he smirked. Things were beginning to look up for him. Now he had the power to change his destiny, and once he returned to Harvard, he was going to destroy O'Connor and regain his Frances.

"It would seem those fickle gods of fortune are finally smiling down on me."

The long walk back to Hotel Monteleone left Magnus famished. Deciding a hearty breakfast was in order, he returned to his room, changed out of his smoky clothes, and left the long cane on his bed.

After being seated in a corner booth in the hotel restaurant, Magnus was served a piping hot cup of coffee and chicory—he was addicted. He had not even taken the first sip of his coffee when a welcomed face graced his table.

"You're up early," Oscar remarked as he took a seat on the bench across from Magnus.

"Yes, I had a good night's sleep to help me get started early today. I have to make arrangements to head back to Harvard."

"Sadly, I too need to make arrangements to return to London." He frowned while waving down a waiter. "I need to get back to my magazine. Women's corset problems and diet secrets cannot be ignored any longer."

Magnus sipped his coffee. "Come and see me sometime at my family home on Mount Desert Island, Oscar. I would love to have the chance to spend more time with you."

"I will make a point of it. Who knows, maybe I can bring you a published book next time we meet. My head is just swimming with ideas." He glanced up again. "Where is the waiter?"

Magnus turned and eyed the restaurant, a rectangular shape dotted with white-linen tables lit by brass chandeliers and walls decorated with scenic paintings of the city. At the entrance, next to the podium, several red-vested waiters stood around and stared at the hotel entrance.

"What is going on?" he muttered.

Oscar shook his head. "Probably gossiping about one of the patrons. Hotel staff are very gossipy. I should know. I get my best tips from those in the hospitality trade."

A waiter standing with the men noticed Oscar staring at him. He hurried to their table, adjusting the white towel draped over his left arm.

"I beg your pardon, Mr. Wilde. We were just informed of the fire."

"Fire? What fire?" Oscar demanded.

"In the city. Over on Basin Street. One of the houses of ...." He dropped his eyes, searching for the right words. "A house belonging to a lady of ill repute is on fire."

Magnus's hand tightened around his coffee cup. "Any idea who?"

Their waiter nodded. "Madam Simone Glapion, sir. Her house is completely engulfed, and the fire department is fighting to make sure it doesn't spread to the rest of the city. Fire is feared in the French Quarter."

"How extraordinary!" Oscar extolled. "Madam Simone, did you say?"

"Yes, Mr. Wilde."

Oscar pointed at Magnus's coffee cup. "Be a good man and bring me one of those. And whatever pastries you have today. I'm famished."

The waiter bowed. "Yes, sir." He scurried away.

Oscar thumped the table with his fist. "Can you believe it? Our Madam Simone. I do hope she is all right. I would hate to think anything happened to her."

Magnus lifted his coffee to his lips. "What would it matter, Oscar? She is, after all, a whore."

"I'm surprised at you, Magnus. That's a very unchristian thing to say."

"Coming from a man who likes to sleep with young men, that isn't saying much, Oscar."

"Yes, well." He dipped his head. "I'm not a saint, Magnus."

Magnus chuckled and took another sip of coffee. "Neither of us are, Oscar."

Oscar eyed him suspiciously. "You didn't happen to go to her house last night? Perhaps to let off a little steam after all the excitement of that ritual at Bayou St. John? Those dancers were very seductive." He eased back in his seat. "Lord knows I could have used some companionship in my bed last night."

Magnus kept his eyes deadlocked on his friend. "I spent the entire night asleep in my room."

From the entrance of the restaurant, a young porter called out Magnus's name. "Magnus Blackwell, Mr. Magnus Blackwell."

Magnus waved down the boy in the bright red velvet suit.

The lad trotted over to the table with a silver tray in his hands. On top of the tray was a single, yellow slip of paper. "A telegram for you, sir," the boy said holding the tray out for Magnus.

Trepidation flowed through him. Telegrams were never good news.

Taking the telegram from the tray, he reached into his pocket and pulled out a nickel for the boy.

After taking the money, the young boy tucked the silver tray under his right arm and jogged back to the restaurant entrance.

Opening the telegram, Magnus felt his heart skip a beat. As he read the brief message, the impact of the words hit him like a wall of water.

"Is everything all right?" Oscar implored, the worry shining in his eyes.

Magnus kept any hint of emotion from his face as he handed the telegram to Oscar. "It seems my father is dead. I am to return to Altmover Manor and take up the family business."

Oscar read the telegram and reached out an encouraging hand. "My dear friend, I am so sorry."

Feeling as if a weight were lifting from his shoulders, Magnus casually reached for his cup of coffee. "I'm not sorry, Oscar."

"He was your father, Magnus; surely you must feel something."

Magnus flashed back to the previous night and to the spirit that beckoned to him from the bayou. "Last night, I saw someone or something coming out of that bayou. Madam Simone stopped it from getting close to me. I remember she said something about the creature I saw being a messenger of the dead."

"When did this happen?"

"When I left the bonfire and went to the water's edge, I thought I saw a woman. Madam Simone claimed it was a spirit."

His eyes lit up, and Oscar edged forward to the table. "What do you think you saw, Magnus?"

Magnus tried to picture the woman he had seen, her tattered

nightdress and her empty eyes, but the only image he could conjure was that of smoke and dust. "What do you think happens to us when we die, Oscar?"

Oscar tossed up his hands, appearing as if he were at a loss for words. "I wish I knew, my friend."

Magnus ran his finger around the rim of his coffee cup. "I know where we go, and it isn't heaven or paradise."

"What kind of end do you envision?"

Magnus raised his green eyes to Oscar, grinning with a profound certainty. "That's just it. I don't see death as an end. For me, it's turning into a whole new beginning."

Chapter Twelve

Altmover

Jacob O'Connor fashioned his vest and checked his stiff shirt in the mirror. Before reaching for his frock coat, he saw her brown eyes stare back at him in the mirror.

"What is it?"

Frances rose from the bed, her deep blue dressing gown trailing behind her. "I just love watching you dress." She came up to him and adjusted the collar of his shirt. "Almost two years of marriage and I am still entranced by you."

He wrapped her in his arms. How had he been so lucky to win the heart of such a captivating creature? He admired her porcelain skin and the lovely way she had twirled her honey-blonde hair atop her head. "Perhaps you will change your mind about me come our third anniversary. What do think?"

She ran her arms around his neck. "I just hope we aren't still living here."

His arms dropped from her waist. "Frances, please. Let's not start that again. It's a good position. Do you want to go back to the ratty apartment in Boston? You know I can make three times what I was making at Fogle, Hardwick, and Hillman."

She backed away, and her high forehead furrowed with worry lines. "I told you, father said he would help us. He offered to pay for a place for us so you wouldn't have to worry about rent."

His irritation rose in his belly—the same way it always did whenever she spoke of getting help from the judge. "How many times do I have to tell you, no!" His voice shook with anger. "I will not take a penny from your father. It was hard enough having him help pay for our expenses when I was at Harvard. I will not take any more handouts from him."

She pointed to the oak bedroom door with the brass doorknob. "You would take a handout from him but not let my father help us? Why, Jacob?"

He went to the dark walnut dresser and scooped some coins on top of it into his change pocket. He then picked up the gold pocket watch Frances had given him as a wedding present.

"Magnus has given me a job, not a handout."

She folded her arms over her chest and stared at him. "I don't trust him."

He let out a long breath between his pursed lips. He was getting tired of having this conversation with her. "Frances, Magnus is my friend. He hired me to renovate his family home because he trusts me and believes I'm very good at what I do. When I finish with Altmover Manor, I can get a job at any of the top firms in Boston. We can go back and have a fine house and have parties for your friends like you've always wanted." His arms went around her slender waist. "And we can start that family you always talk about."

She sighed and rested her head against his chest. "I would like that, Jacob."

He stroked her hair, amazed at the silkiness of it and the way it always smelled of honeysuckle. "Just give me the time I need, sweetheart, and I promise it will be worth it."

She eased back from his embrace. "I just hate living on this godforsaken island. There is nothing in West Tremont but a few shops, the general store, and the post office. It's all so boring."

He chuckled as he stood back from her. "Most wives would be thrilled that they did not need to go into town to shop. Magnus has provided everything for us." He waved his hands about the brightly painted bedroom with its lovely antique furnishings and four-poster bed. "He has been very generous."

"He has ulterior motives for bringing us to Maine, Jacob. Why can you not see that?" She went back to the bed and sat down on the cozy, yellow comforter. "He's not the man you knew in college. He's changed."

Jacob turned for the door. "Of course he's changed, Frances. When his father died, and he had to take over the family business, he had to grow up, practically overnight." He stopped at the door. "Why do you continually bring that up?" He walked out of the room.

Frances followed him out the door. "Because he has changed, Jacob."

As he strode along the narrow hall with its family paintings of Magnus's younger brother and his mother, he could hear Frances's footfalls behind him. Glancing briefly at the picture of the dainty woman with the sad brown eyes, dressed all in black, Jacob rushed ahead.

The hallway opened into a wide living room with knotted pine floors, hued pine ceiling beams, and white wainscoting running along the pale blue painted walls. More family portraits covered the walls, but Jacob did not know the names of these Blackwells. Magnus made a point to ignore his questions when he had asked shortly after moving in a few months before.

Frances stopped above the blue throw rug in the center of the room and faced her husband as he went to the stone fireplace.

"When he never returned to Harvard to finish his senior year, he never contacted you. Never once sent a telegram or message to inquire about his good friend and his wife. Then, almost two years with no word, and he sends a man around to Fogle, Hardwick, and Hillman and requests a meeting."

Jacob placed two more logs on the fire burning in the hearth. "What's so odd about that?"

"Why didn't he come in person?"

Jacob wiped his hands together. "He's a busy man now, Frances. He has an empire to run."

She stomped her foot on the floor. "Why you, Jacob? Of all the architects along the East Coast, why did he want you?" Her husband glared at her. "You have no experience with renovating older homes; you told me so yourself the day he offered you the job. Admit it; even you were baffled by why he chose you."

Jacob briefly admired their wedding photograph in the silver frame on the mantel. "I can't get into this again, not now, darling. I have to get to the manor house."

Frances pouted her heart-shaped lips together. "What about breakfast?"

He laughed as he walked up to her. "You are a wonder with a needle, amazing with debating me on any subject, a fine

125

horsewoman," he nuzzled her cheek, "and a fantastic lover, but you, Mrs. O'Connor, are a terrible cook."

She ran her finger over his freshly shaved cheek. "I'll make it up to you tonight." Frances nipped his neck.

His hand went to her right breast, and he suddenly ached to rip the dressing gown from her body and take her in the living room. It never ceased to amaze him how his lust for his wife only grew stronger with time.

Remembering all the work he had waiting for him at the manor, he dutifully kissed her head. "I will take you up on that offer after I get home this evening." He playfully slapped her round butt. "Now stop getting me excited before I have to go to work."

Frances was giggling at him as he hurried to the door. Next to her velvet skin, seductive curves, and graceful hands, her giggle was his undoing. Stepping outside into the brisk cold, he quickly shut the front door, cutting off her laughter.

Climbing down the three, short steps from his gingerbread-accented porch, Jacob walked away from the bright yellow Victorian cottage he shared with his wife. He looked out across the muddy gravel driveway, over the assorted carriages stuffed with building supplies, to the towering stone walls of Altmover Manor.

It always thrilled Jacob a little when he gazed up at the manor. Meant to be Colonial Revival in style with a symmetrical facade, accented doorway, and evenly spaced windows on either side, the original architect had veered dramatically away from such a simplistic design.

At three and a half stories, it dwarfed all the other homes he had seen on the island. With eight bedrooms and six antiquated bathrooms, Jacob reasoned the structure must have been a monumental task and strained the limited resources on the island when it was first constructed by Magnus's grandfather in 1835. Built of stone to protect it from the corrosive Atlantic winds, it had white wood shutters located beside each of the large, colonial windows. The newly installed leaded glass front doors also had shutters to keep out the frequent squalls that blew in from the nearby ocean. Two stone chimneys rose up on both ends of the steeply sloping gray-slated roof, and stone ravens peered down from each corner.

The ravens were particularly confusing to Jacob. Magnus had no idea where they came from. They had not been part of the original house plans and seemed firmly cemented into the masonry on the top floor. A straight stone staircase rose from the ground up to the first-floor entrance, while a portico of white-painted wood sheltered carriages pulling up to the house from the elements. The portico clashed with the Colonial Revival architecture, but had been added by Reynolds Blackwell to keep his guests dry when they arrived at the remote home.

Now, Jacob's job was to remove the portico and change the appearance of Altmover Manor. When Magnus had first approached him with the idea to renovate the house and update the antiquated interior, Jacob had been excited. But what had started out as a simple renovation had snowballed into a nightmare.

Climbing the newly expanded stone staircase at the front of the house, Jacob stepped beneath the scaffolding that had been set up to erect the six Corinthian pillars Magnus wanted in front of the home, along with sweeping balconies that were to open up on the second- and third-floor bedrooms. He had insisted his home was to remind him of a grand Southern plantation, but the house was beginning to resemble something that should have burned down during the Civil War.

"Can't we just plant some big oaks in the garden and call it a day," Jacob had argued, but Magnus had been stubborn.

"Build it the way I want, O'Connor, or I will find someone else," he had threatened months ago when he first announced his plans.

Jacob had no choice but to go along with Magnus's madness. He needed the job and desperately needed the money.

"Mr. O'Connor?" a member of the crew on the scaffolding called out. "When are the iron brackets coming for the balconies?"

"I was promised today, Henry. They should be on the next wagonload of supplies."

The puffy-faced Henry peered over the edge of the scaffolding at Jacob. "You told me that yesterday."

Jacob held up his hand to his brow to block the sun from shining in his eyes. "I'm assured the brackets will make it here today."

Grunting with annoyance, Henry went back to drilling holes in the thick stone to set the balcony brackets.

Jacob refrained from mumbling the expletives on his lips. With the chilly temperatures, frequent storms, the cranky crew, and the overbearing master of the manor, Jacob was about to pitch every warning the nuns of Peter Clement orphanage had taught him about swearing and embrace the gates of hell. At least there it would be warmer than in Maine.

Entering the open front doors, he stepped on the path of plywood that had been laid over the white marble floors to protect them from the workman's boots and headed inside. He glanced up at the plaster ceiling above with its painted medallion of interlocking rose vines. There was the impressive eight-tiered crystal chandelier that hung from a red velvet rope secured to the second-floor landing. The rope allowed the chandelier to be raised and lowered to light and extinguish the candles. The twinkling of sunlight on the freshly hung gold-flecked wallpaper just inside the entrance reminded Jacob of fairy dust from a children's bedtime story. The colorful landscapes of green valleys and lush forests that were ornately framed and spread out on the walls contrasted greatly with the view of the barren rocky land beyond the doors of the home. Jacob always found it oddly amusing that the paintings inside Altmover Manor were more appealing than any of the views from the home's twenty-four giant windows.

"Mr. O'Connor," the soft-spoken Emily Mann called from the foot of the great black walnut staircase just beyond the foyer.

The recently installed fire-breathing dragon on the banister dwarfed the demure figure of Magnus's secretary. Another touch Magnus had insisted on adding to the home. Jacob had personally preferred the winding rose vine motif of the former banister, but Magnus specifically wanted a dragon.

"He needs to speak with you," Emily advised as Jacob came up to her.

Jacob reflexively cringed. Every time Magnus wanted to talk to him, plans changed, contractors got angry, and Jacob was left trying to appease both sides.

He glanced down at the ruby red eyes Magnus wanted added to the dragon's head at the end of the banister. "What is it this time?" he asked the slight woman with the thick glasses.

"I wish I knew. He probably had another one of those dreams of his."

Jacob scratched his head. "Yeah, any chance we could get some laudanum shipped here to stop him from having those crazy dreams."

Emily Mann rocked her head back and cackled. Her laugh surprised Jacob every time. Her plain, almost dowdy looks, unflattering wool dresses, and bucked teeth hid a fun-loving woman.

Emily patted his shoulder. "Just agree with whatever he says. It's the only way I get through the day." She left him at the base of the stairs and went to a dark-paneled door in the hallway behind the staircase.

Jacob peered up the stairway to the second floor where Magnus kept his office. Knowing there was no getting out of their meeting, he grudgingly trudged up the red runner in the center of the white marble-inlaid steps.

Jacob knocked on the carved office door—decorated with more dragons—and waited for the deep voice of his employer.

"O'Connor?"

Jacob smiled, heartened by the fact that Magnus Blackwell had never stopped calling him O'Connor. Jacob pushed the door open and stepped into the former library of the home, which Magnus had converted into an office.

Expensive, leather-bound books filled the oak bookcases, and a rolling ladder with brass trim was able to circumvent the room on a brass rail. Two red leather reading chairs sat before the wide, colonial window that looked out over the steep cliffs to the Atlantic. In the center of the room, Magnus had placed his father's huge, mahogany desk with three lions' heads carved into the front.

Formally attired in his black coat, ascot tie, and starched white shirt, Magnus sat behind his desk. His thick, dirty-blond hair was neatly combed to the side, flattering his square face and firm jawline. Jacob had envied his handsome countenance—the straight nose, carved cheekbones, ridged brow, and uncanny green eyes. He wondered how different his life would have been if he had been born with such stunning looks instead of his swarthy complexion. If only he'd been blessed with Magnus's upper crust features, he would have had the same opportunities.

"How is Frances today? We must make sure we keep her happy," Magnus stated without looking up from the ledger on his desk.

Jacob clasped his clenched hands behind his back. Magnus always started every conversation asking about his wife. In the beginning, he considered it polite; now, it irked him.

"She's well, Magnus, just bored."

He jotted something down in his ledger with his fancy new fountain pen, which was all the rage among the rich. "As she should be. There is nothing to do on this damned island."

"Then why do you stay in this house?"

Magnus blew on the wet ink and slammed the book closed. "Because it's my ancestral home."

"Your home is in Boston, Magnus, not Mount Desert Island."

"My grandfather built this place, my father renovated it, and I am doing as they did." He pushed back in his chair. "It will be here for my sons when the time comes and their sons after that. Hence the term *ancestral home*." Magnus stood from his chair. "I had an odd dream last night."

Jacob's insides trembled.

"I think we should redo the old mantel in the dining room. I want a dragon one." He reached for the tall cane, leaning against his desk.

"More dragons?" Jacob loudly sighed. "What is it with the dragons, Magnus? You never mentioned being fond of them when we were at Harvard, but now you are obsessed."

Magnus regarded how the red eyes of the dragon cane glowed in the light from the windows. "They represent power to me. The power to assert my will over others."

"They represent a pain in the ass to me," Jacob said under his breath.

Magnus raised his eyes to him, looking as if he were about to rip him to shreds. The glare in his green orbs scared Jacob. He had seen the many moods of Magnus Blackwell over the years but never the sheer fury that confronted him at that moment. Perhaps Frances was right. There was something different about him.

Magnus's angry eyes cooled, and he grinned. "I guess all the changes are very taxing on you and your men."

Jacob kept up his stiff posture, afraid to drop his guard. "The men want to be able to complete a project, Magnus, before having to move on to the next. You keep adding and changing things so much that they are getting frustrated."

"And you are getting frustrated as well, aren't you, dear boy?" Magnus strolled up to Jacob while tapping his cane on the red Oriental rug.

Jacob focused on the tip of the long wooden cane. "It makes my job difficult."

"That's why I have made accommodations for you and Frances in my mother's old cottage. I knew this would not be an easy task, but being so close to the job and having Frances at your side must be some consolation."

Jacob nodded, afraid to say what he was thinking. "It is, and thank you for all you have done for me."

"Done for both of you—you and your lovely wife."

Magnus's sneer was not lost on Jacob. He dropped his eyes.

"Is that all you wanted? To change the mantel?"

Magnus ran his fingers along the smooth length of his cane. "When I was in New Orleans, I fell in love with their quaint courtyards in the French Quarter. I was thinking of putting a courtyard in the rear of the home. Perhaps with a dragon tile motif. I've already ordered a dragon fountain perfect for my plans. It's coming all the way from New Orleans. I wanted an authentic piece true to the city."

Jacob felt his face redden. "A courtyard? What about the sheer drop to the cliffs on the right side? It might be dangerous to put a courtyard so close."

"Find a way, O'Connor."

"Don't you think we've put enough Southern accents into the house? Short of tearing it down and starting over, I don't think there is much more we can do without destroying the aesthetic of the manor. Are you sure about this, Magnus?"

"I want to be reminded of New Orleans whenever I see my home. My time there left a deep impression on me."

Jacob inspected the icy glint in his friend's eyes. There was something different about him; he had no doubt. The affable man who had taken him under his wing at Harvard had morphed into a distrusting, leery stranger.

"Is there anything else, Magnus?" Jacob was anxious to get free from Magnus's disturbing gaze.

"The huge lamps you plan on putting outside of the front doors need to be changed. I want them to resemble the flickering gas lamps of New Orleans."

"We don't have gas on the island, Magnus."

"I know, but perhaps you can contact one of the companies that make those lamps in New Orleans and ask them if they have any with candle settings. See to it, O'Connor."

his father died."

Her arms wrapped around his waist. "I guess power and money change people."

"It will never change me."

Frances ran her hands up his short waistcoat. "Wanna bet?"

He kissed her lips, and instantly the drudgery of his day evaporated. She had that ability to wipe away all of his tribulations with a kiss.

Easing back, he let his lips travel to his favorite part on her neck—the one that always made her moan when he kissed it.

"You know what I would really love to do right now?"

She tilted her head further to the side, giving him access to her neck. "I can only imagine."

Her seductive moan was his undoing. Lifting her in his arms, Jacob carried a squealing Frances from the kitchen and into the bedroom.

Magnus stood by a bedroom window on the third floor and looked down on the yellow cottage. He saw the play of shadows from inside the cottage as the couple hurried across the living room and into the back bedroom. When the lights inside the cottage bedroom were extinguished, Magnus lifted the handle of his cane and lovingly stroked the head of the dragon.

"Enjoy her while you can, O'Connor."

Everything was falling into place. His plan was working out just as he'd envisioned. Magnus knew Frances would soon be his. Of that, he had no doubt. He wanted to give the magic in his cane some of the credit for the ease of his manipulations, but Magnus wasn't a fool. He knew his money, more than any magic, wielded the most power over men.

A knock on his door made him turn away from the window.

"Beg your pardon, sir," a waif-like blonde maid said as she furiously curtseyed to him. "I didn't know anyone was in here. I heard a voice and thought ...." She shut her mouth and was backing away when he stopped her.

"It's all right." He motioned her into the room with its giant sleigh bed and paintings of ocean views. "I was just inspecting the work on the bathroom."

The girl's big brown eyes darted about the room. "Yes, sir."

He eyed her black maid uniform. "You're new here."

She curtseyed again. "Yes, Mr. Blackwell. Ms. Emily hired me a few days ago to see to the third floor."

Not interested in her duties, but very attuned to the way her uniform cut across her slender hips, Magnus asked, "What's your name?"

"Regina, sir."

"How old are you, Regina?"

"Twenty, Mr. Blackwell."

Magnus felt his cock stir. He liked her soft voice and puppy-like brown eyes. "Is your family on the island?"

"No, sir. My family is back in Albany."

"So how did you end up on Mount Desert Island?"

She wrung her delicate hands. He liked her hands. They were graceful and mesmerizing—just like Frances's.

"I, ah, I'd prefer not to say, Mr. Blackwell."

He eased up to her. The cane was pulsating. He could feel the power coming from the wood. That always happened when he found something or someone who intrigued him.

"You can tell me, Regina." He set the tip of the cane on the thick, light blue rug beneath him. "I do not betray a confidence."

She shifted on her feet. "My parents arranged for me to be married to a man on the island. A Mr. Dearborn."

Magnus's brows went up. "Casey Dearborn? The owner of the general store in Mount Desert?"

"But when I got to the island and saw my intended ...." Her voice dried up.

Magnus's cruel laugh reverberated around the bedroom. "Oh, my dear girl. I completely understand. Casey is too old and too ugly for such a pretty young thing as you."

Her smooth cheeks blushed. "You think I'm pretty?"

He closed in the last few feet between them, his green eyes scanning her adorable pert nose and heart-shaped lips. "Tell me, Regina, what happened when you refused your intended?"

"He threw me out on the street. He kept all of my clothes and my money. Thank goodness Ms. Emily came along when she did. She gave me a job, a room in the servants' wing, and even got me some clothes."

Magnus was pleased she was under his roof. "Then I am so glad you are with us, Regina." His finger lightly caressed her pink cheek. "Tell me, how do you plan on making your way in the world? You don't want to be a maid all your life, do you?"

"No, sir." Her eyes glimmered with a sprinkling of hope. "I was hoping one day to own a nice shop and sell linens and ribbons. My father had a shop back in Albany. He taught me how to sew and mend clothes. I even got to make dresses for some of his customers." Her eyes dropped to the floor. "That was before I was sent here."

He went to the sleigh bed and sat on the light blue bedspread. Setting the tip of the cane on the floor, he rested his hands on the handle and studied the young woman. "Interesting. You know I own several newly built storefronts in the nearby town of West Tremont. I could help you. That is, if you are willing to help me."

Regina cocked her head to the side, taking a moment to absorb his meaning. When her eyes became like two walnuts, a thrill rippled through Magnus's cock.

"I can't do that, sir. I've never done ... such things. I'm a good girl."

"No doubt you are, but I am not asking to take your virginity. I can show you pleasure without ruining the gift you plan on giving your husband on your wedding night."

The curiosity in her eyes was delicious. Magnus savored it.

"How?" she asked after a brief silence.

His eyes swept down her petite figure. "Take off your clothes."

Regina's hands went to her chest. "Sir?"

He stood from the bed, motioning his cane down her black uniform. "Take off your clothes. I need to see the goods."

Her brown eyes pleadingly peered up at him. "You will give me a shop if I do as you ask?"

"Allow me to take what I want, and I promise to give you what you want."

Her hands trembled. "You won't hurt me, will you, sir?"

Magnus raised his cane and dragged the tip down the front of her dress. "Only if you do as I ask." He tapped the tip on the floor. "Just close your eyes and think of your lovely little shop."

Nodding, she reached behind her back. "Yes, sir."

While Regina removed her uniform, Magnus shut the bedroom door. She dropped the black dress on the floor, and her hands went to the top of her white petticoat.

He waved at her. "Leave that."

Magnus came up behind her and lifted the white petticoat

with the tip of his cane. "Now bend over and show me your ass."

"Sir?"

"You heard me," he growled.

Regina lifted up her white petticoat, revealing her round, white ass.

Magnus cupped her right butt cheek while his cock grew hard. "Get on the bed," he ordered. "And don't make a sound."

Chapter Fourteen

Secrets

The warmer winds of spring whipped the freshly bloomed wildflowers that blanketed the grounds of Altmover Manor. The black iron balcony railings for the second and third floors of the house were in place, and two of the six Corinthian columns were set into the newly fashioned first-floor porch.

Workman gathered on the front steps of the manor, enjoyed a brief break and took in the warm rays of sunlight. On the roof, Jacob met with his head contractor to decide what to do with the two stone ravens perched atop the corners.

"We've got to get them out of the way to be able to put the outside columns in place," Dexter Hartner warned. Readjusting the blue cap on his head, he kicked at one of the ravens with the toe of his boot. "I've got some dynamite we can use."

Jacob gaped at him. "Are you out of your mind?" And then

another thought hit him. "How much do you have?"

Dexter laughed, and his portly belly jiggled up and down beneath his blue overalls. "Why? You wanting to blow up the house already?"

Jacob chuckled as he gazed down at the third-floor balcony. "Almost. No, I may need it to take out some of the rock in the rear of the home so we can finish up the courtyard without endangering the men by getting too close to that cliff face."

Dexter shook his head. "How long have we been working on this house?"

"Almost two years," Jacob returned. "Feels like fifty."

Dexter ran his hands up and down the straps of his overalls. "Yeah, this one has taken on a life of its own. And not in a good way." He gazed around the roof. "If you ask me, we have made this place worse, not better."

"That may be, Dexter, but you and your men have been well paid."

"No argument there, Jacob. Mr. Blackwell has been very generous." The man's gray eyes became distracted by movement on the ground below.

From the yellow cottage across from the manor, Frances emerged wearing a bright blue hat. She was heading toward the stables at the rear of the driveway when a lone figure emerged from the front of the manor.

The man's long legs and the eager kick of his stride were familiar to everyone who had spent any time at Altmover Manor. Magnus strolled up to Frances and joined her as she ambled along the gravel driveway.

Dexter glanced up to see Jacob staring at the interaction between Magnus Blackwell and his wife.

"He sure does dote on your wife."

"They were friends in college," Jacob explained, clutching his right fist.

"Good friends?"

Jacob kicked the stone raven in front of him. "I don't care how you do it, but get rid of these damned things." He spun around to leave and then froze. "Dexter," he called over his shoulder. "If you do have to use the dynamite, do it when he's not home."

Dexter tipped his cap to Jacob, chuckling. "You got it, Jacob."

He went back in the roof door, which led to the winding steps that opened into the servants' quarters on the right wing of the third floor.

Coming out of the small alcove that housed the staircase to the roof, he rounded a doorway that opened onto the main hall. Flying out the door, Jacob ran smack into one of the upstairs maids. Clasping her in his arms, he kept her from toppling to the floor.

The pretty young brunette gasped when she saw Jacob. Realizing who it was, she jumped out of his arms.

"So sorry, Mr. O'Connor."

"Are you okay?" Jacob examined her dainty features.

She nodded, placing a quivering hand on her chest. "I'm fine."

He took in her simple black maid uniform, trying to remember her name. "Regina, is it?"

The young woman smiled sweetly. "Laurie," she corrected. "Regina was the last third-floor maid. She left two months ago."

"Ah, yes. I am very sorry, Laurie." Jacob noticed a bruise on her left wrist peeking out from behind the ruffled cuff of her maid uniform. He pointed to the unusual bruise that circled her wrist like a bracelet. "What did you do there?"

The girl instantly yanked the cuff of her dress over the mark. "Nothing, sir."

The fear he saw in her green eyes was unexpected. It reminded him of a caged wild animal, terrified by its human captors. "It's all right, Laurie. I won't say anything to anyone. Did you hurt yourself?"

She took a wary step back. "Please don't ask me any more questions, sir. If Magnus—I mean, Mr. Blackwell ...." She lowered her eyes. "I need this job. I have nowhere else to go."

He stepped up to her. "Is someone hurting you, Laurie?" He dropped his voice. "Did Mr. Blackwell hurt you?"

"Damn things are secured with iron rods," Dexter said appearing in the alcove doorway. When he saw Jacob standing next to the maid, he stopped. "You might want to consider that dynamite."

Laurie took the opportunity to scurry down the hall. Jacob's eyes stayed on the girl as she trotted away.

"Did you hear me, Jacob?" Dexter demanded.

Jacob's dark eyes returned to his foreman. "What?"

"The dynamite?" Dexter furrowed his thick brow. "You okay?"

Jacob nodded and then remembered why he was heading toward the stairs in the first place. Thinking of his Frances alone in the stables with Magnus suddenly scared the hell out of him.

He took off at a brisk jog, heading toward the main staircase.

"Jacob?" Dexter called. "What about the dynamite?"

Jacob did not stop to give him an answer.

It felt like an eternity to get down the long flight of stairs to the first floor. When he was finally able to make it out the open double doors at the entrance, he saw a single horse pulling a buggy trot past. In the seat of the buggy was his Frances.

Running down the wide, cement steps he waved to her, but she was too far away to see him. As the buggy turned on to the open road, he heard the crunch of footsteps coming up behind him.

"She was anxious to get to town," Magnus said, coming alongside him. "It seems she wants to shop for something for your birthday."

Jacob straightened out his dark brown waistcoat. "Yes, she had mentioned that."

Magnus took in his face. "You all right, O'Connor? You look as if you've seen a ghost."

"I'm fine, Magnus. I just wanted to catch Frances before she went into town."

Magnus slapped his hand down on Jacob's right shoulder. "She'll be back soon enough. It will do her good to get out of that cottage for a while. Frances always was the restless kind."

The comment gave Jacob pause. "How would you know that, Magnus? You two only courted for a short while."

Magnus tapped his walking stick on the dark gravel. "We got to know each other very well in that brief time. I told you how often we talked."

Jacob tried to cool his outrage. He had to keep his job. "Yes, ah, I remember. It's just a little disconcerting to think you knew her so well. She is my wife after all."

"Your wife?" The grin on Magnus's lips sent a chill through Jacob. "Of course, she is your wife. We both know I was not the right man for her at the time."

The odd statement only added to Jacob's unease. Instead of saying anything to reply, Jacob turned his eyes back to the house. "We will have to use a bit of force to get those ravens off the eaves. Might do some damage, but when we put in the columns, you won't see it."

Magnus raised his head to the roof of the house. "Do whatever you can to remove those monstrosities. My father put them there. I could never stand them."

Jacob eyed his cane. "I guess your father favored ravens, whereas you favor dragons."

Magnus spied the handle of his cane. "Favored? Hardly. I like to think of myself as a dragon, O'Connor—to take anything I wish to possess."

"Does that include taking maids, Magnus?"

Pressing the tip of his cane into the muddy gravel, Magnus faced his friend. "What are you talking about?"

Jacob moved closer, mindful of the men still working on the home. "I saw Laurie's wrist. She has a nasty bruise like someone tied her up—and she fought back. Do you know anything about that?"

The flash of fire in Magnus's eyes almost matched the glint of the rubies in the handle of his cane. At least, Jacob thought they were rubies; there were times he swore the stones changed color.

"I don't keep tabs on the after-hours hijinks of my staff, Jacob. Perhaps she has a lover who likes it rough."

Jacob did not like the tone of his voice and swore he was lying, but he had no evidence. Again, he thought of the generous salary Magnus was paying him to oversee the renovations.

"Yes, you're right." Jacob tucked his hands into his trouser pockets. "One can never tell with people nowadays."

"Exactly," Magnus agreed.

The former friends stood outside of the grand home enveloped in an uncomfortable silence. Jacob was about to head back inside the house when Magnus finally spoke up.

"I am very pleased with the way the house is shaping up, O'Connor. You are doing a fine job."

"I'm glad you're pleased."

"What are your plans when this house is finished?"

Jacob glanced up at the manor. He figured they still had a few more months to go before the house was completed. Jacob had too much to worry about until then to add further misery to his mind by obsessing about his future.

"I haven't given it much thought. I guess I will have to find another position back in Boston when we are done here."

"You do know my family owns an architectural firm in Boston. Collier and Keene was purchased by my father and is where I did my internship before attending Harvard. They are currently seeking new architects to take on some projects in the city. Boston is going through a bit of a building boom. I could put in a word for you."

"Architect, not draftsman like I was before," Jacob clarified.

"Full-time architect, yes," Magnus pointed out with a half-smile.

"But I have no experience. All I could get at Fogle, Hardwick, and Hillman was a draftsman's position."

"You have spent almost two years drafting plans, overseeing work, and renovating a huge home. That is all the experience you will need."

Jacob was overcome. The job he had always wanted, and with a very prestigious firm in Boston, was within reach.

"I could even give you and Frances a house to rent; it's not far from my own in Boston. I think she would like it there. It's not far from her father's house, and I will like having you two close by when I return to Boston."

The offer sank to the pit of Jacob's stomach like a stone to the bottom of a river. "Return?"

Magnus surveyed the craggy landscape that was dotted with the occasional twisted trunk of an old elm. "When we're finished here, I need to return to Boston and see to several other ventures. It will be good to get back to a city, go to parties, and meet with friends." He glimpsed Jacob. "Don't you agree?"

Visions of a life under Magnus's control haunted him. If he took Magnus's offer, his life in Boston would not be any different from his life at Altmover Manor. Could he live like that? Could Frances? He could hear her arguments in his head.

"Thank you, Magnus, for the generous offer, but I will have to discuss it with Frances."

Magnus dipped his head. "Of course. Bring me your answer in a few days, and I will get the ball rolling at Collier and Keene. I'm sure when this project is finished, you and Frances will be eager to get to Boston."

"Yes," Jacob concurred. "She misses her home very much."

Magnus smiled, looking as if he had already convinced his friend to take the job. "You won't regret it, Jacob. I promise."

Magnus strolled toward the wide porch steps of his grand home, and Jacob felt his insides turn to dust. How was he going to convince his wife to agree to Magnus's plans? And worse, how was he going to feel spending the rest of his life being under the thumb of the inscrutable Magnus Blackwell.

In town, Frances was invigorated by the quaint shops and the people on the busy main street. She had forgotten how nice it was to talk to strangers on a pretty spring day. She glided along dusty boards with her bright blue parasol in one hand and the few purchases she had made in the other.

She was taking in the sparse offerings of the haberdasher's shop window, unsure whether to buy Jacob a new hat or waistcoat for his birthday when she spied an array of ribbons in the shop window next door.

Excited by the prospects of getting something pretty, she went to the shop entrance. The tinkle of the bell as she entered the inlaid glass door made her smile. She viewed the yards of rich fabrics, rolls of ribbon, and the trays of buttons and hooks. Finally, there was a shop in town with a few frilly, girlish things she could enjoy.

"Can I help you, ma'am?" a faint voice inquired.

Frances spied the young woman coming closer and thought she looked familiar. Then again, it was a very small town.

"Yes, I was looking at the ribbons you have. I could use a selection for my wardrobe."

The woman's puppy-like brown eyes inquisitively brushed over Frances's countenance. "It's Mrs. O'Connor, isn't it?"

Frances was at a total loss for words. How did the young woman know her name?

"Have we met?"

The pretty girl held out her hand. "Yes, ma'am. I used to work at Altmover Manor. I'm Regina. I was the upstairs maid for Mr. Blackwell."

"Of course." Frances took her small hand. "I remember you. You left so suddenly from the house."

Regina peered around the shop. "I was anxious to get started on my business."

Frances marveled at the store tables filled with fabric. "This is your store."

Regina nodded her head of curly blonde hair. "Mr. Blackwell owns the store, but he is renting it to me. I always dreamed of having my place, and ...." Her voice faded.

Frances was dumbfounded. She hardly pictured Magnus as the philanthropic type. She had never known him to do anything without motivation. During their brief courtship, he had promised her wealth and comfort but only after she would bed him. Marriage had never entered the conversation with Magnus, and even though he vowed to want a wife, Frances never believed him.

"You are very lucky. I've known Magnus for a few years, and I can never remember him being so generous."

"I can assure you, Mrs. O'Connor, I worked very hard to achieve my goals."

"What do you mean?"

Regina smashed her lips together as a shadow of worry marred her pretty face.

Guessing what the woman was alluding to, Frances placed her white-gloved hand over the girls tightly clasped hand. "I know how he can be, Regina. I am very familiar with how he treats women."

"Then you know about his ... tastes?"

Frances knew she was treading dangerous water. It was not considered polite to gossip about men of position with their former servants. She had been raised to be above such things, but the terror in the girl's eyes ate at her. There was something wrong, and she needed to know what it was. If anything, she could use it to convince Jacob to hurry and end his employment with Magnus. The sooner they got off that damned island, the better.

"I know Magnus Blackwell can be very charming, especially

with women. He uses his power and money to cajole, to sweet talk, to make you do things that are," Frances peered around the empty shop, "unseemly at times."

Regina's lower lip trembled, and her brown eyes glistened with tears. "Did he make you feel so ugly?"

Frances's heart trembled. "Regina, what did he do to you?"

Before Frances could put an arm around the girl's slim shoulders, Regina was sinking to the floor.

"Oh, Mrs. O'Connor, I'm so ashamed."

Frances sat on the floor and hugged a weeping Regina. "Dear girl, what is it?"

"I have done things—horrible things. He promised I would not be ashamed, but I don't feel that way."

Frances held the girl at an arm's length and pulled out a handkerchief from her blue pouch purse. She dabbed Regina's eyes and waited until she had calmed down.

She took the young woman's hand and helped her to her feet. "Now I want you to start at the beginning and tell me everything."

Regina gulped back her tears. "He told me never to tell. He said he would take away my shop if I did."

Her fury with Magnus burned in the back of her throat, but Frances gave Regina a warm, caring smile. "He will never hear about it from me, Regina. I promise. It will be our little secret."

Chapter Fifteen

Discovery

"We have got to leave this island as soon as possible, Jacob!" Frances cried out as she glowered at her husband standing before their stone hearth. "He's a monster."

Jacob raised his hands, begging for calm from his wife. "You don't have any proof, Frances, just the ramblings of some young woman he set up in a fabric shop."

She rushed toward the mantel. "Jesus, Jacob. Do you know what she told me? The things he did to her—do you honestly want to stay employed by someone like that?"

"If she was so unhappy with what he did to her—if he did those things, Frances—why take the shop he offered her? Why take his charity?" Jacob combed his hand through his wavy black hair as he thought of Laurie and the marks on her wrist. "She

154

was a former employee. Perhaps she had an argument with him. Maybe she blackmailed him into giving her the shop. You don't know. You can't believe the word of a former housemaid over the man who is keeping a roof over our heads." He slapped his pant leg. "Frances, I have a hard enough time keeping good men employed for me; I can't imagine what Magnus goes through with his help."

Frances's eyes widened. "You're defending him?"

"What in the hell is that supposed to mean?" he demanded, raising his voice—something he never did. "He has been good to me—to us. I need him if I'm going to continue in this business. I need a reference for this job. I can't just walk away."

She stared at him, her mouth ajar. "You don't need him, Jacob. You're talented enough to get any position you chose."

"Am I?" He turned back to the fire burning in the hearth and gripped the edge of the mantel.

Frances watched in horror as his fingers turned white on the mantel. She was shocked by his outburst but sensed there was more to his anger than what he was telling her. She knew her husband well enough to figure something was bothering him. Reining in her anger, she closed her eyes and held her hand to her chest. She blew out a breath and then stepped forward.

Resting her hand on her husband's shoulder, she proclaimed, "I believe in you. I always have." She squeezed his shoulder. "Perhaps you're right. The woman in town was probably angry with how she was treated during her employ at the manor house. I shouldn't have been so carried away by her tale."

Jacob stood motionless for a moment, debating if he should tell Frances the news of Magnus's offer. It seemed every heated discussion they had struggled through lately revolved around

Magnus. The man was coming between Jacob and his wife.

"What if I was to tell you I was considering a job offer?"

"What offer?" Her voice sounded so hopeful.

He turned around. "There is a firm in Boston, Collier and Keene. I might be able to get on with them after the manor house is finished this fall."

"Boston?" The smile on her face was so uplifting for Jacob he did not have the heart to tell her who had offered him the position. "We could return and live in Father's cottage behind the main house until we find a suitable place to live."

He set his hands behind his back, hiding his clenched fists. "The position comes with a rental house."

"A rental house?" Her eyes warily searched his. "Who made you this offer?"

He hesitated and then announced, "Magnus."

Her face fell. "No, Jacob. Absolutely not. I will not live like we have been these past few years. I cannot abide being around the man."

"Really?" He rocked forward on his feet. "That's not what I saw."

"What are you talking about?"

"Today, I was standing on the roof and watched the two of you as you walked to the stables. All I could think about was not letting you be alone with him."

She tilted her head quizzically to the side. "Jacob, what are you saying?"

He came up to her. "Do you know what it's like for me day in and day out listening to him talk about you? He's always asking after you." He threw up a hand. "He wants to know if you are happy or bored or if there is anything he can do to make you more comfortable. He is so in love with you; it's killing me."

She laughed, more out of shock than amusement. "Magnus isn't in love with me. He was never in love with me. I was merely a possession to him."

Jacob shook his head, disagreeing. "When we were at Harvard, all he ever did was talk of you. He was obsessed."

Frances nodded her head; her brown eyes intently focused on her husband. "That's right. He was obsessed. Magnus told me once he considered women objects to pursue, win over, and keep brightly polished on a mantel. After that, I knew I had no intention of continuing with him."

"You never told me that." Jacob inched closer. "I thought you broke it off with him because of the other women."

"The other women were another reason to end it, but not the cause." She glided away from him, wringing her hands. "Today, when I was with that young woman, Regina, I began to remember my time with Magnus—I had felt all the things she said to me, all the coldness of him. I realized if I had stayed with him, that woman in the fabric shop could have been me."

"Frances," Jacob cooed. He went to her and put his arms around her. "Magnus may be harsh at times, but he is not the man that woman described to you. I spent almost three years at his side, his companion in all things, and I never once heard or saw him do anything to a woman that would make me question his integrity."

Frances patted his waistcoat. "But that was before, Jacob. After we married, he changed. I think he finally gave in to the evil he has kept hidden inside him."

Jacob snickered and let her go. "You sound like one of those horror books you always like to read—the ones that give you nightmares."

"Some nightmares happen while we are wide awake, Jacob.

Such terror can destroy the soul."

"Please don't be so cryptic." He pointed to their front door. "I get it all day from him; I don't need it when I come home to you."

"What is the matter with you?" She took a step back from him. "First, you tell me you are considering taking a job with this man, and then you describe how his obsession with me is driving you mad. Do you honestly want to spend the rest of our lives tied to Magnus Blackwell? Our marriage will not survive it, Jacob."

"What about the money, Frances? We need money for a house and for a family; he can provide us with all of that."

She determinedly folded her arms across her chest. "I would rather live with my father than take another handout from Magnus."

"I've already told you I will not go to your father."

"But you would go to Magnus, is that it?" She checked her anger and sucked in a pensive breath. "What has happened to you, Jacob? Since we have moved here, we have been fighting more and more. We need to leave this island and Magnus. He will not be happy until he has all of us, can't you see that?"

No, he couldn't, but he couldn't tell his wife that. Jacob was tired of arguing with her. Instead of helping to ease the flurry of worries in his head, Frances was just creating a whole new set of problems. "I can't talk to you about this anymore, Frances. I'm going for a walk to clear my head."

"A walk? Now?" She stomped her foot on the knotted pine floor. "Jacob O'Connor, if you go out that door without finishing this discussion, you can," she gazed around the room, "you can sleep on the sofa," she blurted as she pointed to the floral sofa by the hearth.

"Fine." He stormed toward the door as he heard her footfalls heading to their bedroom.

Just as he opened the front door, the bedroom door slammed closed.

"Mr. O'Connor?" Emily Mann stood outside the cottage door. Wearing her usual dowdy black frock with long sleeves and a high collar, she held out an envelope.

"Ah, Ms. Mann," Jacob said, sounding rattled. "I didn't know you were out here."

She gave him an encouraging smile, showing the slight dimples in her cheeks. "I heard nothing, Mr. O'Connor. I assure you."

He breathed a sigh of relief. "I know that." He motioned to the envelope. "What is this?"

"An invitation to dinner this weekend at the manor. Mr. Blackwell has a friend visiting, and he would like you and your wife to attend a dinner party in his honor."

"Magnus has a friend?" Jacob joked.

Emily chuckled and adjusted her glasses. "Apparently so. He's a writer from England Mr. Blackwell met in New Orleans."

He took the envelope from her. "A writer? Who?"

"Oscar Wilde."

Jacob was unimpressed. He had never heard of the man, but made a mental note to ask Frances later—if she was still speaking to him. Then again, he reasoned he had better wait until morning.

He held up the envelope to her. "Tell Magnus thank you, and we will be there."

She nodded. "The time is on the invitation."

Jacob waved the envelope in front of him. "We needed an invitation?"

Emily playfully raised her dark brows. "Apparently so."

She was about to turn from his door when he asked, "Ms. Mann, do you remember a girl that used to work for you named Regina?"

"Ah, yes, Regina Lionel. Why?"

Jacob struggled to find a way to word his question. "Did she, ah, ... was there a problem with her?"

Emily pushed her glasses back on her nose. "Not that I'm aware of. Mr. Blackwell liked her. He told me she was very bright and wanted to own a fabric shop. He felt she was a sound investment and set her up in town. He tells me she is doing quite well."

Relief snaked through Jacob. He never thought of Frances as gullible, but maybe the years she had been cooped up in the cottage were starting to get to her. Then he remembered Laurie and the terror he had seen in her face.

"What about the new girl, Laurie? How is she working out?"

Emily's small mouth grimaced. "He is not so pleased with this one. It looks like I will be searching for a new third-floor maid soon."

"What's wrong with her?"

Emily casually shrugged. "Who knows? I find most of the girls in town. They arrive on the island looking for work. I hire them, but soon they do or say something to anger Mr. Blackwell, and I have to get rid of them."

"He never gives you a reason?" he probed, hoping for more.

"He suspected one of stealing the silver. Another one was drinking while on the job. That's all I know."

"I understand. It's hard to find good help." He held up the envelope again. "Thank you for dropping this off."

Emily curtly nodded. "Have a good evening, Mr. O'Connor."

After he shut the door, he opened the envelope and read the formally written invitation card.

You are requested to attend a dinner party for Oscar Wilde
Hosted by Magnus Blackwell at Altmover Manor.
Formal attire.
Cocktails are at six.
Dinner service is at seven.

"You think the man could have just told me about the dinner in the morning."

Chuckling, Jacob took the card to the mantel and set it beside the wedding photograph of Frances and him, hoping she would find it. Suddenly regretting their heated row, he glimpsed the closed bedroom door.

"Maybe a formal night out is just what we both need."

Chapter Sixteen

A Wilde Time

Oscar Wilde burst into Magnus's office with all the gusto he had possessed during their time in New Orleans. Wearing an outer coat trimmed in fur, a shiny gold bob chain across his red silk vest, a tall black hat, and finely polished leather shoes, he reeked of wealth and success.

"Magnus," he called, coming up to Magnus's desk with an extended hand.

Coming around his desk, Magnus caught Emily Mann's smile as she shut his office door—no doubt pleased he had company.

He gave Oscar's hand a firm shake. "Oscar, it is good to see you. After all of your wonderful letters, it is going to be a joy to endure your biting commentary in person."

"I only write the bitter truth to those I know well." Oscar

removed his fur-trimmed coat and tossed it onto a red leather chair by the library window. "I told you once I wanted to come and see you when I was back in the states. And here I am." He held up his index finger. "And I come bearing gifts."

He went to his coat and reached into the outer pocket. When he returned to Magnus, he was holding a black, leather-bound book in his hands.

"My new book." He held it out to Magnus. "I hope you like it."

Magnus took the book and read the title in gold on the cover. "*The Picture of Dorian Gray.*" He glanced up at Oscar. "What is it about?"

"You." Oscar pointed at him. "Or my interpretation of you. A man so obsessed with his greatness he thinks he is above sin. During our time together in New Orleans, I kept telling you that you would make a great character in one of my books. I based the main character, Dorian Gray, on you."

"Me?" Magnus sounded genuinely surprised. "I don't know what to say."

Oscar took a seat on the corner of his desk. "The more I wrote him, the more he reminded me of you."

Magnus put the book on the desk. "I shall treasure it along with your letters. If you ever become famous, I can sell them and make a fortune."

Oscar's eyes fell on the dragon head cane leaning against the desk, and he froze. "I had hoped my suspicions in New Orleans were wrong about you." He pointed to the cane. "Now I know they were not."

Magnus picked up the cane, twirling it in his hands. "It arrived at our hotel the day of the fire at Madam Simone's house. I assumed it was from her."

Oscar shook his head. "You expect me to believe that?" He pointed to the book on the desk. "When I wrote that, I thought I was too harsh; now I know I was being kind."

"I didn't touch the woman, Oscar."

"I'll take your word on that."

"You have it, my friend. I do not kill innocent women."

"You and I both know Madam Simone was never innocent, but her death was not for us to determine. That was for God to decide." Oscar gestured to the walking stick. "The eyes have changed."

Magnus glimpsed the changeling stones. "Yes, I noticed after it arrived."

Oscar climbed off the desk. "You do realize she was a powerful woman and, in death, could become a vengeful spirit."

"In Maine? I doubt she would like our cold winters."

Oscar's donkey-bray laugh filled the library. Magnus smiled, pleased to hear the disturbing sound once again. He had missed that laugh and the man who wielded it.

"Enough said about the topic. May Madam Simone and all her voodoo spirits rest in peace." Oscar clapped his hands together. "I see you have been doing a great deal of work on the old place. Will you be reenacting the Civil War, too?"

Magnus's laugh sounded unusually pleasant. "I wanted to be reminded of all things Southern. A sort of tribute to my time there."

"Yes, but most people simply buy a souvenir, Magnus, not renovate a house."

"My architect is also updating the old bathrooms and adding a courtyard in the rear of the home."

Oscar went to the window and peered down at the sheer cliffs. "Frightening view."

"Only if you are not used to it."

Oscar rested his hand on the back of one of the red leather chairs. "Who is the architect you hired to redesign your home?"

"Jacob O'Connor."

Oscar turned to him, a deep frown marring his happy-go-lucky face. "O'Connor? Not the same O'Connor you told me of in New Orleans?"

Magnus went back behind his desk, resting the cane against it. "Yes."

"And the beautiful woman he stole from you?"

Magnus motioned to the door. "Staying in the yellow cottage across from the manor. Surely you saw it on the way in."

Oscar approached the desk, his head bowed. "Is that wise, Magnus? You professed such deep hatred for the man, and yet you have employed him to redesign your home. Why?"

"How else can I keep him and his wife close to me?" Magnus sat down in his desk chair.

Oscar's stare was bitingly cold. "You think now that you have the cane you will win the woman you desire? Is that it?"

"Who knows?" Magnus lovingly caressed the cane's handle. "But it might help."

"What do think this O'Connor will do when you try to steal his wife away?" Oscar's snort carried around the office. "If he's like most men, he will not go quietly."

"You can find out what kind of man he is tomorrow night. You will meet O'Connor and his wife at a dinner I have planned in your honor."

"My honor?" Oscar lightly chuckled. "Well then, I will have to attend." He went to collect his coat from the chair by the window. "I'll head to my room to do some unpacking, so you get back to work. Brandy and cigars later?"

"Of course." Magnus stood from behind his desk. "I'll have Emily take you on a tour of the house."

"Sounds delightful." He flipped his coat over his arm. "Read some of my book before we meet up later. I want your brutally honest opinion."

"Brutally honest?" Magnus called as Oscar moved to leave.

"Perhaps not that brutally honest." Oscar reached for the brass doorknob. "Just lie and tell me I'm a genius like all the rest of London." He eyed the dragon-carved doors. "Intriguing. Self-portrait?"

"I'll see you tonight, Oscar."

Oscar left the room, and Magnus returned his gaze to the cane leaning against his desk. Initially, he'd hoped the magic of the cane would help weave some spell to win over Frances. But with time, he considered all the strange events he'd witnessed in New Orleans as nothing more than a show put on for the tourists. For Magnus, magic was just a bedtime tale told by parents to teach their children how to dream.

In the quiet of his office, Madam Simone's last words came back to him. Magnus recalled the thrill of taking her life, and was more excited than appalled by his actions. Since his departure from New Orleans, no evil had befallen him. If anything, his luck had changed for the better.

"So much for your voodoo, dear lady. I just hope your baton juju lives up to its promise."

Jacob was putting his gold watch in his tuxedo pocket when he saw Frances emerge from their bedroom. For an instant, he forgot about his job, his future, and the constant squabbling with his wife. He simply basked in the vision of her.

Her dress was an underskirt of white satin covered with pink silk. It was pleated in front and trimmed with Mechlin lace and a garland of pink satin roses. The low neck and short sleeves showed off the creaminess of her skin, and the flowers in her hair matched those in her dress.

"Do I look all right?" she asked, patting the arranged coif of honey-blonde curls on her head.

"You are stunning, Frances, truly." He went up to her side. "I am the luckiest man alive."

She brushed away a piece of lint from the lapel of his black jacket. "I'll bet you weren't thinking that last week when you weren't speaking to me."

"I was giving you time to calm down."

"I am calm. Are you still considering his offer?"

Jacob took his wife's elbow. "Let's not talk about it anymore tonight. Get your wrap, and we'll head over to the house."

She ambled across the knotted pine floors of the living room to the coat rack where she had left her white shawl.

"Not speaking about it is not helping the situation, Jacob." She flung the white lace wrap around her shoulders. "We need to make some decisions."

He strode across the room. "And we will. Tonight, let's just have some fun. When was the last time we went to a dinner party?"

She sighed, recalling the event. "You were leaving Fogle, Hardwick, and Hillman, and Mr. Fogle gave us a going away dinner. Over two years ago."

He adjusted the wrap around her shoulders. "Reason enough for us to enjoy the evening. I want to show off my beautiful wife."

She pressed her white-gloved hand to his cheek. "No matter how much we fight, you do know I still love you."

He held her hand to his face. "I know, my precious. That fire inside of you only makes me love you more."

"Fire?" She giggled. "I thought it was tenacity. That is what my professors always called it at Radcliffe."

He opened the front door for her. "Your professors never knew you like I do, Frances. Otherwise, they would have seen what I see now—a breathtaking woman."

She sashayed toward the door. "Careful, Jacob. I might just have to let you sleep with me tonight instead of on the sofa."

Jacob followed her out the door. "And I was just getting used to the sofa."

The great brass lamps newly mounted on either side of the leaded glass front doors were lit, and the long recently finished porch freshly swept.

Emily Mann answered the door in a blue and pale gray evening gown trimmed with lace and a stylish array of blue feathers in her mousy brown hair. Her pale gray gloves and blue dress made her white skin appear a sickly ash color.

"Ms. Mann, how wonderful you look," Jacob lied.

The dour-faced secretary bowed her head. "Thank you, Mr. O'Connor. Mrs. O'Connor, it is good to see you again."

"Ms. Mann, I am so glad you will be joining us this evening," Frances confided while walking inside. "I was afraid I would be the only woman here tonight."

"Mr. Blackwell asked me to join you this evening."

Jacob removed the wrap from Frances's shoulders. "Will anyone else will be attending?"

"Judge Atherton and his wife are already here along with the Mayor and Mrs. Gauge. Mr. Blackwell wanted Mr. Wilde to meet some of the locals."

"Then it should be a grand party," Jacob admitted.

"Let us hope so, Mr. O'Connor."

They were shown to the main living room to the right of the grand staircase, and the sound of wood crackling in the fireplace was the first noise to greet them. The walls, paneled in a rich oak, had rosettes sprinkled along the seams, and the ceiling was white plaster with a vine of roses circling the border. Furnished with white and peach floral sofas and chairs and heavy wood tables, the room had a quiet sophistication to it. Above the mantel, decorated with more carved rosettes, was a framed portrait of Magnus wearing a long black coat, red vest, high cut black boots and holding his prized dragon cane. Every bit the aristocrat, his thick dirty-blond hair was a tad longer than he currently wore it, and his flashing green eyes looked out over the room. Jacob thought the portrait was a good likeness, but it had not captured the malevolence of Magnus's mouth or the distrust ever present in his eyes. The artist had painted the image of Magnus Blackwell, but had not captured the man.

"O'Connor," Magnus called, as he extended a tapered hand to his friend. "Thank you for coming." His eyes shifted to Frances. "Hello, my dear. You look wonderful tonight."

Frances graciously accepted the kiss he planted on her left cheek. "Thank you, Magnus."

Jacob's protective instincts stirred for his wife as Magnus kissed her.

"Jacob and Frances O'Connor," Magnus went on as he broke away from Frances. "I would like to present the mayor of Mount Desert, his honor Ben Gauge and his lovely wife, Gloria."

The mayor was a very tall man with gaunt features, hollow cheekbones, and pale blue eyes. His thinning fair hair was brushed to the side to hide his growing bald spot. When they shook hands, Jacob was surprised by the strength he felt in the mayor's hand.

His wife was half his height, plump, and had a cherubic red face that contrasted against her husband's cadaverous appearance. Around her neck was a choker made of diamonds and rubies that matched the bracelet on her right wrist. Her fingers glittered with more diamonds and gold.

"Magnus was just telling us what a wonderful job you are doing on the manor. I must say what we have seen has been overwhelming," Mrs. Gauge twittered in a perky voice. "Perhaps you might take a look at our house in town. I keep telling Ben it needs to reflect his importance."

"I would be happy to offer some suggestions," Jacob graciously replied.

"I am warning you, Mr. O'Connor, my wife will probably want to turn it into Buckingham Palace," the mayor declared in a nasal voice.

"Well, first he must finish with Altmover Manor," Magnus insisted. He waved to another couple approaching. "This is Judge Wentworth and his new bride, Natalie. They also have a house on the island, O'Connor, so consider yourself warned."

The judge's brisk chortle matched his portly appearance. Decked out in a red vest beneath his black tuxedo, which matched the color of his bloodshot eyes, the older man's handshake was even firmer than the mayor's.

His attractive wife appeared to be years younger than he was. Jacob guessed she was barely twenty; she seemed very shy and socially awkward in the room full of grownups.

When the young woman stepped forward and gave a slight curtsey in her bright yellow dress, Jacob tried not to snicker when he saw Frances's brows go up in alarm. He took her hand and squeezed it, trying to remind her to save her outrage for when they were alone.

"And finally our guest of honor, Oscar Wilde." Magnus motioned to a man in a dashing black tuxedo trimmed with black silk down the sides of his trousers and along his lapels.

To Jacob, he looked nothing like a writer. He had always believed writers to be sophisticated and very charming, but this man had a rather plain appearance. If anything, his long face, small brown eyes, and oversized nose reminded Jacob of one of the horses in the stables.

"O'Connor." Oscar came forward. "I have heard so much about you."

His ardent handshake left Jacob reeling. "Thank you, Mr. Wilde."

"Oscar, you must call me Oscar. I feel as if I have known you forever."

Jacob's eyes darted to Magnus. "I didn't realize Magnus had told you about me."

"My dear fellow, when we were in New Orleans, all he did was talk about you."

"You're exaggerating, Oscar," Magnus scolded. "I'm sure I did not talk about O'Connor the entire time."

Oscar gave Magnus a shifty side-glance. "Why you went on and on about him, my good man."

"Is that where you two met?" Frances piped in. "New Orleans?"

"Why yes." Oscar took her arm. "And when he wasn't talking about your husband, dear lady, he was lamenting over losing you to another."

"Oscar, please." The chill in Magnus's voice was palpable.

"You see there?" Oscar waved at a glowering Magnus as he escorted Frances into the room. "He only gets that way when I am right."

The loud, obnoxious laugh that emanated from the lumbering man shocked everyone in the room. Jacob noticed how Magnus seemed to delight in his guests' reactions.

"O'Connor, what will you have to drink?" Magnus slapped him on the back. "Your usual whiskey and soda?"

"Yes, Magnus, thank you."

"So tell me, Mr. Wilde, what was New Orleans like?" Frances inquired as she took a seat on one of the sofas. "I've always wanted to go there."

"Since when?" Jacob grilled.

"All of my life."

"She was quite obsessed, O'Connor," Magnus affirmed as he went to a bar in the corner of the room. "She went on and on about it when we were at college. Even made me go to a little coffee shop filled with pictures of the city."

"I'm confused. How did you three meet again?" Judge Wentworth implored.

"Frances was at Radcliffe College while O'Connor and Magnus were at Harvard," Oscar explained.

"Oh, you were a college girl?" Gloria Gauge took a seat next to Frances on the sofa.

"Yes, I was studying teaching." Frances nodded to the woman. "I gave it up when my husband had to return to Boston for work."

"I never thought it was a good idea for women to get too much education," the judge extolled. "I've read that it ruins them for child-rearing."

"Perhaps it might make them better mothers because they

will know more to pass on to their children," Frances shot back. "Knowledge is never a bad thing to have, Judge."

"Yes, but all that study is wasted on women. They eventually marry and have children, and you don't need a college degree for that."

"Can you imagine if it were required; the country might be in a much better state than it is," Frances said.

Magnus chuckled, Jacob beamed with pride, and Oscar applauded.

"Oh, I like her," Oscar professed. "You should have married her, Magnus."

Magnus brought a drink to Jacob. "The better man won her heart, Oscar."

Jacob saw the hint of jealousy in his eyes. It wasn't the first time he had noticed it. Jacob had seen it repeatedly since the first day he had announced his intentions to marry Frances.

"I wanted to go to college," the demure Natalie Wentworth blurted out.

The room was awash with anticipation as everyone waited for her to go on. When she didn't, Oscar redirected his attention to Frances.

"So tell me, Mrs. O'Connor. What would you like to know about New Orleans?"

"I've heard the food is quite good."

"The food?" Oscar closed his eyes as if caught up in a dream. "It is divine, but the whole essence of the city is unique. Wouldn't you agree, Magnus?"

"It's an amusing town," Magnus spoke up from the bar as he poured out a glass of sherry.

"Touring the streets and seeing the quaint homes was a wonderful way to spend our time," Oscar went on.

"What else did you do?" Gail Gauge inquired. "Surely you didn't dine out and sightsee the whole time."

Oscar's eyes went to Magnus as he brought the glass of sherry across the room to Frances. "Oh, we found other ways to amuse ourselves."

The men in the room snickered except for Jacob.

"What of the people?" Ben Gauge posed. "I've heard it's a very unusual blend of cultures there."

"French, Spanish, Caribbean, African—they are all represented there and blended into something resembling gumbo, one of their famous dishes. The religion followed there is especially interesting. It's called voodoo."

"Voodoo?" Frances took the glass of sherry Magnus gave her. "What is that?"

"A religion brought over by the slaves and mixed with the Catholic traditions of the French and Spanish. They have rituals and cast spells to bring luck, fortune, and love." Oscar's eyes followed Magnus. "Magnus and I befriended a local practitioner of the religion when we were there. A high priestess named Madam Simone."

"Spells, rituals—sounds like witchcraft to me," Judge Wentworth scoffed.

"What was this high priestess like?" Gail Gauge begged. "Was she hideous like an old crone?"

"Far from it," Oscar confessed. "She was of mixed blood and had beautiful skin the color of café au lait. She was refined and well-versed on many subjects."

"What on earth could she have been well-versed in?" Judge Wentworth went to the mantel and put down his drink. "I mean, if she was of mixed blood and a heathen, what could she have had to talk about?"

"The plight of the soul, my good man," Oscar expounded with a perturbed grin. "She knew a great deal about it. She even professed it can never die."

Gail Gauge let out an incredulous snort. "The Bible tells us that."

"Perhaps, but the Bible puts everything in such black and white terms. With Madam Simone, everything was more like shades of gray and much more interesting."

"What did you think of this woman, Magnus?" Judge Wentworth waved to him. "Is she as Mr. Wilde describes?"

Magnus collected his glass of whiskey and soda from the bar. "Very much so. She was very entertaining."

"Oh, she adored Magnus." Oscar chuckled as he motioned to Magnus. "I think she took quite a fancy to you."

"We got along."

"Got along? Good lord man, she gave you her prized possession after all."

Jacob's ears perked up. "What prized possession?"

"The cane he has." Oscar waved to the portrait. "That one with the dragon's head for a handle. She sent it to him right before she died."

"She died?" Gail Gauge gasped.

Oscar nodded, eyeing Magnus. "In a fire at her place of business on Basin Street. It was all very mysterious."

"Any idea why she sent you the cane?" Jacob pressed, his curiosity nipping at him.

"Yes," Oscar joined in, smirking at Magnus. "Why did she send you that cane?"

Magnus lifted one side of his mouth in a coldhearted grin. "I have no idea. Perhaps she sensed her coming demise and wanted the cane given to someone who would cherish it as she did."

Oscar clapped his hands while smirking at Magnus. "Oh, bravo."

"What was so special about this cane?" Natalie Wentworth beseeched, shocking everyone with her sudden loquaciousness.

"What was it, Magnus?" Oscar peered upward. "It was carved from a branch of the Sang Noir Tree from some cemetery in the city. I can't remember which one."

"Holt Cemetery." Magnus moved away from the bar, carrying his drink. "It is a black cemetery in the city, and the tree grows in the middle of it. Sang Noir means 'black blood.'"

"How creepy," Frances commented.

"The stones in the eyes of the dragon's head are called shifter stones, I believe," Oscar offered.

"Changeling stones," Magnus corrected, gripping his glass. "They change color to reflect the heart of the owner."

"And it's magical, too," Oscar continued. "It can send out the feeling of the heart of the person who owns it, and return that feeling into their life. Love for love, hate for hate, and so forth."

Gail Gauge sat up on the sofa. "Oh, can we see it?"

At that moment, Emily Mann walked into the room. "Excuse me, Mr. Blackwell; dinner is served."

Magnus put his drink down on the thick oak coffee table with carved roses in the center. "I hope everyone is hungry. I had my chef prepare something special for tonight."

"What, no gumbo?" Judge Wentworth chortled.

"No, but I have imported some of the coffee from New Orleans, Judge, to have with our dinner. Coffee and chicory. You will love it."

"Sounds very sinful," the judge added with a grin.

The tolerant smile Magnus flashed the man told Jacob his patience was wearing thin with his dinner guests. Jacob had never known Magnus to tolerate obnoxious men like the judge for very long.

The party moved farther down the wallpapered hall, which was decorated with lovely paintings of waterfowl taking flight. When they came to the open door to the dining room, Jacob marveled at the shiny array of china and crystal on the long oval table. With an intricately woven Irish linen tablecloth and two silver candelabras set in the center, the table garnered *oohs* and *aahs* from the guests.

After being seated in the mahogany carved chairs, Magnus waited for the young man wearing formal tails and white gloves to finish filling the wineglasses of his guests with the heady Bordeaux.

Lifting his wineglass to Oscar on his right, Magnus could not help but grin when he saw his friend eyeing the good looking young man pouring the wine. "I would like to propose a toast to my friend Oscar Wilde on the release of his novel, *The Picture of Dorian Gray*. I wish you every success."

The rest of the party rang out with, "Hear, hear," and raised their glasses. After everyone had tasted their wine, Magnus motioned for the soup service to begin.

"What is your novel about, Mr. Wilde?" Frances asked as a bowl of what appeared to be chowder was placed on her white and gold dinner plate.

Oscar kept his eyes on the sharply dressed man setting out the soup. "It's about a man who has a portrait painted of him in his youth. He wishes for the portrait to grow old and ugly while he remains young and handsome forever. Soon, he notices the picture changes. The painting takes on his age but also his sins: his lies, his manipulations, and ultimately his acts of murder. The picture becomes a grotesque monster he has to hide away in his attic until his secret is discovered."

"It sounds like the kind of horror stories my wife likes," Jacob added.

"I read some of it this afternoon," Magnus admitted, selecting a silver soup spoon from the array of silverware to the right of his plate.

Oscar chuckled. "And?"

"I don't see me in it at all."

Oscar scrunched his brows together. "You're joking. I fashioned the main character after you."

Seated on Magnus's left, Frances grinned across the table at Oscar. "Perhaps if you told us more about the main character, Mr. Wilde, we could determine if it sounds like Magnus or not."

Gail Gauge, who was seated next to Oscar, clapped her hands. "Yes, like a game."

From his chair to the right of Gail Gauge, Jacob could see the anger building in Magnus's green eyes.

"Well, where to begin?" Oscar lifted his wineglass to his lips. "Dorian Gray is so many opposites at once. He's good and bad, beautiful yet ugly, perfect but also terribly flawed. He is literally two things at once—he's a human being, and he is also the portrait that reflects the state of his soul."

"Maybe we should keep a close eye on that picture above the mantel in your living room, Magnus? See if it grows old instead of you," Judge Wentworth threw out from the end of the table.

Frances dipped her spoon into her chowder. "But does the character in your book see the ugliness in his painting and change his ways? I would think being able to see your sins in a painting would be enough to make you want to change."

Oscar set his wineglass on the white tablecloth. "Actually, Dorian takes a kind of perverse delight in seeing just how depraved and corrupt his secret soul can become. He knows he is evil, but he doesn't want to do anything about it. He enjoys being evil. Throughout the novel, he is given opportunities to change and embrace the good in him, but he doesn't. In the end, he is beyond salvation."

"I think it's a sad story," Mrs. Gauge lamented. "Tell me, Mr. Wilde, does your character go to church?"

Oscar snickered. "God doesn't save men, Mrs. Gauge. Men must save themselves. God merely shows them the way."

Jacob turned his eyes to Magnus. "What about you, Magnus? Are you beyond salvation?"

Magnus put his soup spoon down and wiped the corners of his mouth with his linen napkin. "No man is beyond salvation, O'Connor. The question is, is every man worth saving in the first place?"

"But like the character in the book, you did have opportunities to take a different course in your life. To be a different way, a kinder way, but you never took it."

"Jacob," Frances whispered across the table to her husband.

"No, Frances," Magnus chided. "Continue, O'Connor."

"Back at Harvard, you thrived on pushing the boundaries with classmates, professors, even the women you courted."

Oscar's eyes volleyed from Magnus to Jacob. "Do give us an example, O'Connor? I would very much like to hear what he did to the women he courted."

"Me, too," Gail Gauge mused.

Jacob sat back in his chair, his brown eyes challenging his friend. "I remember this one beautiful woman you were very much infatuated with. You strung her along with promises of fidelity, but you would do nothing of the kind. You toyed with her affections, and when she finally had enough and called it off, you pretended to be indifferent. I've always wondered why. Why did you treat her so coldly if you cared for her?"

Silence settled over the table like a heavy fog. Magnus took in the eyes of every one of his guests staring back at him, and beneath the white collar of his starched tuxedo, he seethed.

"I think I know to whom you are referring, and I must confess, I did care for the woman. But when confronted by the inevitability of marriage, I decided she was not the one for me." He lifted his wineglass. "I never promised fidelity to any woman I courted, especially not her. What you may have interpreted as uncaring was simply my giving her the opportunity to call it off first and save herself any embarrassment."

The hard stare Magnus gave him made Jacob's palms sweat. "And have you continued to be that way with other women, Magnus? Hard-hearted, I mean."

"Unlike the character in the book, O'Connor, I do not revel in being onerous with anyone. I cannot help it if some misconstrue cruelty as nothing more than asserting my authority."

"Of course," Jacob agreed. "Powerful men are often misunderstood."

Jacob noticed the flush on Magnus's cheeks, the way his lips were smashed together, and the tight grip on his wineglass. Jacob had done something he had never done before: he had challenged Magnus. The encounter invigorated Jacob.

"So what happened to the young woman? The one who was spurned?" Mrs. Gauge pestered, her brown eyes agog.

Jacob retrieved his soup spoon. "I heard she married another."

Oscar took another gulp of his wine, almost draining his glass. "I'll bet the painting you hid of yourself in the attic is much better looking than my own." He lifted his empty wineglass for the handsome young man to fill.

The tittering's around the table lifted the tense vibration in the room, and the guests returned to their soup.

While Jacob enjoyed the creaminess of his chowder, he saw Magnus watching him out of the corner of his eye. He had crossed a boundary tonight, but he didn't care. He was getting tired of the man's manipulations, and it was time to fight back.

Chapter Seventeen

Beyond Obsession

After sending his guests on their way home, Magnus shut the leaded-glass front doors. The boom of the heavy doors coming together thundered across the foyer.

"You should send O'Connor and his wife away," Oscar advised.

Magnus turned from the doors. "But my house isn't finished, Oscar."

Oscar warily shook his head. "This will not end well, Magnus."

"Nonsense. When the house is done, I will be returning to Boston. I have businesses to see to. I will open my house there and stay away from this island for a while."

"Why not go now?"

Magnus removed his jacket. "Because I am not ready to go."

Oscar took a few steps across the white marble floor to Magnus. "If they stay, you will only end up like the character in my book. Evil will tempt you, and eventually, you will give in to it."

"What is so wrong with evil, Oscar? I think a little evil in a man is a good thing. It makes him competitive, strong, and able to command his destiny."

"Love can do the same thing for a man. I suggest you find a woman of your own. Frances O'Connor is in love with her husband, and such love can never be broken—no matter what spells you try to weave."

"Madam Simone said the same thing once," Magnus confessed.

"Well, she was the expert, not me." Oscar turned for the staircase. "I will see you in the morning before I leave."

"There is a going away present in your room."

Oscar turned to him. "A present? What kind of present?"

Magnus grinned as he looked up the stairs. "A nice bottle of wine and someone to pour it for you."

The thrilling smile that spread across Oscar's long face was beguiling. "You are too good to me."

Magnus motioned up the stairs. "Go on; he's waiting."

After Oscar had disappeared around the second-floor landing, Emily Mann emerged from her office door right past the stairs. The skirts of her formal gown brushed against the cool marble as she came up to him.

"I have the new invoices you requested. Do you still want to go over them tonight?"

He slung his jacket over his arm. "Yes, and make sure you tip the young man well when he leaves Oscar's bedroom. I think he is going to earn every penny."

"I have sent Laurie on her way with a nice severance. She left the island earlier today."

"And her replacement?"

"Annie."

"Is she docile?"

Emily Mann nodded. "Yes, Mr. Blackwell. She is what you are looking for."

"Just make sure this one stays away from O'Connor. The last thing I need is him making inquiries of all my maids."

"She's been warned not to speak to him. I told her if she discussed anything that went on in the house with anyone she would be sacked. This one desperately needs the work, so she will comply."

He studied his secretary's cool brown eyes. "If I didn't know better, I would swear you enjoy your job, Ms. Mann."

"I like what you pay me, sir."

"Some people cannot compromise their integrity for money. Let me know if you ever become one of those, Ms. Mann

"You outlined my duties from the moment I arrived, Mr. Blackwell. I told you I could handle it, and I still can."

"Good." He started toward the stairs. "Bring those invoices up to my office."

His hand touched the dark wood of the dragon's head on the banister and Magnus felt his energy drain from his body. It had been a long night, and he still had more work to get through. Trotting up the steps, he recalled Jacob's words during dinner. It would seem his formerly quiet friend was finding his voice.

His hand tightly gripped the banister. "I'll put a stop to that soon enough."

"Do you think you should have challenged him like that?" Frances was pulling down the blankets on their bed as he finished hanging up his tuxedo in their small closet.

"I couldn't help myself. The way Oscar Wilde talked about his book and the character. It sounded exactly like Magnus."

She sat down on the bed, wrapping her dressing gown around her body. "I know. I found the whole thing eerie. And that story about the cane! No wonder he is so obsessed with it. He probably thinks it gives him magical powers."

"Well, it explains why he has been so insistent on the dragon theme around the house."

"What if he fires you for what you said at dinner?"

Jacob chuckled and sat down next to her, tucking his robe under his legs. "He won't fire me. We are so close to finishing. I figure we have two good months, three if the weather acts up, and we are done."

"Then?" she asked hopefully. "Are you going to take his job offer?"

Jacob stared into her brown eyes and something inside of him stirred. How could he subject her to more years under the scrutiny of Magnus? She had stuck by him so far, but he was not foolish enough to believe they could continue living under such stress.

"I was going to start making inquiries with other firms in Boston and other parts of Massachusetts. I have no interest in continuing with Magnus once we are done here."

Frances flung her arms around his neck. "Really?"

The happiness he felt from her was something he had not sensed in a long time. He had made the right decision. They needed a fresh start.

He pulled her to him. "Does this mean I get a reprieve from the sofa?"

"Absolutely, Mr. O'Connor."

He kissed her cheek. "Thank God. I was beginning to think you had forgotten me, Mrs. O'Connor."

Her hands went to the front of his robe. "Never." She pushed the lapels of his blue robe open and reached inside to caress his chest.

As his kisses traveled down her neck, Jacob pushed aside the robe, eager to feel her soft skin. The smell of honeysuckle on her was driving him mad. Soon her robe was open down the front, exposing her luscious body. His hands luxuriated in the feel of her breasts and slim hips. When he pinched her right nipple, the sweet moan from her lips sent him over the edge.

Pushing her back on the bed, he ripped the robe away from her body, desperate to have her naked beneath him. He was amazed how every time with her was as exciting as their wedding night. His desire for her had never waned; if anything, he wanted her more than ever before.

Frances pushed back his robe, and her hands caressed his wide shoulders and muscular back. The touch of her fingertips was like tendrils of electricity on his skin. Her hands ran over his round ass, and when she dug her nails into his butt cheeks, he almost groaned with delight.

His cock ached to be inside her. He knelt between her legs and dipped his fingers into her. She was so wet he did not know if he could wait to enjoy her, but he tempered his need and traced his fingers along her folds, wanting to make sure she was ready. As his thumb worked back and forth over her clit, he enjoyed watching her writhe beneath him. There was nothing more wonderful for Jacob than making Frances come. The two other women he had been with before his wife had taught him the importance of pleasing a woman, but he had never enjoyed giving such pleasure until Frances. He had always found sex awkward, but that all changed with his wife. In the bedroom, they had always found harmony.

"Jacob," she cried out just as he felt her body buck beneath him.

She settled back on the bed, sighing with contentment, just as he opened her folds for him. Slipping slowly inside of her, Jacob curled his arms around her. Her hands went to his shoulders as he pulled out and thrust deeper into her wet flesh.

"Harder," she murmured against him. "Do it harder. The way I like."

The next time he rammed into her, he went in deep and hard.

Frances gasped, and her nails cut into his flesh. He loved that part when she completely let go and handed herself over to him. Pounding into her, he grunted into her neck as the climax climbed his spine.

"Frances," he whispered into her cheek as he felt himself teetering on the edge.

With one last powerful penetration, he came inside of her. Spent, he settled on top of her, a light film of sweat breaking out on his brow.

"I liked it when you stood up to Magnus tonight," she softly said while running her fingers through his wavy hair.

"I just couldn't keep silent anymore. He looked so damned smug. I wanted to wipe that smirk off his face."

"Why was tonight any different than the years you have spent with him?"

Jacob sat up and gazed into his wife's eyes. "Because tonight, for the first time, I saw him for what he really is—a monster."

Chapter Eighteen

Dilemma

The work on Altmover Manor was nearing completion. The exterior resembled a Southern plantation with six Corinthian columns in place, sweeping balconies and wrought iron railings installed, and stone ravens blasted into oblivion—thanks to Dexter's dynamite.

There were just a few touches left on the interior of the house. The plumbers were finishing up with the bathrooms, making sure the newfangled water heaters were operating and the new fixtures were fully operational. The last detail Jacob was overseeing was in the courtyard.

Enclosed on three sides by a newly built stone wall, Jacob felt the structure was very close to the New Orleans courtyards he had seen in several books he had bought as references. The only feature that still troubled him was the sheer drop to the ocean on the right.

Strolling up to the black fountain in the center of the courtyard, he sighted the paunch of his plumber sticking out from beneath the fountain.

"What's the problem, Max?"

"I'm having trouble getting the dragon's mouth to spurt water from the top of this fancy piece of shit. We should never buy anything from the South. They're just waiting to get even with us for losing the war."

Jacob snickered while shaking his head. "Try filling the pump again, Max. Perhaps you didn't have it primed with enough water."

"I've already tried that," Max griped from beneath the stone base of the triple-tiered fountain.

"Where is Eddie? He was supposed to fasten the iron railing around that open edge of the courtyard today."

"Haven't seen him," Max grumbled from underneath the fountain. "I'm here to handle the plumbing, Jacob, not oversee the help. That's your job."

"Thank you for that, Max. I can always count on you to keep me in line."

"O'Connor," Magnus called from the entrance of the conservatory at the rear of the home.

"Ah, Christ," Jacob muttered under his breath.

"Better go on and see what he wants to change now," Max encouraged. "But if he wants to move this damned fountain again, I'll kill him."

As of late, hearing Magnus call his name had started to get on Jacob's nerves. Spying the walking stick, Jacob shuddered. Ever since he had heard how Magnus had acquired it, he'd been uncomfortable looking into the blood-red eyes of the dragon's head. The damn thing was creepy enough without knowing its history.

Rushing across the green dragon mosaic in the courtyard floor, Jacob went to Magnus. As soon as he stood before the man, he could tell something was wrong. His perturbed sneer was back, and the light in his green eyes was hostile.

"We need to talk." Magnus turned away and entered the conservatory.

When the two men came to rest under the great glass roof of the wide room, Magnus faced him. "I have just heard some rather disturbing news." He tapped the cane on the stone floor of the conservatory. "Have you been making inquiries into positions at architectural firms in Boston?"

Jacob gulped back his dread. How had he known? "Ah, yes, I have. I've been exploring my options."

Magnus gave him a tolerant snicker. "You have no other options, O'Connor. You need to understand Boston is a small town as far as business is concerned. I have already put it out there that you were going to come to work for my architectural firm in the city, and when you began to make inquiries to other firms, well, they immediately contacted me."

"I told you I would consider the job, Magnus, not that I would take it."

"You will take it, O'Connor. You have nothing else, especially now that all the other firms in town know you will be working for me. They will not want to hire you."

Stunned, Jacob was silent. How was he going to tell Frances? She had been so happy over the past few weeks knowing their time with Magnus was coming to an end. She had even been talking about going to Boston to start house hunting. The news would crush her.

"Why are you doing this, Magnus?"

He gazed around the bright room decorated with white wicker furniture and potted green plants. "Because I want to keep you around, O'Connor. I have great plans for us in Boston. You are a very talented architect, and I know you will make me a great deal of money."

"What if I don't want to work for you?"

Magnus leveled his angry eyes on Jacob. "But you will work for me; you have no choice. No matter where you go, I will ruin any hopes you have of employment. In the end, you will come to me. Better to avoid all those problems and just say yes to me now. I will make it well worth your while. You and Frances will want for nothing—ever."

Jacob wanted to rip Magnus apart with his bare hands. He had never been prone to violence, had never wanted to kill a man before, but he had been pushed too far. Instead of acting on his impulse, he clenched his jaw and pushed his fury back to the depths from which it had emerged.

"You have given me a lot to think about."

"There is nothing left to think about, O'Connor." Magnus's malicious grin was back. "In two weeks, I will have a party to celebrate the renovations on Altmover Manor. After that, you and Frances will relocate to one of my houses in Boston. I've already notified the staff at Collier and Keene that you will be starting on the first of next month. If you have any special requests for the move or your home in Boston, give them to Ms. Mann. She will see to it." Without another word, Magnus strolled out of the conservatory, swinging his long walking stick as he went.

Standing in the middle of the all-glass room, Jacob rocked his head back, closed his eyes, and stifled the scream rising up

had planned for them. She would insist they fight him and find their way. To take Magnus's job would be beneficial for his family, but what was best for his family was sticking to his dreams.

"Darling, there is something I need tell you."

"What is it, Jacob?"

"There you are." Magnus's voice grated against Jacob's skin.

Wearing a black tuxedo with tails and diamond studs in his white silk shirt, he cut a dashing figure. His dirty-blond hair was neatly combed to the side; his sharp features radiated charm, and his green eyes twinkled as they took in Frances.

"You look beautiful tonight, my dear."

"Magnus, what a wonderful party." Frances was putting on her best fake voice; Jacob could tell. "Where's your beautiful cane?"

"My cane is upstairs in my office for the night. I didn't want to misplace it with so many people in the house. Someone might accidently walk off with it."

"Yes, it's too valuable to lose," Frances concurred.

"I am afraid I have to steal your husband away for a bit." He motioned behind him to the gloomy face of Emily Mann. "Ms. Mann has some last minute accounting she needs you to check over."

Emily stepped forward in a lovely gown sewn with pearls and trimmed with antique lace. In her fashionably curled hair, a row of white feathers swayed as she moved her head. "I'm sorry, Mr. O'Connor, but it won't take long."

Jacob looked from Emily to Magnus. "Can't it wait until morning?"

"Afraid not, O'Connor. I need the books closed out for the end of the month."

Jacob was about to say something to Frances when Magnus

intruded. "I will entertain Frances while you're gone. We'll take a spin about the ballroom. What do you say, Frances?"

His eyes connected with his wife. "Go on. I'll be fine," she told him.

Encouraged by her smile, he kissed her cheek. "I'll be right back."

Allowing Emily to lead him from the ballroom, Jacob glanced over his shoulder at his wife in time to see Magnus inching up beside her. Silently vowing never to leave her alone with that man again, Jacob picked up his pace to catch up to Emily. He was suddenly anxious to be done with whatever financial matters loomed so he could get back to his Frances.

Finally, he was alone with her. Magnus planned for Emily to keep O'Connor tied up for hours so he could spend the evening with Frances. After a long deliberation about how he would win over Frances, Magnus had left his treasured walking stick in his office. He wanted her without the benefit of magic. Even though he thought the cane was nothing more than a showpiece, Magnus needed to make sure his charm, and not voodoo, seduced Frances. When he held her in his arms and danced with her, Magnus had to know Frances was there because she wanted to be. After all he had done to obtain the baton juju, in the end, Magnus did not feel he needed it to steal Frances's heart.

Convinced he had enough ammunition to drive a wedge between them, he would tell her of O'Connor's plans to take the job in Boston, how excited he was to go, and how he was devoted to Magnus. It would infuriate Frances even more. He knew they were fighting; he had heard their rows. All he needed was to add more fuel to the fire, and then she would need someone to turn to.

"You do look stunning in that dress." He took in her curves beneath the fabric.

"You've seen it before, Magnus. At the dinner for your friend, Oscar Wilde." She rolled the flute of champagne in her hands. "I read his book about you. The one we discussed at dinner."

"What did you think?"

Her light chuckle was music to his ears. How had he lived so long without it?

"I don't think you're quite as bad as the man in the book. After all, you haven't killed anyone, like Dorian Gray. Or have you?"

The playful expression on her face made him want to kiss her. "No, not yet, but the night is still young."

She was laughing again. Good. His plan was working.

In the corner of the room, the music changed and strains of "Three Little Maids from School" filled the air.

"Do you remember this?" Magnus waved his hand in the air.

"The Gilbert and Sullivan play you took me to in Boston. *The Mikado.*"

He took the champagne from her. "You kept humming it the entire ride home from the theater."

Frances watched as he placed her flute on a passing waiter's silver tray. "I thought you hated that song."

Magnus held out his white-gloved hand to her. "I did, but now every time I hear it, I think of you."

Frances gazed down at his hand, unsure of what to do.

"Dance with me for old time's sake," he pleaded.

With a pleasing smile, she took his hand and let him lead

her to the open floor. As he escorted her along, his hand discreetly behind her back, Magnus was in heaven. It was as if the years had slipped away, and they were once again in college.

When she faced him, he eased his arm around her waist and held out his right hand, waiting for her to take it. As soon as she moved in close, he guided her along in time with the upbeat tempo. They were laughing together as he twirled her about, their merriment shining back in long mirrors' reflections around the ballroom. She'd always been a wonderful dancer, and holding her close made Magnus feel so strong, so virile. The sensation was the same as when he carried his long walking stick. The Sang Noir wood made him feel just as powerful, but it had never made him this happy.

As their dance came to an end, he longed for the small orchestra to play the tune again and again, but when they changed to a slow waltz, Frances pulled away.

"I am out of practice," she admitted, sounding winded.

Concern crossed his handsome face as he saw her pale before him. "Do you need some air?"

She nodded. "Yes, for a minute, if you don't mind."

Magnus took her elbow and quickly escorted her through the crowds building in the room. Outside the arched doorway, he motioned with his head to the rear of the house. "I'll take you to the courtyard."

She abruptly stopped beside him. "You don't need to do that, Magnus." She waved inside the ballroom. "You have guests to attend to. I can find my way."

His hand went to her elbow once more. "Don't be silly. You are the only guest that matters to me."

After showing her through the conservatory, Magnus led her out to the courtyard behind the home. The night sky was clear,

difficult to traverse. His secret was safe, for the time being.

Straightening out the sleeves of his jacket, he brushed away the crease or two her grip had made on the fine cloth. Raising his head, he smelled the sea salt in the air, and then slowly strolled back to the conservatory, ready to return to his guests.

At the conservatory doors, he spotted his face in the reflection of the glass. Frances had made a mess of him. He raised his hand to the scratches on his cheek, and touched the blood. Before his eyes, he saw the cuts on his face heal and the blood vanish. Within seconds, there was not a trace of what Frances had done. No evidence that any crime had occurred.

"So dear Madam Simone was right, after all. The cane does have magical power."

Chuckling as he passed through the doors, Magnus thought ahead to how Jacob O'Connor would react when he discovered his wife's dead body at the base of the cliffs.

"Have you seen Frances?"

Magnus held up the champagne glass in his hand as he turned from the round gentleman he had been speaking with and confronted Jacob. "No, I haven't, dear boy. We danced, and she wasn't feeling well, so I escorted her out of the ballroom."

"I can't find her."

"Did you check your cottage? Maybe she went back there."

Jacob's heart thudded like a terrified deer. He felt sick to his stomach, and there wasn't enough air in the room. Sweat beaded on his upper lip.

Magnus stepped away from his guest and took ahold of Jacob's arm. "You look a fright."

"Something is wrong, Magnus. I can feel it."

Magnus let go of his arm. "You're exaggerating, O'Connor. I'm sure she just went back home after we danced. She said the exertion did tire her out a bit."

Jacob nodded. "Yes, she must be at home," he muttered.

When Jacob burst through the door of his cottage, he expected to see the lamps lit and Frances in the kitchen making cocoa like she did every night before bed. But the house was dark and empty. He tore through the small cottage and looked in rooms, closets, even outside the back door and around the grounds surrounding their home.

Returning to the cottage, he lit one of the oil lamps to take with him to search more of the grounds. He was convinced she had to be somewhere. It was so unlike Frances. She would never just walk off and not tell him where she was going.

Outside, he searched around the manor, went down to the main road, and back again, carrying his lamp.

As the guests left the party in the wee hours of the morning, he was still at it. His bright lamp, shining through the black night.

Magnus was standing on his porch and waving to the last of his guests on their way home when he saw Jacob stoically marching to the stables; his lamp held high.

"Don't worry, O'Connor. I am sure she is all right." He called from the porch. "Tomorrow we can make inquiries in town. Maybe she went there and stayed the night."

But Jacob knew in his heart that she was gone. Without his Frances, he was lost.

Chapter Twenty

A Sad Affair

The next morning, Jacob was curled up on the front porch of his cottage, wearing his tuxedo and clutching the gold watch Frances had given him. The oil lamp was by his side, still burning.

"Mr. O'Connor," a voice called into the blackness of his dreams. "What did you do? Tie one on last night?"

Jacob bolted upright. "Have you found her?" came out of his mouth before his eyes even focused on the person before him.

The very large man in front of him was wearing blue coveralls and a white cap. His face was scarred across the left cheek, his nose looked as if it had been broken a few times, and his skin was dotted with pock marks.

"Mr. O'Connor, it's Eddie. I came to put in that railing you wanted around the courtyard this morning, and I found.... Sir, you better come and see for yourself."

Jacob was on his feet and running toward the house before the massive bulk that was Eddie had even stepped from his porch.

The sun had just crested the horizon as Jacob ran around the back of the house to the courtyard. He was hoping they had found her, trapped during the night somewhere outside. But as he came to the end of the courtyard and peered down at the rocks along the shoreline, his heart fell.

He tumbled to his knees as he made out the traces of pink and white of her dress in the sunlight. Even the ringlets of her honey-blonde hair were visible.

"I'm sorry, Mr. O'Connor," Eddie panted behind him, catching his breath. "I tried to get here sooner to finish the railing, but my missus was ill, and I couldn't leave her."

"Frances!" Jacob screamed over the ledge. "Frances, speak to me."

A massive hand came down on his shoulder as he hung over the edge of the cliff, reaching for his wife.

"I'm sorry, Mr. O'Connor, but she's dead."

Eddie dragged him back onto the courtyard and held him as Jacob called out for his wife again and again.

"Any idea what happened?" the police officer asked.

Magnus shook his head, pulling his red satin robe closer around his body. "She wasn't feeling well and left the party last night. I assumed she went home."

The officer, dressed in his bright blue uniform with the shiny silver badge, made a few notations on the pad in his hand. "Have there been any fights between the couple that you know of? Any reason she may have wanted to end her life?"

Magnus stared at the officer and was about to defend Frances, but he stopped. "Yes," he divulged with a sigh. "They had been fighting a lot recently. My secretary overheard them a few weeks ago. Mrs. O'Connor admitted to me last night she wasn't happy with her husband."

Magnus spotted Jacob huddled over on a bench in the conservatory. "I believe there were money problems. He was going to start another position with me in Boston at the beginning of next month, but she wanted him to search for something with better pay."

The police officer nudged his blue hat back on his head. "Do you know if he was having an affair?"

Magnus tried to contain his grin. "I know he had an unusual interest in one of my maids. Her name was Laurie. He seemed infatuated with her. I let her go when I suspected she was lying to me about her relationship with Mr. O'Connor. Frances was a friend, and I did not want to see her betrayed like that."

The police officer scratched the tip of the pencil in his hand and under his hat. "That should be about it then, Mr. Blackwell. It all seems pretty cut and dry."

"It does?" Magnus questioned, amazed.

"It was obviously a suicide. She must have thrown herself over the edge of the courtyard when she found out her husband was having an affair."

Magnus directed his gaze to Jacob. "What will you do with O'Connor?"

The police officer shrugged. "Nothing. Having an affair isn't a crime. Not yet, anyway." He tipped his hat to Magnus.

"Thank you for your time, Mr. Blackwell."

The police officer went back to the edge of the courtyard to check the progress of the men sent to recover Frances's body.

"Do you think it was suicide?"

Emily Mann came up to him. Already dressed for a day in her office, Magnus wondered if the woman had even gone to sleep after the last of the partygoers had left earlier that morning.

"Yes, I believe it was suicide." He pulled his robe closer, fending off the morning chill. "She admitted to me last night she wasn't happy. I sensed she'd wanted to speak to me for a while. It was the reason I needed you to keep him occupied last night."

"He seemed very nervous about getting back to her. Do you think he suspected she was confiding in you?"

Magnus raised his eyes to the broken man sitting in the glass conservatory. "Yes, I believe he did. He was always jealous of our former relationship. You see, she was still in love with me. I tried to tell her it was over, but she could never be convinced. O'Connor was my friend, and I never wanted to see him hurt by her."

Emily gave him a reassuring pat on the arm. "It wasn't your fault, sir. She was just a very sad woman." Nodding to the conservatory, she asked, "What do you want me to do about Mr. O'Connor? Is he still to take the position at your firm in Boston?"

Magnus felt his blood race. "No. I think considering the circumstances that would be a very bad idea. Give him his notice and tell him he has twenty-four hours to move out of the cottage."

"Twenty-four hours? But his wife just died, sir."

"Yes, but it was his fault, wasn't it? Reason enough to get him out of my sight."

The funeral for Frances Beatrice McGee O'Connor happened on a cold, drizzly day a week later in the beginning of October. The main road into Forest Hills Cemetery, located just inside the Boston city limits, was lined with a procession of closed black carriages and open buggies.

There were quite a few mourners gathered at the graveside; not as many people as had attended her wedding, but enough to show she had been well liked. The freshly dug grave held her white oak casket covered in yellow roses. Jacob had insisted on the yellow roses, claiming they had been her favorite.

Standing to the side of the grave, next to her father, Jacob felt the cold, wet weather seeping under his skin. He wondered if he would ever feel warm again.

The cleric wearing black robes spoke at the head of Frances's grave. He droned on about ashes and dust, but Jacob paid no attention. His eyes seared into the man he blamed for his wife's death—Magnus Blackwell.

Surrounded by other mourners, Magnus stood out to Jacob. In a long black overcoat and tall black hat, the dragon-headed cane at his side, he was just like the day Jacob had met him at Harvard: brash, bold, and still arrogant as hell.

He was still glaring at Magnus when he felt a nudge from his father-in-law. It was time to put his wife to rest. Picking up a handful of dirt from the side of the grave, he tossed it on top of Frances's casket. The thud of the clumped mud against her coffin turned his stomach.

After his father-in-law had repeated the same gut-wrenching sound, the cleric made one last prayer of deliverance for

Frances's soul and then sent the mourners on their way.

But Jacob could not move; he was still bound to his spot next to her grave, fearing that if he walked away, he would lose her forever.

"Jacob, leave the men to bury her," Judge McGee implored with an urgent tug on his elbow.

"Give me a moment to say good-bye."

Judge McGee pushed up the lapels of his black coat against the cold and dipped his head to Jacob. He went to the gravestone of Frances's mother next to them. Kissing his hand, he touched it to the headstone of Agnes Claire McGee and walked away.

As the rain began to fall a little harder, the mourners quickly scattered for the shelter of their carriages. But Jacob did not mind the rain. He liked the solitude it brought him. Better than people coming up to him and expressing their condolences. Such a gesture was meaningless to him. What did they know of his loss or his pain?

The heavy raindrops made small puddles in the piles of mud around her grave. Jacob became fascinated with the way the rain pooled and moved the mud aside, showing its mastery over the earth.

"I'm sorry, sir," a beefy man in a cap and overalls said to him. "We need to bury her now before the rain gets too heavy."

Jacob saw the shovel in his hands, and slowly the gravedigger's words set into his brain. Nodding his acquiescence, he stood off to the side as the men began their grim task.

The horrible sound of the heavy globs of mud beating down on her coffin made Jacob turn away from her grave. He could not stand to see her covered up. Jogging away from her gravesite, he went to a row of nearby tombstones and, overcome with emotion, fell to his knees.

seed? Turning his back on her grave, he hurried to his carriage, eager to put her behind him.

After climbing inside his black carriage, Magnus removed his wet overcoat and placed it to the side. Glancing out the window, he saw Jacob moving in a mad stagger amid the tombstones. Shaking his head, Magnus sat back in his seat.

"The poor boy has lost his mind." Raising the cane in his hand, he tapped the carriage roof, signaling for the driver to move on.

"Do you think he blames himself?" Emily Mann asked from the seat opposite him.

Magnus swept his eyes over her wet, black clothes. "Of course. In time, I am sure he will be just fine. O'Connor always was a resilient fellow." He gazed out at the passing tombstones as the carriage left the cemetery. "Have you made arrangements to close up Altmover Manor?"

"Already done, sir. I've let most of the staff go and kept a skeleton crew on to keep the house in order."

"Very good, but I doubt I will be going back there for quite a while. I want to spend some time in Boston to forget the whole unhappy affair."

"I understand, Mr. Blackwell. I have already begun interviewing staff for the house here in Boston."

His eyes skirted across her depressing little face. "Just make sure you get what I like, Ms. Mann."

"I know your taste, sir. No need to be concerned. I will find the perfect maids to appease your specific requirements."

Magnus tipped his head back against the seat. "I'm so lucky to have found you, Ms. Mann. Sometimes I feel you know me better than anyone."

Emily Mann just nodded her head.

Magnus closed his eyes, pleased she wasn't one of those chatty women. He hated the women who never shut up; then again, he didn't like the ones who were too quiet, especially when he was having his fun with them. Yes, he needed to find a woman who was obedient, docile, yet he also wanted her to be outspoken and interesting. Sort of like his Frances. If he could just find another one like her, he could be happy. He would have to save himself for another. To stay faithful until just the right woman came along.

Chapter Twenty-One

Road to Revenge

Jacob O'Connor sat in a corner at the End of the Line Bar drinking from his third whiskey and soda and staring at the gold pocket watch Frances had given him. Wearing dirty brown coveralls and a cap with *B&M* stamped in black across it, he looked like the other men who crowded into the popular watering hole after a long day. The drab-looking bar, with faded portraits of steam engines covering the walls, resonated with the hum of men deep in conversation and the occasional hoarse chuckle.

With a shaky hand, Jacob raised his glass to his chapped lips. He was much leaner, his muscular body more defined from hours of hard labor, and his once shiny brown orbs were now listless and dull. The dark circles rimming his eyes spoke of the many sleepless nights he had endured, while his scarred and greasy hands were the ever-present reminders of his new vocation.

"Still drinking alone, Jacob?"

The fat man that took a seat at his round table wore brown coveralls similar to Jacob's, but his accentuated his protruding gut. He was bald, his fingernails were black from dirt, his round face tanned from the sun, and his blue eyes bloodshot.

"Why do you ask me that, Mac? You know I always drink alone." Jacob took another sip from his watered down whiskey.

"I've been working with you for almost three years on the Boston and Maine Railroad, and every night after work, you come in here and drink. Always alone and always at this stupid table." Mac slapped his gnarled hand on the table.

Jacob eyed his hand. "You got a problem with that?"

"I'm not looking for a fight, Jacob. I'm wondering about your story. Why do you sit here every night and drink until you damn near pass out?"

Jacob slipped the gold watch into his pocket. "You know why, Mac. I already told you."

"You told me you were married, your wife died, and you went to work on the railroad. But that don't drive a man to drink, not like you do." Mac wiped his hand over his bald head. "Men that I know drink because they are either real sad or real angry."

"Maybe I'm sad." He toasted his friend with his glass.

Mac wrestled the glass from him and banged it on the table. "I've asked you time and time again to come to my house and dine with my Hattie and me, but you always turn me down. Instead, you come here to swill this piss." He motioned to the glass. "Now I think you're a man in need of some help. I'm offering. Are you willing to take it?"

"I'm beyond help, Mac."

Mac leaned across the table and patted his arm. "No man is beyond salvation. The good book says so."

A memory of Magnus telling him the same thing jolted Jacob. "I know one man who might disagree with you there, Mac."

Mac pointed to Jacob's drink. "Is he the one who drove you to this?"

Maybe it was the alcohol, or perhaps the years of loneliness were catching up with him. Jacob had lived inside of his shell for so long that he almost forgot what it was like to talk to another person—what it was like to unburden his soul.

"I thought he was my friend," he whispered, while his unsteady hand reached for his drink.

Mac pulled the drink out of his reach. "What did he do?"

Jacob watched his glass of courage move farther away from his grasp. "Do? He destroyed me."

Mac leaned in closer to the round wooden table. "Talk to me, Jacob, before you have no one else willing to listen."

Mac waited, but Jacob said nothing; he only stared at the glass of whiskey.

"If you won't tell me who he is, then tell me what you did before?" He pointed to his hands. "You ain't missing no fingers yet, so you're not an old-timer working on the railroad like me." He held up his left hand and proudly showed his missing middle finger. "I watched you when you first arrived on the crew. You could barely swing the sledgehammer to set the rail ties; you weren't used to any hard labor. So what were you?"

Convinced he was not going to get his drink back, Jacob decided maybe it was best to play along. "I was an architect. I got my degree from Harvard." Jacob pointed to his glass. "Now can I have my drink?"

Mac stared at him, his bloodshot eyes round with wonder. "You went to Harvard? What happened? Were you rich or something and lost it all?"

"No, I didn't come from money. I was born an orphan."

"But you went to that fancy school?"

"I went to Harvard on a scholarship I got with the help of a benefactor. It was also the place where I met my wife."

"Frances," Mac chimed in. "You told me a little about her."

Jacob nodded as the tears gathered in his eyes. "She was pregnant when she died. It was going to be our first."

The sadness that registered on Mac's face mirrored Jacob's. "Me and my Hattie lost our two boys to typhoid fever many years ago. I know your pain. Hattie got it after our sons. I almost lost her, too."

"Typhoid fever?" Jacob's foggy mind tried to recall who else he had known that had lost family to typhoid fever. "I knew someone who lost his brother and—" His mouth clamped shut when he remembered.

"Who lost their brother?" Mac pressed.

Jacob shook his head. "He was ... never mind."

"What was his name, Jacob? Just tell me his name. That's a start."

His name was on the tip of his tongue, but something kept holding him back, and then he saw Frances in his mind's eye. He saw his Frances in her pretty pink and white gown dead across the rocks.

"Magnus Blackwell," he hissed.

Stunned, Mac pushed his drink back in front of him. "The rich guy in Boston? He was just in the papers a few weeks back. Something about him getting married to some society girl."

Jacob snatched up his drink. "Yeah, that's him. He married

Katherine Parker of Parker and Mills Banks. Her grandfather started the bank, and now her father, Miles Parker, runs it."

Mac looked at his friend with a newfound appreciation. "I don't get it. How did you go from being his friend," he waved around the dark bar, "to this?"

Gazing down at the dirty cement floor, Jacob tried to find the answer but couldn't. He remembered the day of Frances's funeral and how he had stumbled about the graveyard until his father-in-law had taken him back to his home. He had stayed with the judge for a few days, but then one morning, he got dressed and walked out the front door with no idea where he was going.

"After my wife died, I took a job with the railroad. I wanted to walk away from my former life. Walk away? That's a joke. More like run. I had nothing left, no home, no wife. I signed up with B&M and never looked back."

Mac chuckled, sounding like a throaty version of Santa Claus. "You've been doing nothing but looking back, if you ask me. You're so attached to the past, son, you're burying your heart in a bottle to forget it. Would your wife want this life for you?"

Jacob shook his head and wiped his grimy hand over his face. "No."

"Then fix this. You're still young, Jacob. Put the past in the past."

"How do I do that, Mac?"

"Start with this rich guy in Boston—Blackwell. Now, what do you think he did to you that was so bad?"

Jacob looked the fat man in the eye. "I think he killed my wife."

Mac's face fell. "Shit. Really?"

Spurred on by Mac's reaction, Jacob tossed back the last of

his drink. "I've been mulling it over for three years, Mac. Every day I am on the railroad, pounding spikes into the ground, I think about what he did to her." Jacob slammed his glass into the dented table. "He was the last to see my Frances alive. He told the police she committed suicide. He claimed she was unhappy with our marriage. But Frances never killed herself. She was pregnant. A woman wanting a child would never consider such an act."

The fire of rage showed in Mac's dark brown eyes. "If he did that to her, then there is only one thing left for you to do."

"What is that, Mac? Revenge?" Jacob snickered. "I thought you were a God-fearing man."

Mac drummed the table with his three fingers. "What does it say in the bible, Jacob? 'An eye for an eye.' If this man wronged you, if he killed your wife, then you need to do something about it." He motioned to the drink on the table. "Otherwise, that is where you will end up. To save yourself, you're gonna have to sacrifice something or someone."

Jacob's shaky hand stretched for his glass. Mac quickly took the glass away. "You're coming home with me. Hattie and I are going to get you sobered up and cleaned up, and then send you back to where you came from."

Jacob held his shaking hands together. "Why do you give a damn about me?"

Mac rose from the table. "Because I'm not going to see you give up everything you worked so hard to get." He went around and helped Jacob get to his feet. "Come on."

"I can't go back to Boston," Jacob mumbled as held on to Mac's shoulder.

"You have to go back, Jacob." Mac guided him to the bar entrance. "You don't belong here anymore."

Chapter Twenty-Two

Return

The ferry to Mount Desert Island wasn't very crowded that day. Then again, it was too cold for some to want to make the trip across the rough water. Jacob watched the island come into view as he pulled his coat tighter around his neck. He had forgotten about the cold. He had forgotten about the smell of the sea and the sound of the ocean.

Holding his only suitcase in his hand, he slowly departed the ferry, his limp slowing him down. When he finally reached the first street in the town of Mount Desert, he put his suitcase down and took a look around.

Not much had changed since his time at Altmover Manor. It was still the idyllic small town with a smattering of shops and homes along the main thoroughfare. Collecting his suitcase, he forged on. Passing the open doors of a bar, he smelled the liquor inside and was surprised to discover he had no yearning for alcohol anymore. His need to bury his sorrows had been replaced with another more urgent desire—his lust for revenge.

Knowing he could never make the trek to Altmover Manor on foot, Jacob spent the little money he had to hire a carriage. After telling the driver where to go, he climbed into the cab and sat down on the hard bench.

The ride was shorter than he remembered, maybe because he had always been in such a rush when he traveled the road to town. Anxious to get supplies for the manor, he had never noticed before how beautiful the island was. Jacob remembered it as rocky and barren, but lush trees and foliage that hugged the dirt road reminded him of the land he had seen when he worked on the railroad.

Jacob thought it funny how the years had changed his perspective—and his body. Rubbing his sore right leg, he winced when he hit the spot where the bone had come through his calf. It was months before he could walk again after the loose railcar ran into him. The doctor had told him better to have a limp than no leg at all. At the time, he had been in so much pain he thought he might have preferred taking his leg. Now he was glad the doctor had spared it.

When the manor house rose up from the road ahead, Jacob forgot about his discomfort. The churning in his belly suddenly outshined all his aches and pains.

"You sure you don't want me to bring you up to the house, Mr. O'Connor?"

The young boy he had hired to run errands around the manor construction site had grown into a strapping young man.

"No thanks, David. I'll be fine."

"Why don't you let me carry the bag up to the house for you, at least?" David urged.

Shaking his head, Jacob started down the dusty road to the manor door. "I need to do this alone."

The sweat was dripping onto his long coat when he finally reached the front of the home. Gazing up at the thick columns, wide porch, and shady balconies, a surge of pride swelled through him. He had done this; he had turned the dreary manor house into a grand home.

The front doors unexpectedly opened, and Jacob felt unprepared. He had rehearsed his speech to give to Magnus, but only after he had presented himself at the servant's entrance. He needed to appear humble.

A woman all in black emerged from behind the doors, and when she saw Jacob standing on the gravel driveway, she jumped with surprise.

"Oh, I never expected to see—" Emily Mann went instantly silent. She moved closer to the edge of the porch, her hand rising to her throat. "Mr. O'Connor?"

Jacob removed his black hat and bowed his head. "Hello, Ms. Mann."

In a shot, she was reaching for the skirts of her dress and trotting down the steps. "Oh, Mr. O'Connor, it is good to see you."

When Jacob took a step forward, her small eyes went to his limp. "What happened to you?"

"There was an accident." He put his hat back on his head. "When I was working for the railroad."

Her face soured with revulsion. "Railroad?"

"It is a long story. I came ...." He hesitated when he spotted the little yellow cottage out of the corner of his eye. When Jacob appraised the structure, his heart ripped in two.

It was just how he had left it the day after Frances's death. Still quaint, still a pale shade of yellow, and still filled with a thousand memories.

"I came to wish Magnus well," he began as he turned away from the cottage. "I read about his wedding. I wanted to come and wish him every happiness as he did on my wedding day."

Emily moved closer and took the suitcase from his hand. "He will want to see you. He's not the man you remember, Mr. O'Connor. He's changed."

"Changed how?"

Emily shrugged as she backed up. "He's happy." She spun around and headed up the porch steps.

Mustering his strength, Jacob followed her. "Good," he muttered under his breath. "Soon you will know how it feels to be miserable, my friend."

The grand foyer had changed very little, and the wide staircase with its dragon banister was still there. The ruby-red eyes he had placed into the beautifully carved head, just as Magnus had wanted, were still gleaming.

He followed Emily into the home, and when they reached the living room doors, she pushed them open for him. "Wait in here, and I will get him."

Jacob peered into the fine room. It was the same one he'd been in the night Magnus had invited him and Frances to meet Oscar Wilde. His eyes went to the masterful portrait of Magnus above the hearth, and his insides burned.

"His new wife, what is she like?" he asked, before entering the room.

"She's a lot like ... well, you'll see."

After she had returned to the main staircase, Jacob went to the mantel and gazed up at the portrait of his former friend. In his mind, he repeated the speech he had prepared, the words he had precisely chosen, and the way he would put himself at his friend's mercy.

"O'Connor?"

This time, when he heard Magnus say his name, all the anxiety it used to cause in him was gone. His apprehension had turned to rage.

Turning slowly, Jacob took in the man he had waited years to see. When his eyes came in contact with Magnus's face, the change he noticed was astounding. The malevolence he'd always associated with his grin was gone and a warm, welcoming smile had replaced it. Even the coolness of his reproachful gaze had warmed. His thick dirty-blond hair was shorter, his waist a little thicker, and perhaps a line or two of worry had become a little more embedded in his forehead, but he was still Magnus—the man who had taken away his Frances.

"My God, it is you." Magnus came barreling toward him with open arms; something Jacob never thought he would live to see.

Magnus gave him a heartfelt embrace, patted his back, and moved away. Jacob noticed the smell of coffee lingering in the air around him. "Where have you been? How have you been? I made inquiries after ... the way we left things. I am sorry for—"

Jacob silenced him with a wave of his calloused hand. "It's the past, Magnus. I wasn't in my right mind after Frances died. I've done a lot of soul-searching since then, and I was wrong to blame you."

His relieved smile almost had Jacob convinced of his sincerity.

"I'm glad you've come back." He looked him over. "How fit you appear. Where have you been for the past few years?"

"Working the railroad." Jacob held up his head. "After the

funeral, I took a job with B&M. I started out as a coal bin loader, and after a few months, they put me to work doing railroad repair and building new lines." He gazed down at the polished oak floors. "I liked the hard work. It helped me forget."

Magnus placed his hands behind his burgundy dinner jacket. "You should have contacted me, O'Connor. I could have helped you. Gotten you work as an architect instead of menial labor." He went to the plush floral sofa and sat down. "But you're back, and we can begin again."

Jacob took a few steps toward the sofa, pronouncing his limp. He watched as Magnus's eyes widened with concern.

"What happened? Are you injured?" Magnus stood up.

Jacob smiled, patting his left thigh. "An accident on the rail line. I was pinned between two cars. The bone broke in two places and poked through my calf. It still bothers me when I walk, but at least I have my leg."

"I'll get you the best doctors to look at it. We will make you as good as new."

Jacob wanted to shout out that he could never be whole again, not without his love, but he figured there was no point in explaining that to Magnus. Such devotion was beyond him.

"I didn't come here for a handout, Magnus," Jacob began, citing the speech he had committed to memory. "I read about your nuptials in the paper, and I wanted to come and give you my best wishes. You did the same for Frances and me, and I know she would want me to come and convey our congratulations. I only wish my wife had lived to see this day; I know she would have been so pleased."

Magnus cockily rocked back and forth on his toes, smiling like a silly schoolboy. "I am a very lucky man, O'Connor. My Katie is the most remarkable woman. Sweet, smart, beautiful, and she comes from an affluent family in Charleston."

"You married a Southern girl?" Jacob feigned a smile. "How appropriate, considering your love of all things Southern."

"And she adores this house," Magnus asserted. "We end up spending more time here than in my home in Boston. We are even considering purchasing a home in Charleston to be near her family during part of the year." He rolled his eyes. "I am still debating the hazards of that."

Both men chuckled, the awkward air in the room lifting a little.

"You must come and meet her." Magnus motioned to the living room doors. "She's in the conservatory. She is an absolute magician with plants. Katie has turned the entire conservatory into a nursery."

"She sounds wonderful, Magnus, but I am ...." Jacob lowered his head to his dusty, second-hand coat and wrinkled pants Hattie had traded a friend two fine hams to obtain. "I am not presentable."

"Nonsense." Magnus came up to him and took his elbow. "You are like family, O'Connor. Katie isn't the sort to care about what you wear. She is very down-to-earth and practical."

"She sounds like Frances."

Guiding him to the doors, Magnus nodded. "She is very much like her in many ways."

The hall that led to the conservatory had not changed since the last time Jacob had walked down it that horrid day. The paintings of forests, glens, and babbling brooks still crowded the walls, and when he spied the bright daylight of the conservatory through the wide archway at the rear of the home, he steadied himself for the memories that were sure to inundate his mind.

The conservatory was indeed very different than he

remembered. Shelves of potted plants and flowers covered the walls and rose up the side of the glass panes that looked out over the courtyard. He spotted the green dragon mosaic on the courtyard floor and the black fountain with the gold dragon on top. All that was as he remembered, and then his eyes drifted to the end of the courtyard.

"Darling," Magnus called in a sweet voice that Jacob found strange. "I have someone I want you to meet."

A dainty oval face with bright pink cheeks, a pointy nose, and slightly dimpled chin surrounded by honey-blonde curls peeked out from behind a shelf of miniature red roses.

When she stepped out, her petite figure was wrapped in a green apron that protected her gown. Giving Jacob the prettiest smile, she began pulling off her long green gloves.

"Well, hello," she said in an angelic voice.

She held out her hand to Jacob, and he was instantly reminded of his Frances. She had the same elegant manner as his departed wife, the same hair, but her features were more childlike and delicate.

"I am Katherine Blackwell."

"Katie, meet Jacob O'Connor."

She eagerly took Jacob's hand. "The O'Connor?" Her blue eyes brightened. "My husband has gone on and on about you, dear sir. It is a great pleasure to finally shake your hand."

The feel of her small hand in his gave Jacob an unusual strength, as if his years of toil had come to an end, and his purpose had suddenly become very clear.

"Mrs. Blackwell, it is an honor." Jacob attempted to bow, but his injured left leg hindered him.

"None of that formality, O'Connor," Magnus scolded. "I want you and my Katie to be friends."

"Katie?" Jacob inquired. "A nickname."

"Growing up I was always Katie to my parents and two sisters. Magnus adores the name and calls me nothing else."

Magnus came alongside his wife, putting a protective arm around her. "It suits her. She is something delicate and precious to be protected, don't you think, O'Connor?"

Jacob cleared his throat, and his eyes shot to the tiled floor, embarrassed by their show of affection. "I think all husbands feel that way about their wives. We want to protect them from all harm."

Katie moved out from under Magnus's arm and came up to him. "Magnus told me about your poor wife." Her hands clasped his. "I am so sorry you have suffered such a loss. Know that the love you had for your wife lives on in the next world. I am convinced of that."

"Katie is very much into spiritualism," Magnus explained.

Katie giggled. Jacob was astounded by the sound. Her laugh was exactly like his Frances's. "My husband makes it to be a fad or something equally as fleeting. I am a student of the writings of Emanuel Swedenborg, one of the founding fathers of the spiritualist movement."

"I'm not sure I am familiar with that movement," Jacob confided.

"They are into the afterlife and ghosts, dear boy." Magnus winked at him.

Jacob stared at the diminutive figure of Katie Blackwell once more. "Ghosts? You?"

"The afterlife is very real, and not in the biblical sense." She glowered playfully at her husband. "Despite my husband's skepticism, I can assure you, Mr. O'Connor, the world that comes beyond this physical plane is of great comfort to the soul.

We can reach out to those we have lost and communicate with them. Many esteemed men believe in this practice. Why, did you know the famous writer Arthur Conan Doyle was a member of The Ghost Club in London? It was founded to focus scientific study on paranormal activities to prove the existence of paranormal phenomena. Famous members of the club included Charles Dickens."

Jacob hid the surprise from his face. He had not expected Magnus's wife to be so radical. "I did not know that, Katie."

"Why yes. Magnus and I learned a great deal about the spiritual movement when we honeymooned in London. We even met with an old friend of Magnus's. What was that writer's name, darling?"

"Oscar Wilde." Magnus came up behind her and placed his hands on her slender shoulders. "I am sure O'Connor doesn't want to be bothered by your fascination with the realm of the hereafter."

"Actually, I am very interested in what comes after this life." Jacob nodded to Katie. "I would like to hear more about it."

She gripped his arm. "You must join us for dinner tonight so I can go on and on about my interest. Where are you staying?"

Jacob bowed his head. "I have not yet found a room to rent in town. I have limited means and was hoping to return to the mainland this evening."

Katie's eyes went to her husband, pleading. "Magnus, we cannot leave the poor man in such a dire state."

Magnus nodded, coming up to Jacob. "You will stay with us, O'Connor."

"I can't take your charity, Magnus. I will be fine."

"It's not charity, dear boy." Magnus held out his hand. "We will get you better, and then you will come and work for my architectural firm in Boston. It's time to get you back where you belong."

Jacob eyed his outstretched hand and thought of Mac. His friend had been right. "Thank you, Magnus. I accept. And you're right; I've been away long enough. I'm ready to come home."

That night, in their grand bedroom trimmed in royal blue wallpaper, Katie and Magnus prepared for bed. As Katie excitedly talked about her treatment for Jacob's ills, Magnus changed into his red silk robe.

"I will send word to Dr. Dinsmore in the morning to come out and take a look at his leg," she proposed. "There must be some special exercises or herbal remedy we can use on him."

Magnus had a seat on the bed and watched as she brushed her hair at her dressing table. It still shocked him at times how obsessed he'd become with his Katie. In the beginning, her quirky ways had been cute, but with time, he had found her utterly addictive.

"I liked the way you fussed over him at dinner."

"He will need assistance getting around the house. That bad leg of his is weak." She faced him through her oval mirror. "Perhaps you can give him that old cane of yours, you know, the one with the dragon's head. You never use it anymore."

"Since I met you, I haven't felt the need to use it."

Magnus almost chuckled at his disclosure. His happiness with Katie had swept aside his desire for the power the baton juju gave him. Love had superseded his need for magic.

"Then it's settled." Katie wheeled around on her red velvet cushion. "You can present it to him in the morning. I always hated that old thing."

"You did?" Magnus knitted his brow. "You never mentioned anything before."

"Yes, it always made me feel uncomfortable. I never liked touching it."

"Then it is O'Connor's from now on." Magnus stood from the bed and went to her dressing table. "He has had a pretty rough time of it from what I can gather. Working on the rails was never an easy life, and Jacob wasn't raised like other orphans to endure such toil. He was taken in by a good family and educated." He picked up the atomizer filled with her favorite perfume and enjoyed the scent. "I'm surprised he pursued such a difficult job."

She put her silver brush down on the table and swept her long honey-blonde hair around her shoulder. "You said he was devastated after losing his wife. Such sadness can drive a man to do things he would never think possible."

Magnus put the atomizer down and fingered the intricate lace sleeve on her nightgown. "Frances was everything to him, just as you are everything to me."

The seductive grin she gave him made his cock grow hard. "Even when I am bad?"

He slid the lace sleeve off her shoulder. "Are you saying you've been bad?"

She rose from the bench, running her hands along the lapels of his burgundy silk robe. "Yes, sir. You need to punish me. A long hard punishment." Her right hand dropped to his cock. "Don't you want to punish me?"

He roughly twisted her around as he pulled the sheer fabric of her nightgown up her legs. "You do know what my punishments entail, don't you?" Magnus shoved his hand between her legs, feeling her silky wetness.

"I want it tonight. Hard, make it hard, Magnus."

Her words turned him on. She always did that to him—begged to be fucked like a whore and not a wife. It had been one of the things that had made him fall in love with her. Katie had adored his games.

Magnus shoved her toward the bed, ripping the sheer nightgown from her body as he went. By the time her knees hit the edge of their king-sized, four-poster mahogany bed, she was naked. He bent her over the side of the bed, bringing her round white ass up to the perfect position.

Katie was wiggling with anticipation as he raised his hand above her right butt cheek. The crack of his slap against her pure white skin was heavenly. She squirmed and moaned as her butt cheek pinked. He slapped her again a little harder, and she squealed. It never ceased to amaze him that no matter how hard he spanked her, Katie reveled in his punishment.

She had first professed her desire for punishment when they had been courting. A simple kiss had led to heavy petting and ultimately her confession. Katie enjoyed being spanked by her father and had daydreamed about finding a man to do it to her. Magnus was all too happy to indulge her fantasy. By the time he had proposed, she had become addicted to his spankings.

The globes of her butt had reddened nicely, and a light film of sweat covered her body. Satisfied she was ready for him, he positioned her hips as he reached for his cock. Tonight, he wanted to feel all of her. She wanted it rough, and he was more than willing to oblige.

He rammed his cock into her wetness, pumping hard and going as deep as he could. Wanting to hear her beg for him, he spread her butt cheeks apart and slipped two fingers into her.

She was panting as he rhythmically thrust with his cock and his fingers at the same time. Katie was backing her hips into him, begging for him to go deeper. He grunted as he shoved deeper, feeling as if he were splitting her in two. He eased a third finger into her butt, and she called out his name.

Her wet walls felt so good; he wanted to come inside of her, to pound into her again and again. His climax was rising fast. She was quivering on the bed, gripping the blue bedspread in her hands. When she screamed his name, he felt her insides clamp down in one hard orgasm. Then that wonderful tingle shot up his spine, and his body jerked as he spilled into her. With her name on his lips, he finally collapsed on top of her.

They were lying on the bed; his robe loosely gathered around him as Katie curled into his chest.

"I hope that time it worked." She sighed against him. "I want to give you a house full of sons."

He patted her thigh. "You will, Katie. Be patient."

Her blue eyes pleaded with him. "Can we do it again—but the other way?" She kissed his chest. "It feels so much better."

"I can't get you pregnant that way."

Her lips moved down to his stomach. "I know, but I want you inside of me again." She let her lips linger over his cock. "This feels so much better than your fingers."

He sat up and pulled her to him. "Say the magic words."

"Please hurt me, Mr. Blackwell."

His erection came to life, and he flipped her over on her stomach. "We were meant to be together, my love."

Chapter Twenty-Three

Setting the Stage

"I think we can relieve a lot of your discomfort with some poultices of willow bark and devil's claw," Dr. Dinsmore announced.

"Devil's claw? That sounds ominous," Jacob remarked, rolling down his left pant leg.

The short doctor with the freckled face pushed his wire-rimmed glasses up his hooked nose as he moved his chair back from Jacob's bed.

"I assure you the herbs are quite safe. Mrs. Blackwell has the herbs in her greenhouse. I'll leave her directions on what to do." He pointed to Jacob's left leg. "You had a skilled surgeon."

Jacob nodded as he rubbed his calf. "I was almost six weeks in the railroad hospital. The rail line I worked for took good care of me."

The doctor stood from his chair. "You'll need to strengthen that left leg. The muscles are atrophied. When they get stronger, it should help your limp."

Jacob sat up in the large four-poster bed. His room was decorated with accents of gray and deep green in the wallpaper and fine gray linens on the bed. He had found the paintings of hunting scenes on the walls somewhat disturbing, but the luxury of a personal bathroom had made up for it. For almost three years, he had been sharing a communal bathroom with the men in his boarding house. Jacob had almost forgotten the luxury of not having to share his sink.

"I'll be back in another week to check on your progress." Dr. Dinsmore clapped his black bag closed. "In the meantime, gain some weight and take daily walks, twice a day if possible. The exercise will be good for you."

In the open doorway of his bedroom, Magnus appeared, carrying the dragon cane in his hand. The eyes of the dragon were glowing bright red. "How's the patient?"

"He'll be fine, Mr. Blackwell. Nothing that time and some good care can't fix."

"He will get that here, Dr. Dinsmore."

Dr. Dinsmore patted Magnus's arm as he met him in the doorway. "I'll see myself out."

"Thank you, Doctor." Magnus watched the short man with the hurried gait leave the room. Directing his attention to O'Connor still sitting on the bed, he held up the cane. "For you."

"I can't take that. You love that thing. I remember the night you told us the story of the woman who gave it to you. That voodoo priestess from New Orleans."

"Yes, Madam Simone."

"You went everywhere with it." He held up his hands. "No,

Magnus, you have done enough for me. I will not take such a treasure."

Magnus approached the bed while holding out the cane to Jacob. "It's not a treasure anymore. I do admit I was fascinated with it. I even swore it had some hold over me—maybe that was just my imagination or the voodoo. But since I met Katie, I have lost interest in it."

Jacob took the cane, and the second his hand touched the dark wood on the handle, he felt something disturbing. Gripping the handle tighter, the odd sensation climbed his arm.

His eyes rose to Magnus. He wanted to ask him about the strange feeling but decided against it. Better to not let the man know what he was thinking.

Setting the end of the cane on the gray throw rug in front of his bed, he got to his feet and put his weight on the cane. The ballooning sensation surged throughout his body. In the blink of an eye, he felt stronger. It was as if the cane had given him some unearthly power.

"How does that feel?" Magnus asked.

Jacob wanted to laugh at the question but instead, put on a reassuring smile. "Good."

Magnus nodded with approval. "It will help you get better. When you're stronger, I am sure you won't need it at all."

"I hope you're right." Jacob lowered his eyes to the cane. "I want to thank you, Magnus, for helping me."

Magnus waved off his comment. "I am happy to help you, my friend." He paused, and his green eyes appeared conflicted as if he were debating some grave concern. "I'm sorry, O'Connor. Sorry I was not there before when you needed me. I'm sorry for Frances and what happened. I'm sorry for the man I used to be."

"I never expected that, Magnus. You weren't the kind of man who apologized for anything."

"Katie has changed me. Loving her has made me realize how empty my life was before."

Jacob gripped the cane handle tighter. "Where did you two meet?"

The hearty laugh Magnus uttered was not like the one Jacob remembered. It was softer and filled with emotion. "I was in Charleston on business. I was coming out of my hotel when I bumped into her on the street. I stepped on her foot. I offered my apologies, and she proceeded to tell me I was no gentleman, and a proper Southern gentleman would have proposed marriage by getting so intimate with her. I thought she was serious. Then she began to giggle."

"She reminds me of Frances when she laughs," Jacob divulged.

"That was what endeared me to her on the steps of that hotel." Magnus tossed up his hand. "My two-day visit turned into a four-week stay, and we attended parties and plays together." Magnus sighed, clasping his hands together. "Soon I could not stand to be away from her. She filled a void in my life. One I never knew existed. When business matters begged me to return to Boston, I asked her to be my wife."

"And her family?" Jacob inquired, knowing Magnus would never just marry anyone. "What are they like?"

"Her father owns a bank, and her mother is from one of the oldest, most socially notable families in Charleston."

A burst of power from the cane vibrated throughout Jacob's body, and flashes of his Frances on the broken rocks overtook his mind. "I'm happy for you, Magnus." His voice was flat, emotionless.

Katie's bright face appeared in the doorway. "I just spoke with Dr. Dinsmore, and he says you should be leaping around in no time." She pointed to the cane. "It looks good on you." Her smile fell as she continued to stare at the stick in Jacob's hand. "That's funny. The stones in the eyes of the dragon. They were red before." She pointed to the handle. "Now they're green."

Both men looked down at the handle.

"So they are." Jacob glanced up at Magnus. "What did you say these stones were again?"

"Changeling stones."

"I thought they were rubies," Katie confessed.

Magnus eyed the handle of the walking stick. "No, the woman who gave me the stick said they were stones that were meant to reveal the heart of the person who possessed it or something like that. It was so long ago."

"What does the green mean?" Jacob inquired.

"I can't recall," Magnus admitted. "Red represented anger, I think."

"Why were you angry?" Katie moved up to her husband. "I have a hard time picturing you as angry."

His arm went casually around the corseted waist of her blue and white dress. "I was an angry man when I was younger. And then I met you. You changed me."

"It's true. I have changed him, Jacob." Katie tucked her head into her husband's chest. "He had so many nasty habits when we met. I've broken most of them, but I am still working on his coffee addiction."

"I have grown obsessed with the coffee and chicory from New Orleans. I import it by the pound now."

Katie's eyes dropped back to the cane. "Perhaps green means luck," she blurted out. "The cane is predicting that Jacob is going to be very lucky in life."

Magnus smiled, indulging his wife's childish notions, but his distrustful heart was not so readily convinced. He searched his memory for what Madam Simone had said about the color of the stones, but he could not recall her ever mentioning the color green. Knowing the dark history of the baton juju, Magnus guessed the color green was not for luck, but something much more sinister—envy.

"When I was working on the rail line, I did a good bit of reading on voodoo," Jacob revealed. "Very nasty stuff."

Magnus cautiously studied him. "Why did you do that?"

"I guess after everything I went through renovating this house—all the New Orleans accents you wanted to add and such—I became interested in the culture of that city. Besides, there isn't a lot to do at night in a boarding house. Frequenting the local libraries kept me sane."

A tweak of distrust snaked its way through Magnus. Somehow Jacob's words did not ring true. First the change in the eyes of the dragon cane, and now his confession about studying voodoo made Magnus uncomfortable. He would have to keep a close eye on his friend.

Katie walked up to Jacob. "Now, sir, if you will come with me, I will apply your poultice." She rested her hand under his left elbow as he leaned on the cane with his right hand. "Dr. Dinsmore said we should get started right away on your treatment."

"Am I going to regret this?" Jacob softly inquired of Magnus as Katie urged him along.

"Absolutely," Magnus joked.

"You cannot believe a word my husband says, Jacob. I am a very skilled poultice maker."

Katie's warmhearted giggle followed them out the room while Magnus's fake smile washed away. His concerns were once again taken up with O'Connor's intentions.

"I might have to send him on his way sooner than expected," he whispered, turning to the door.

Katie had insisted on a lavish dinner of roasted lamb, mashed potatoes, biscuits, and a sweet nut pie for dessert to get Jacob fattened up. While they were enjoying their coffee and chicory around the oval dining room table, Emily Mann came into the room.

"Everything has been prepared as you requested, Mrs. Blackwell."

Magnus returned his white coffee cup to the saucer. "What have you done, Katie?"

Taking one hurried sip from her coffee, she put her cup down and pouted at her husband. "I thought we could do something special for Jacob, darling. It might help him with his recovery."

Magnus cautiously glanced over at Emily Mann. "Should I be worried, Ms. Mann?"

His plain secretary, usually with a sullen face, cracked a slight grin. "Not to worry, Mr. Blackwell."

Katie fidgeted in her seat like a child, making her honey-blonde curls bounce around her face. "I asked Emily to prepare my special room."

Jacob pushed his cup of coffee away, feeling quite full. "What special room?"

Magnus drummed his fingers on the white linen tablecloth.

"Katie has a séance room. I had the staff convert one of the third-floor bedrooms for her. She uses it to talk to spirits."

Jacob sat back in his chair, awestruck. "You're joking."

"The spirit world is very real, Jacob," Katie insisted. "We can communicate with the spirits if we like by reaching out to them. They only need a dark, quiet room in which to be heard."

"I think Katie means to contact Frances for you." Magnus dropped his white linen napkin on the table. "Isn't that right, darling?"

Katie twirled one of her curls around her finger. "I promise no harm will come to you, Jacob. I'm quite skilled at it."

Magnus crossed his legs beneath the table, appearing unamused. "Yes, she had several séances when we returned from our honeymoon. Katie wanted to get in touch with any spirits in the house."

"What happened?"

"No one was home," Magnus jested.

The two men chuckled while Katie pouted. "I just thought now that Jacob is here, Frances might come through."

Magnus rested his hand on the table, attempting to temper his reply. "Darling, I told you before I am uncomfortable with such demonstrations in this house. Involving Jacob is something you should have discussed with me instead of springing it on both of us, especially after that enormous meal."

"I want to try. Magnus, please?" she whined.

He motioned to Jacob. "You see, now that I have spoiled her and denied her nothing, she will hound us both until she gets her way."

Jacob reached for the cane against his chair. "Then we had better give it to her."

Clapping her hands, Katie turned to Emily Mann. "And

Emily will be joining us?"

Magnus's eyebrows went up. "Ms. Mann? Are you ready to speak to the spirits?"

Emily dipped her head in agreement as she waited at the dining room door. "After dealing with your accountants all day, sir, spirits will be a refreshing change of pace."

Magnus stood from his chair. "My God, Ms. Mann, was that a joke? I don't think I've ever heard you joke before."

Jacob easily got up from his chair, amazed at his strength. Just yesterday, standing had been such a trial. "Ms. Mann always joked with me, Magnus."

"About what?"

Emboldened by the power running through him, Jacob replied, "You, of course."

The old Magnus would have snapped like an alligator on the attack, but this version simply smiled.

Genuinely confounded by the change in his former friend, Jacob chucked up the lack of a good tongue-lashing to the presence of his wife. He might pretend to be something he wasn't for Katie's sake, but underneath the sincere gestures and kind words, Jacob was sure the cruel Magnus Blackwell still existed.

After a slow climb to the third floor on the immense black walnut staircase, Katie showed Jacob to a room just off from the landing.

As the door creaked open, the mood of the party changed from jovial to eerie.

The interior had been emptied of all furniture except for one round table in the middle of the room with four chairs set around it. In the center of the table was a flickering white candle. Along the green marble mantel, several more candles had been lit, and black curtains hung in front of the two long windows, shutting out the light from the full moon. All the paintings had been removed from the eggshell painted walls except for one. Hanging above the mantel was a full portrait of Katie. She looked radiant and very young, wearing a white lace gown with a full hoop skirt and lace shawl about her milky white shoulders. In her hand was an open white fan.

"Lovely painting," Jacob commented.

"My father sent it to us after our honeymoon," Katie explained. "Magnus always admired it."

"So why is it in the séance room?" Jacob probed.

"Her choice, not mine, dear boy." Magnus gestured to the portrait. "She said the painting would pass on her essence to the spirits."

With a reproachful glance at her husband, Katie folded her hands together. "I plan on putting pictures of other spiritualists on the wall."

"To help the spirits, I assume." Jacob looked to Magnus, who simply rolled his eyes.

"Enough talk. Take your seats," Katie ordered, sounding unlike her easygoing self.

She directed the group to sit boy-girl, boy-girl, and insisted the spirits would prefer it. Jacob was trying to keep a straight face the whole time. He did not want to offend the woman, but he did not want to believe his Frances could come back to him either. He had hoped for years she was in a better place, and the last thing he needed was to find out that she was not.

After the door was closed, everyone sat and Katie asked the group to join hands. Jacob was surprised at how soft Emily Mann's hands were. He had always thought of her as cold and distant, but the warmth of her hands in the dim light of the room said something else about the aloof woman.

"We call on the spirits to join our circle," Katie began in a very dramatic voice. "We wish to communicate with all those who have moved across the bridge to the other side."

Jacob felt Emily Mann's grip on his hand getting tighter.

"We are here for you. We wish to speak to you. Are there any spirits who want to communicate with us? Send us a sign."

Silence.

Jacob wanted to ask if there should be something happening but decided against it. Katie seemed to be intent on contacting somebody.

"Do not be afraid. Come forward. We only wish to speak to you," she went on.

More silence.

Emily Mann's hand was starting to get sweaty. Jacob swore the room turned colder and shifted in his chair.

"Did you feel that?" Katie's voice was bursting with excitement.

"I felt a chill," Emily admitted.

"I think it did get a little chillier," Jacob confirmed.

"It always gets colder when the spirits are near," Katie affirmed.

Jacob swore he heard Magnus sigh. Through the dim light, Jacob could see the bored expression on Magnus's face.

"Spirits, come to us." Katie's voice was growing stronger. "We want to communicate."

This time, the cold draft that floated past Jacob's left arm was unmistakable. It felt as if someone had touched him. He wanted to pull away, but Emily's grip was so firm he couldn't without causing a commotion.

"Can you tell us who you are?" Katie pleaded. "Tell us your name."

Now the chill was all around Jacob. He was officially getting spooked. He sucked in a deep breath to calm himself, and as he did, the hairs on the back of his neck stood up.

In the middle of the table above the candle, a smoky essence materialized. At first, it moved about, changing shape and morphing into nondescript figures.

"That's it," Katie encouraged. "I can see you trying to get through. Keep going. We are here for you." Katie gasped. "What was that? What did you say? Beware ... beware of who?"

"Katie, are you all right?" It was Magnus, sounding concerned.

"They're warning me," she came back. "The spirits are telling me something is not as it seems. No, someone is not what they seem."

A chill drifted by Jacob's cheek and the shape above the candle captured his attention. He was mesmerized by it. The smoke quickly got thicker, and a face began to emerge. It was the face of a woman.

Jacob was terrified. He wanted to run out of the room, but as the face came into focus, his breath caught in his throat. It was his Frances.

She was as he had seen her in life. Vibrant, beautiful, and giving him that wonderful smile that always made him feel blessed.

He waited, enraptured by her image. Her lips moved, but he could not hear any words coming from her mouth, and then, as if someone had opened a door, he could hear her voice in his head.

"Magnus, stay away from Magnus, Jacob. He is evil."

"Did he do this to you?" He heard himself asking in his head. "Tell me, Frances. I have to know."

She hesitated and then, slowly, she nodded. "Yes. The night of the party—he was the one who killed me."

Magnus could not believe what he was seeing. Jacob was frozen, his eyes glued to something above the candle, but he could not see anything other than smoke.

The look of terror in Jacob's eyes alarmed him. Magnus was about to stand from the table and end the silly game when the smoke above the candle grew thicker. The way the smoke shifted and twisted was intriguing, and Magnus was about to call Katie's attention to the phenomenon when he thought he saw a face appear.

He had to squint to make it out, but then the image focused. The face was of a woman with finely carved features, and her hair was a shiny dark brown. Then, he saw her eyes. They were green and brimmed with the same hatred he had seen when he left her to die in her house on Basin Street.

"Spirits do not die, eh, Magnus."

Madam Simone's voice was in his head. He could hear her.

"Go away," he muttered.

"My blood will be avenged, boy. You shall see. And then your soul will be mine."

"No, get out of my head," he yelled.

He broke free of the hands holding him to the table and jumped from his chair.

"Magnus," he heard Katie call.

The door opened, and the light from the sconces in the hall shone into the room.

"Magnus?"

He spun around. Katie standing behind him.

"What is it? Did you make contact?"

Shaken to his very core, Magnus held his trembling hands together, not wanting his wife to see them. "I thought I saw a face in the smoke from the candle."

"So did I," Emily chimed in as she stood up. "I thought I saw my mother. She was trying to say something to me, but I couldn't hear her."

Katie held her hands to her chest, overcome with relief. "I, too, saw someone in the smoke. My little sister, Elise. She died when I was ten. We were very close." She grasped her husband's arm. "Who did you see, Magnus?"

He stared at her small hand on the sleeve of his black coat. "I, ah ...." He regained his composure. "I think I saw my brother, Edward."

Katie was beside herself. She was practically jumping up and down in place. Then she saw Jacob, still in his chair, his face in his hands. She went to him.

"Jacob?" She eased closer to him. "Did you see anyone?"

He lowered his hands from his face, the tears evident in his eyes. "Yes. Yes, I saw someone. I saw my Frances."

Katie dropped to her knees. "Was she all right? Did she tell you she was well?"

Jacob's eyes honed in on Magnus. The fury Magnus saw in Jacob's dark eyes rattled him.

"She's fine," Jacob said, keeping his eyes locked on Magnus. "She told me everything was going to be all right."

"We all saw different spirits," Emily surmised. "How is that possible?"

Katie rose from Jacob's side. "We each saw the person we wanted to see. The person we felt most connected to on the other side." She came around the table to Magnus, grinning like a proud peacock. "Do you still doubt my abilities?"

"No." Magnus blew out a long breath. "I think we should not do this again, though. I got the impression what happened tonight may be only the beginning."

"The beginning of what?" Emily pestered.

Magnus straightened his coat as he turned for the door. "Something very dangerous."

Chapter Twenty-Four

The Unraveling

Later that evening, Katie and Magnus prepared for bed. He watched her out of the corner of his eye as she unlaced her corset, removed her long white stockings, and changed into her sheer nightgown. He could feel his anger stirring as he went over the words he had heard from the image in the smoke. In the back of his mind, he wondered if Katie had something to do with the appearance of the dead woman. Had she known about Madam Simone and her fate?

"You've been very quiet since the séance, darling." Katie came up to him on the bed. "Are you sure you're all right?"

He pulled his white dress shirt over his head. "I'm fine."

Her hands went to his naked chest. Her fingers went over the ripples of muscles in his abdomen, seemingly fascinated with their feel. "We could talk about it. Sometimes it helps to resolve the emotions a séance can dig up."

He grabbed her arms, pulling her to him. "Did you do that?"

Shocked at his tone and the painful grip of his hands, Katie fought against him. "Magnus."

He brought her to within inches of his face. "Tell me. Did you do that tonight?"

"Do what?"

"Did you make that woman appear and say those things to me? How did you know?"

Her lower lip trembled. "What woman, Magnus? You said your brother appeared to you."

He threw her to the bed and climbed on top of her. "Tell me the truth."

The panic in Katie's childlike blue eyes did something to him. He knew he should have stopped, should have let her go, but there was something strangely arousing in her fright. He had loved it when the women he had taken before had fought back. And although Katie had been a willing participant in his games, the excitement he felt taking her this way was so much sweeter.

He ripped the hem of her nightgown. "You will tell me, Katie, or I will fuck it out of you."

"Magnus, please," she whimpered beneath him. "Not like this. I don't like this game."

His fingers went to her folds, and he wasn't surprised to find her dry. Flipping her over, he pressed his arm into her back. "Did you summon that woman?"

Katie was kicking now, trying to push him away.

Magnus had her nightgown up above her hips, her round white ass wiggling beneath him. Spitting onto his fingers, he thrust them into her.

She cried out beneath him.

She was tight with fear. Perfect. It was just the way he liked it.

Hurriedly undoing the buttons on the fly of his black trousers, he reached inside for his hard cock. "Tell me you like me like this." He rubbed the tip of his cock between her butt cheeks.

"Please Magnus," she begged.

"Tell me you want me." His arm pressed harder into her back. "Say it!"

"I want you," she gasped between sobs.

"Good girl." He dove into her, forcing her flesh apart as he pushed his cock as far as it could go.

She was whimpering beneath him as he rammed into her, but he didn't care. Ever since seeing Madam Simone's face in the smoke, all of his old anger had returned. He thought he was done with that life, but it appeared he was wrong. The old Magnus Blackwell, silenced by his marriage to his adorable wife, had suddenly awakened.

Katie wore a green apron over her lavender gown—the one with the poofy ruffles in the sleeves. She carefully applied a poultice to Jacob's left calf. He sat back on a white wicker chair in the conservatory, taking careful note of her puffy eyes. He guessed she had been crying. That was good. Things were beginning to unravel.

Around them, a collection of potted plants had been placed on shelves, long work tables, and were even growing from planters on the floor. The late morning sun shone in through the panes of glass that made up the ceiling and walls, warming the chill in the room.

Jacob admired her delicate hands as they smeared the thick, gooey white paste on his skin. "Where did you learn about this?"

"My mother taught me." She worked the poultice into his calf. "She grew up during the Civil War and learned about the medicinal properties of plants from her family slaves. Momma always claimed they knew more about treating disease than the doctors."

"And where did you learn about summoning spirits?"

She put the pot of white paste to the side. "That was my older sister, Margaret. She was fascinated with ghosts and introduced me to books about spiritualism when I was a girl. She even married a practitioner of the arts and moved to Rochester." Katie picked up a long white strip of linen hanging from the arm of his chair.

"Katie, what happened the other night at our séance? I'm still not certain of what I saw."

She began wrapping the linen around his calf. "You tell me what happened, Jacob. What did you see in the smoke?"

He reached out for her hand, halting her progress with the bandage. "I thought I saw my wife. She spoke to me in my head. Now was that real, or just my imagination?"

Katie rested her hand over his. "You saw what you needed to see, Jacob. That's what each of us saw that night. The people we loved and needed to know were well on the other side."

Jacob knew this was his chance to further the wedge between husband and wife. He collected his thoughts and planned an approach. "There is one thing that bothers me," he said after a brief interval. "I find it odd Magnus saw his brother, Edward. In all the years I've known him, he only mentioned his brother once. I got the impression they were not close."

She went back to work, covering his calf with the linen. "Just because he never mentioned him, doesn't mean he wasn't thinking about him. My husband is a very quiet man when it comes to his emotions. As his friend for all those years, surely you noticed how he kept everything to himself."

Jacob dipped his head to the side in agreement. "He was always secretive."

"With me as well," Katie conceded. "I thought he would never open up to me. Then as we began to discover things in common, he started to trust me. Eventually, his trust turned into showing me his true feelings. I consider it a precious gift."

"It is. There was only one other person I know who made him show his emotions," Jacob offhandedly remarked.

She tied off the end of the bandage. "Your wife?"

He sat back in his chair, astonished by her admission. "You knew?"

Katie wiped her hands on a towel by the bowl of paste. "He told me about her and him. He said he was stupid to let her go, but then again, she would never have gotten the chance to make you happy, and I would never have met him. You see, the universe had a plan."

Jacob's eyes dropped to his clenched hands. "Do you believe that?"

She rose from the cement floor. "Yes, I do, with all my heart. The universe has a plan for each of us. Good or bad, it does not matter."

Jacob rolled down the leg on his trousers. "There has to be more to it than that." He reached for the cane and relished the zap of strength he felt from it. "I can't believe we are put here to carry out some divine purpose. What about our hopes, our plans?"

"Are they truly yours, or has the universe put them in your head?" Katie debated. "Maybe your thoughts are dictated by another."

Jacob's upper lip curled into a brief sneer. "Not my thoughts. I very much doubt your universe would take kindly to the things that go on in my head."

Katie patted his knee. "What the universe needs you to do is for the greater good, not for yourself." She picked up the bowl of paste. "Stop looking for answers, Jacob. They will only lead you to more questions. Just accept what is."

"Katie, a package has arrived for you from your father," Magnus called, entering the arched doorway of the conservatory.

She set the bowl down on a nearby work table covered with potted herbs. "That must be the books I wanted from my old room."

"What books?" Magnus came up to her side and smelled the poultice, making a face at the stench.

She untied her apron. "More books on spiritualism. I need to check my references."

With a concerned frown, Magnus placed his hand under her chin. "I told you, no more séances for a while. I think we were all frightened enough the last time."

Katie pushed his hand away while glaring up at him. "I know. I just want to read up on a few things."

Jacob could not help but notice the chilly demeanor between them. The fun-loving, happy couple had disappeared.

Before heading to the entrance of the conservatory, she pointed to Jacob's left leg. "Let's give that poultice half an hour to dry, and then we will go for our walk."

"Of course, Katie."

Without giving her husband a second glance, Katie hurried

from the glassed-in room. Jacob noticed how Magnus's worried eyes followed her.

"She appears distracted this morning," Jacob commented.

Magnus wiped his hands together as his eyes dropped to the floor. "You two seem to be spending a lot of time together these past few days."

The hint of jealousy in his voice almost made Jacob smile. "She's been helping me, Magnus. That's all."

"Is it, O'Connor?"

Jacob sat back in his chair, trying to read Magnus's face. "You always did this. Attack others when your life wasn't going according to plan."

Magnus angrily pointed at him. "I never attacked you, O'Connor."

"You're not the type to set out on a full frontal assault, Magnus. You always preferred to sneak up on a man and catch him at his most vulnerable."

The cruel chuckle he had remembered returned, filling the conservatory with the unholy sound. "Well, well, this is a new side of you I have never seen, O'Connor. Since when did you stand up to anyone?"

Jacob clutched his cane, the power from it encouraging his desire to fight. "Why do I get the impression my visit is coming to an end?"

Magnus flung his hands behind his back and inspected the assortment of herbs on the work table. "Perhaps it would be for the best if you recovered in Boston instead. Your position is waiting for you at Collier and Keene. I suggest you make plans to go there in a few days." He raised his surly green eyes to him. "You will tell Katie you are better and anxious to return to work."

A little unsteady on his feet, Jacob rose from his chair. "I'm not a threat, Magnus. She's in love with you."

"I know. I just don't like sharing her with you, O'Connor. We did this before with a woman, and the results did not turn out in my favor. I do not wish for that to happen again."

The old Magnus he had known was back. The stiff posture and scowling eyes were there once again, teasing Jacob. Only this time, he was not going to back down and appease his friend. Those days were long gone. The churning hatred in his gut would never allow the likes of Magnus Blackwell to beat him down ever again.

"What if your wife is not convinced I am ready to leave?" he proposed with a smirk.

Magnus came up to him, his fists clenched. "You will convince her, O'Connor. You will make it a very fine performance."

Jacob hid the glee from his face. "Whatever you want, Magnus. I have no wish to cause you any discomfort."

Magnus marched from the room, and Jacob could not help but grin. Things were moving along. A vision of a destroyed Magnus rallied Jacob's resolve to push ahead with his plans.

Plans. Jacob recalled Katie's insights into the plans of the universe and her belief that he was being driven by a mystical force. Tapping his cane on the cement, he quietly chuckled at the notion. There was nothing otherworldly about revenge.

"The universe be damned. This is just between Magnus Blackwell and me."

Dinner that night was a rather subdued affair. The growing tension between Katie and Magnus was stifling. Their conversations were stilted, her previously bright face and perpetual smile were gone, and Magnus seemed to be at a complete loss.

Jacob, on the other hand, enjoyed the brooding looks, long silences, and numerous sighs that accompanied dinner. The more the couple appeared at odds, the happier he became.

"I heard from Bob Keene today," Magnus said after a very long lapse in conversation. "The head of my architectural firm, Collier and Keene."

Jacob felt a prickle of interest in his gut. "Yes, I remember you telling me about him."

Magnus finished cutting into his piece of rare roast beef. "He is anxious to get you started at the firm. He said they are in desperate need of help."

"So soon?" Jacob feigned surprise. "I didn't expect that."

The clang of Katie's knife on her plate made both men turn to her. "He is not well enough for that, Magnus. The poor man hasn't even been with us a week."

Magnus patted his white linen napkin against the corner of his mouth. "I know, darling, but he could continue his treatments in Boston. I can provide him with the best of care, and he can stay in my home until he finds a place to let."

"No," Katie huffed. "I will not let you toss the poor man out on the street before he can get around better." She flopped back in her chair. "Besides, I have enjoyed his company. With you up in your office all day, Jacob has given me someone to talk to and take long walks with."

The red hue in Magnus's cheeks almost made Jacob laugh out loud. "Dear Katie, this is business, and Jacob cannot stay with us forever. He has to start his life."

She banged her fist on the table like a spoiled child. "I know

261

that, Magnus. I'm not an idiot, so please stop treating me like one." She paused and took in a calming breath. "At least let him stay until the party. It's only two weeks away, and I would very much like to have Jacob here for it."

Jacob stabbed a few of his peas with his fork. "What party?"

Avoiding his eyes, Magnus picked up his knife. "Our one-year anniversary party. I have planned a big party with over a hundred guests. I even have a photographer coming to immortalize the event."

Jacob reached for his wineglass. "I'm sure Mr. Keene can hold on for two more weeks, Magnus. After the party, I will go to Boston. Two weeks will give me plenty of time to mend, and I can help Katie plan the event."

"Yes, please, Magnus?" Katie's bright smile returned as she clapped her hands. "Do let Jacob stay just until the party. Then I will be all yours again."

Like a cornered rat on a sinking ship, Magnus gave his old friend a searing gaze of pure hatred that made Jacob's stomach summersault with happiness.

"If that is what you wish, Katie," Magnus finally relented. "I cannot deny you anything, my love. But after the party, O'Connor must take up his position at Collier and Keene."

"Agreed," Katie jubilantly returned and, then, with a vigor she had not yet shown that evening, attacked her plate of roast beef and peas.

Sipping from his glass of very tasty burgundy, Jacob smiled. Two weeks was all he needed. "An eye for an eye," Mac had once told him. Jacob O'Connor had used the phrase as his mantra ever since hearing it from his friend. Soon, the happy little life Magnus had created would come crashing down around him.

Chapter Twenty-Five

Justice

Hundreds of candles bathed Altmover Manor in flickering lights while the frigid November winds from the Atlantic swept in through the open front doors. With guests arriving on horseback, in buggies, and grand covered coaches, the drive was jam packed with horses, drivers, and stable hands.

Jacob stood on the wide porch he had designed, his cane in his hand, as he sucked in the refreshing, cool air. The house overflowed with people, more than he had ever seen before. Katie's sphere of influence must have been quite extensive; friends came from as far south as Georgia. She had been bubbly and happy during the days before the event, caught up in the menu planning and decorating of the great ballroom. Jacob had indulged her requests for him to accompany her to town to shop for party supplies. Magnus had been suspiciously absent during those last few days, adding to Jacob's delight.

Now with the guests clogging the hallways and spilling over into every room of the first floor of the house, Jacob was suddenly not in the mood for the company of strangers. Resting his shoulder against one of the wide columns he had struggled to get into place when renovating the home, he enjoyed the peace away from the party.

"What are you doing out here?" Katie asked, coming alongside him.

Her dress had been imported from Paris, a surprise from Magnus for the affair. Trimmed in gold ribbon, it shimmered beneath the great lamps Jacob had spent numerous hours of correspondence tracking down in New Orleans. The bodice was done in gold silk, while the underskirt and full sleeves were antique lace. Two gold doves had been placed precariously on her head as if nesting in her honey-blonde hair.

"There were so many people in the house; I just wanted to get some air," he told her.

She tugged on the black sleeve of the tuxedo Magnus had loaned him for the event. "What is it, Jacob? You've been very quiet all day."

He glanced back at the open leaded-glass front doors; the noise of the party wafted through. "I'm just not very much into parties."

She let go of his arm. "The whole affair reminds you of the night your wife died, doesn't it?"

He glimpsed the array of horses hitched to posts in the drive. "Yes, it does. It was very much like tonight. Not as many people of course." He chuckled. "But it was very much the same."

"You saw her at the séance, so you know she is at peace."

"I don't know anything of the kind, Katie."

"Yes you do, Jacob." She placed her hand over his heart. "You know it here."

"Thank you, Katie, for all you have done."

A happy group of men carrying large cigars in their hands stepped out on the porch. As they began lighting their foul-smelling stogies, Katie scrunched up her face in revulsion.

"Let's go dance. I feel like celebrating. It's our last night together, Jacob. Who knows when we will be together again?"

Taking his arm, she walked slowly with him as he used his cane. While strolling past the men gathered around her front door, Katie waved away their cloud of smoke with her gloved hand.

Crowded with people, most of them drinking champagne, the foyer was a colorful rainbow of bright women's dresses and men in black tuxedos. Katie pushed aside guests, allowing room for Jacob to follow behind her. After a lot of bending, twisting, shimmying, and darting around partygoers, they stood at the entrance to the ballroom.

An orchestra, larger than the one Magnus had hired before, was spread out over a wide swath in one corner of the room. They played a lively tune, and Katie bounced up and down on her gold shoes, anxious to join the swirling couples in the center of the fair hardwood floor.

Her exuberance was contagious, and Jacob laughed as he set the cane to the side of the door. "I'm not sure how good of a dancer I will be, Katie." He took her arm. "You will catch me if I fall, won't you?"

"Always, my friend."

Once at the edge of the dance floor, Jacob put his arm around her waist. "I apologize ahead of time for stepping on your toes."

He rocked back and forth in time with the music, and then, spotting an opening in the array of waltzing couples, he swept her across the floor and joined the dancers.

Katie's blue eyes grew wide with astonishment. "Why, you are an excellent dancer, Jacob."

Jacob kept nodding his head in time with the music. "My wife taught me. Frances was very keen on dancing."

They followed the flock of couples taking to the floor like a group of migrant birds carried by the whipping winds. Jacob was surprised to discover that dancing was easier than walking; then again, maybe it was just the thrill of the moment.

After circling the ballroom a few times, Jacob's left leg began to tire. The pull of his aching muscles was getting too hard to ignore when he finally winced.

"I think I've had enough," he said in Katie's ear to be heard above the music.

With a worried frown, she helped him from the dance floor and back to his cane. "I have tired you. I'm sorry."

"No, Katie." He reached for the cane, and his energy instantly returned. The thrill of holding it quickly wiped away all of his aches. "I'm just not quite ready for an entire night of dancing."

She guided him to the ballroom doorway. "Let's get you a place to rest."

After more shoving through the crowded hallway of the house, they emerged in the conservatory. Katie showed him to a white wicker bench by the doors that led out to the courtyard.

"That's better," Jacob muttered as he pulled his stiff leg up under him after sitting down. "Go back to your party. I will be fine here."

"I could do with a break myself." She sat down next to him.

Jacob smiled. "You remind me of Frances. She was like you. I think you even have her laugh."

"Magnus told me that once when he spoke of her. I know he cared for her a great deal."

Jacob's anger bubbled to life. "Maybe he cared too much."

Katie turned to him. "What is it, Jacob?"

His eyes fixated on the edge of the courtyard where the iron railing stood. He had tried to picture a thousand times what happened—what Magnus must have said and done to Frances, but the images had always been too painful to confront.

"Did Magnus ever talk to you about the night Frances died?"

Katie rose from the bench, wringing her hands. "No. He refused to discuss it. He said it was a suicide and speaking about it would do neither of us any good."

His body was strengthened by his anger, and Jacob used his cane to rise easily from the bench. "Do you believe that?"

Katie shook her head. "I think sad experiences need to be revisited; otherwise, their energy can never be set free from a place. Frances's energy has never been set free from this house."

"Her energy?"

Katie went to the glass doors that opened onto the courtyard. "She is still here, Jacob. Her energy haunts that courtyard. I think I saw her one night from my bedroom window walking around the dragon fountain in the center."

He went up to her grabbing her right shoulder with his free hand. "Why haven't you told me this before?"

"Would you have believed me?"

He let her go. "No."

"Not before the séance. Now you believe me, don't you?"

Jacob went to the doors that led to the courtyard. He pushed them open with his shoulder and went outside.

The wind from the Atlantic whipped his black hair about his head as he headed for the edge, wanting to peer down at the rocks where he had seen his beloved Frances. When he reached the black iron railing, he stopped.

He hesitated before looking down, afraid he would see the same vision that had haunted his mind since the day her body was discovered. He finally found the courage to peek over the edge, but the darkness hid the rocks below.

"Do you have any idea why she would have done such a thing?" Katie asked while gripping the black railing.

"She didn't kill herself," he admitted. "She was murdered."

Katie faced him, her eyes bulging with fear. "Who would do such a thing?"

The tingle of cocky arrogance that had awakened in Jacob since arriving at Altmover Manor raised his lips in a grin. "Your husband killed my wife."

The horror that twisted Katie's dainty features was strangely satisfying to Jacob. The pain he had endured was now being paid back in kind.

"Jacob, you can't mean that. Magnus may be many things, but he is not a—"

"Your husband is a liar, a cheat, and was known to enjoy raping housemaids before you came along. I suspect my wife was not the first person he murdered." Jacob moved closer to her, pinning her against the railing. "Did he ever tell you about what happened to Madam Simone in New Orleans? The woman who gave him this." Jacob held up the cane. "I did some digging about her. Apparently, she was pretty famous in the city. I found an old newspaper article about her in Boston. She was murdered in her whorehouse by someone the police suspect she knew. Did you know your husband frequented whorehouses, Katie?"

She tried to push him away. "Stop this! Enough, Jacob. I will not have you speak ill of a man—"

"Frances came to me that night of the séance, Katie." Jacob pushed her against the railing. "She told me Magnus killed her. She told me to stay away from him. She said he was evil."

Katie struggled against him now, pounding her fists against his chest. "Get away from me."

Jacob dropped the cane from his right hand and reached for her. "He took away the only person I ever loved."

"You're mad!" She fought against him as he grabbed her arms. "Magnus!" she screamed. "Help me!"

Afraid her cries would reach her husband, Jacob had to silence her. He put his hand over her mouth, but she bit him. His fury kicked in, and he shoved her into the railing. To get away, Katie tilted backward and was precariously perched over the side of the cliff. The terror in her eyes told Jacob she must have realized her mistake. The slightest nudge and she would fall onto the rocks.

Jacob wanted to laugh at her, warn her to enjoy her last moments on earth, but he didn't. Katie stretched for his tuxedo jacket, and he slapped her hands away. He was tired of toying with her. Time to end it.

Lifting her in his arms, Jacob calmly tossed her over the rail.

Her scream echoed all the way down to the rocks. Then there was a *thud*, and she was quiet. Jacob's first emotion was one of relief. It was over, and then he realized what he had done. But he knew there was no room for regret when setting out for revenge. Besides, he was not done. There was still one more to destroy.

Gazing once more over the cliff, a flash of green to the side caught his eye.

On the ground next to the railing, the green eyes of the dragon cane glowed.

"O'Connor," Magnus called as he came out onto the courtyard. "What are you doing out here? I've been searching everywhere for you." He rubbed his arms. "It's freezing." He gaped about. "Is Katie with you? I thought I heard her voice."

Jacob smiled as a ribbon of satisfaction coursed through his veins. "She's gone."

Magnus came up to him at the rail. "Gone? Gone where?"

Jacob directed his eyes to the rocks below.

"Where is my wife, O'Connor?" Magnus grabbed his arm, spinning him around to face him.

Jacob pried Magnus's hand off his jacket and squeezed it with all of his might. "She's with my wife now."

Magnus yanked his hand free and tried to land a blow on his face, but Jacob was too fast and ducked out of the way. Before Magnus could strike at him again, Jacob's hands went around his neck. Magnus clawed at him, but the years Jacob had spent driving ties on the railroad had hardened him against pain. Jacob registered the horror in Magnus's green eyes as his grip tightened.

"I know you killed Frances," Jacob snarled. "I know you pushed her over this cliff and took her away from me. For three years, I have been waiting for this day, Magnus. How does it feel to lose the only person you've ever loved?"

Magnus fought against Jacob's hold around his neck, but Jacob was too strong for him. He began punching at Jacob's chest and arms, desperate for air. In a bold move, Magnus twisted his shoulder upward, and finally broke free.

Magnus fell backward and gasped for air. "You pathetic bastard." He coughed and cupped his hand over his throat, his voice still very weak. "How dare you strike out against me. I made you."

Jacob spied the cane on the ground and picked it up. "Yes, you did make me, Magnus. You turned me into this pathetic bastard when you murdered my wife." Jacob raised the cane over his head. "Give Frances my best when you see her."

Magnus held up his hand to fend off the assault, but Jacob landed the handle of the heavy cane in the middle of his skull. The *crack* resonated throughout the courtyard. Dazed, Magnus stumbled backward, but Jacob came after him and whacked him over the head once more. Magnus dropped to his knees. His hands went up to protect himself from another attack, but he was wavering on his knees and clearly stunned.

"Please, Jacob, not like this," Magnus mumbled as the blood trickled down his face.

Unmoved by his plea, Jacob lifted the cane once more and mercilessly brought the handle down on Magnus's head again and again. Every time Jacob hit his mark, the green eyes of the dragon glowed even brighter.

Magnus's face was a bloody mess by the time Jacob stopped. He took a moment to catch his breath and then dropped the blood-covered cane to the ground. He gazed down at Magnus's body, smiling.

"An eye for an eye, my friend."

Jacob easily lifted Magnus's body from the ground and tossed it over the railing. When he heard the *smack* on the rocks below, Jacob casually picked up his walking stick and hobbled to the conservatory.

Chapter Twenty-Six

It Begins

Inside the all-glass room, Jacob found a few watering cans that still had water in them. He dipped the cane handle into one of them and washed off the blood and brain matter. With a few scraps of linen cloth left over from Katie's poultice applications, he wiped down the handle and stuffed the linen into his trouser pocket.

Composing himself, he was about to leave the conservatory and return to the party when Emily Mann came up to him.

"Is everything all right, Mr. O'Connor?"

Jacob tapped the tip of his cane against the cement floor, smiling. "Perfectly wonderful, Ms. Mann. Why do you ask?"

"You looked flushed. I was just wondering if you are well."

"I've never felt better." He glanced inside the house. "How is the party going?"

Emily Mann rubbed her hands together. "Several guests are asking for Mr. and Mrs. Blackwell. I've searched all over, but cannot find them. Do you happen to know where they went?"

"Yes, I know exactly where they went," he announced, fixing the cuffs of his wrinkled tuxedo jacket.

Emily appeared relieved. "I'm so glad. I was beginning to worry."

"They are fine." He motioned to the courtyard beyond. "Follow me."

Jacob stepped out the glass doors of the conservatory and into the courtyard while Emily followed behind.

Anxiously searching the courtyard, she grabbed his arm. "They are not out here, Mr. O'Connor."

"Yes, they are."

He casually strolled over the green dragon mosaic on the courtyard floor, past the black fountain with the golden dragon on top, and when he reached the black iron railing that overlooked the cliffs, he pointed the tip of his cane at the rocks below.

"You will find Mr. and Mrs. Blackwell down there— together."

At first, Emily appeared confused. "I don't understand. Where are they?"

Jacob insistently pointed his cane, yet again. "Down there."

Emily peered over the edge of the railing, squinting. "I can't see anything. It's too dark."

"They're there. Trust me."

Emily faced him. "How do you know this, Mr. O'Connor?"

He arched closer to her, grinning. "I put them there. I've killed your Mr. and Mrs. Blackwell, Ms. Mann. I murdered them both."

Her scream was deafening. Jacob thought it overly dramatic.

Gripping the railing, Emily cried out, "Why? Why did you do this?"

Amused by her theatrics, Jacob shrugged. "Payment for what he did to my Frances."

The sheer terror in Emily's pug-like face took him by surprise. He had never thought her capable of such emotion.

"You're mad!" she yelled.

He chuckled, feeling that resolute sense of strength his cane gave him. "Correction, my dear Ms. Mann, I used to be mad. Now I'm sane."

Emily backed away and turned to the house. Running away as fast as her little black shoes could carry her, she went screaming into the conservatory. Jacob thought the noise a bit excessive. Katie and Magnus were already dead. Why the fuss?

Taking one more gander over the railing, he struggled to make out the dim form of a couple resting within a few feet of each other at the base of the cliff. Twirling the cane in his hand, he walked away from the railing and headed back toward the house.

In the conservatory, he spotted the strips of linen Katie had left in a small pile on her work table. Stopping at the table, he took a moment to tie several of the long strips together. After checking the integrity of the knots, he wrapped the long rope of fabric around his left arm.

Humming as he went, he ambled back inside the house.

The guests still frolicked about, drinking, dancing, and completely unaware that their hosts were no longer among them. Amid the peals of laughter, loud conversations, music, cheers, and celebration, Jacob made his way to the grand staircase.

Leaving the revelers on the first floor, he slowly went up the steps. He felt happy—happier than he had been in a very long time. Taking his gold watch from his inner jacket pocket, he kissed it and then slipped it back inside. On the second-floor landing, he went to the tie where the massive eight-tiered crystal chandelier was secured. Undoing the knot, Jacob pulled on the velvet rope and swung the chandelier toward him. Resting the cane against the black banister shaped like a dragon, he unwound the long linen rope from his arm. He secured one end to a circular rod inside the chandelier. The other end he tied as a noose around his neck.

Jacob stared down at the partygoers completely oblivious to his actions. From his vantage point, the women's colorful dresses reminded him of a rainbow cutting across a stormy sky.

"We will make this a party they will never forget, eh, Magnus?"

As if carried by a passing breeze, Jacob swore he heard a cruel chuckle answer him.

He ignored his inner voice, questioning the uncanny sound, and chalked it up to the party below. Jacob glanced up at the mammoth chandelier and smiled. He was ready. Using all the strength he could muster, Jacob pushed the chandelier out over the white marble floor of the crowded foyer and jumped over the black banister.

Numerous screams from men and women roared up from the floor as Jacob O'Connor's body swung from the crystal chandelier. The cane he had left resting against the banister toppled over. The changeling stones briefly radiated a brilliant green light, and then, slowly, the eyes of the dragon faded to black.

Other Titles from
Vesuvian Books

KILLING JANE

STACY GREEN

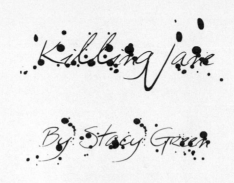

Killing Jane

By Stacy Green

What if everything you've ever heard about Jack the Ripper is wrong ...

A young woman is brutally murdered in Washington D.C., and the killer leaves behind a calling card connected to some of the most infamous murders in history.

Jack the Ripper.

Rookie homicide investigator Erin Prince instinctively knows the moment she sees the mutilated body that it's only a matter of time before someone else dies. She and her partner, Todd Beckett, are on the trail of a madman, and a third body sends them in the direction they feared most: a serial killer is walking the streets of D.C.

The clock is ticking.

Erin must push past her mounting self-doubt in order to unravel a web of secrets filled with drugs, porn, and a decades old family skeleton before the next victim is sacrificed.

The only way to stop a killer is to beat them at their own game.

SOUTHERN GOTHIC

A NOVEL

DALE WILEY

SOUTHERN GOTHIC
A NOVEL

By Daley Wiley

Aspiring author Meredith Harper owns the hottest bookstore in Savannah.

Michael Black is her favorite writer—long thought dead—until he mysteriously approaches Meredith with a new manuscript, and a most unusual offer. Meredith can keep the manuscript to herself, or publish it under her own name.

Her decision results in a bestseller, but the novel contains a coded secret; one that will put her on trial for murder and in hiding from "the blood stalker," proving too late that making a deal with the devil comes at a heavy price.

CHILDREN OF THE FIFTH SUN

2012 WASN'T THE END
IT WAS THE BEGINNING

"A bit Tom Clancy, a hint of Dan Brown"
—Charity Scripture, Amazon

GARETH WORTHINGTON

COMING 2.28.17

CHILDREN OF THE FIFTH SUN

By Gareth Worthington

Genre: "Science Faction" - science fiction, action and adventure with fact-based science, theories and mythology

IN ALMOST EVERY BELIEF SYSTEM ON EARTH, there exists a single unifying mythos: thousands of years ago a great flood devastated the Earth's inhabitants. From the ruins of this cataclysm, a race of beings emerged from the sea bestowing knowledge and culture upon humanity, saving us from our selfish drive toward extinction. Some say this race were "ancient aliens" who came to assist our evolution.

But what if they weren't alien at all? What if they evolved right here on Earth, alongside humans ... and they are still here? *And, what if the World's governments already know?*

* * *

Kelly Graham is a narcissistic self-assured freelance photographer specializing in underwater assignments. While on a project in the Amazon with his best friend, Chris D'Souza, a mysterious and beautiful government official, Freya Nilsson, enters Kelly's life and turns it upside down. Her simple request to retrieve a strange object from deep underwater puts him in the middle of an international conspiracy. A conspiracy that threatens to change the course of human history.

www.childrenofthefifthsun.com